PEANUT BUTTER PICKLEBA

PEANUT BUTTER PICKLEBALL AND MURDER

BOOK 1 OF THE PICKLEBALL CHRONICLES

BY: ROB MUNDEN

Copyright: 2022

Rob MUNDEN

Randall Baines, a divorced white man in his early seventies, was forced into retirement from his career as a detective in Wichita, Kansas. Randall becomes a grumpy, hot-tempered lost soul. He often takes his anger out on his neighbor, Keisha, a young African American recent high school graduate. Randall is agitated most by his next-door nemesis due to her insistence on taking an oversized ping-pong paddle and banging a rock-hard Wiffleball against her garage during his early morning reading time. Randall struggles to find his purpose in life until a psychotic murderer, known as the Peanut Butter Killer, takes the life of a treasured elderly lady in his neighborhood. Randall is not the type of guy to stay passive under such circumstances and decides to investigate the case himself.

   Randall soon develops the theory that peanut butter may not be the key to the murders, but rather, the key may be a game involving the very same equipment used by his neighbor to disturb his peaceful reading time. Randall must swallow his pride to team up with neighbor foe Keisha to try

PEANUT BUTTER PICKLEBALL AND MURDER

to catch a crazed madman that Randall suspects is a professional athlete in the fastest growing sport in America – PICKLEBALL!

PREFACE

Although the book is fiction, most of the story-driven points during the matches presented are based on actual points in matches that I have played. The novel refers to 5.0 players as professional pickleball players. I recognize that most pickleball players at a 5.0 level are not on the PPA or APP tour. I feel as though the common pickleball player reading the novel can identify with the term 5.0 more so than the term PPA or APP.

If you ask me, I will tell you that I am a higher-end 3.5, borderline 4.0 player. But if you ask those with whom I have played, they will tell you that they invented a special category for me called negative 1.5.

Is there any basis of truth to this novel that there is a serial killer pickleball player on the loose? Probably not, but if you're a pickleball player and you find yourself in a town that you rarely or have never been to, and you and your partner take to the foreign courts for your first match of the day,

Rob MUNDEN

ASK YOURSELF,

DO I REALLY KNOW WHAT'S ON THE OTHER SIDE OF THE NET?

PEANUT BUTTER PICKLEBALL AND MURDER

CHAPTER 1

Cluck Putoo Puh - Cluck Putoo Puh - Cluck Putoo Puh

7:33 AM: Randall Baines sat by the window in his bedroom on the second floor of his old, but well-maintained, gray Victorian home. He looked down at the teenage African American girl hitting the Wiffleball back and forth against the metal garage door of her house next door. Her home was also designed in a Victorian style and sat just a few yards from his. Stranger yet, she continuously struck the Wiffle ball with what appeared to be a gigantic ping-pong paddle.

Randall just wanted some peace and solitude as he read his novel, but instead, he could not ignore the banging sound of the Wiffle ball hitting the garage door.

Cluck Putoo Puh - Cluck Putoo Puh - Cluck Putoo Puh

"It's 7:33 in the damn morning. You are a teenage girl, for Christ's sake. Sleep until noon like any other newly graduated youngster would before starting a new adult life!"

Cluck Putoo Puh - Cluck Putoo Puh - Cluck Putoo Puh

This wasn't the first time that Randall had to endure the Wiffle-ball-garage-door banging noise. He had tolerated the noise many times in the past, but this was different. The Wiffle-ball-garage-door banging noise was severely disrupting his morning reading time. Although Randall was short-tempered and hotheaded, he initially ignored his impulse to act. His restraint was made possible by purely deductive reasoning.

"A: It's a girl so bored on a Saturday morning that she's using an odd-looking ping-pong paddle to hit a Wiffle ball continuously against her garage door. How long could that possibly last before she went on to more important post-graduate things, such as texting her friends, painting her fingernails, combing her hair for the nine hundredth time, or simply going back to bed?"

"B: It's a damn Wiffle ball. A Wiffle ball will break by dropping it onto a grassy lawn, let alone smashing it a hundred times with the largest damn ping-pong paddle the world has ever seen. "

"C: No need for a C. Either A or B would most certainly eliminate the problem. "

Cluck Putoo Puh - Cluck Putoo Puh - Cluck Putoo Puh

7:47 AM: Neither, A nor B has yet played out. Randall turns to page 82 of the Follett novel. Not much of an accomplishment since he started on page 77.

7:33 AM: The logic in his former detective mind stayed the path. Deductive reasoning: A may not pan out, but if the tortured toddler sphere lasted more than two more minutes, Randall himself would think of calling the Guinness Book of World Records to introduce the world's most brutal Wiffle ball.

Cluck Putoo Puh - Cluck Putoo Puh - Cluck Putoo Puh

8:03 AM: The window slides up, and Ken Follett and all his 1046 pages of historical fiction take flight, darting just two feet from the teenage Reynolds girl's head.
The Reynolds girl's immediate reply? A middle finger that rose to the sky aimed right at the bitter old man's face.

....

To say the least, Randall was having a difficult time adjusting to life as a retired Wichita police detective. Sure, Wichita, a town of 550,000, didn't bring about the excitement and danger that being a part of the NYPD would. But Kansas's largest city could provide an officer with plenty of thrills to fulfill a forty-two-year career. In fact, he had chased enough bad guys, climbed enough trees to save a few felines, provided more than his share of sobriety tests, and investigated enough crimes to be more than ready for a simpler life.
Well, so he thought. Sure, the first two years weren't so bad. He enjoyed sleeping past 6 AM, although he still found himself up by seven. He occasionally met some of his fellow retired

police buddies at the nearest Starbucks, but you can only tell the same police war stories so many times.

He visited his only child, Samantha, in St. Louis every so often. She and her husband, Rudy, enjoyed his company the first couple of days, but eventually, he would sense that he had overstayed his welcome. When they would visit him, they generally made an excuse that they needed to stay in a hotel for reasons that seemed much more imaginative than logical. After all, Randall's Victorian home held four bedrooms. During their Wichita stays, Samantha and Rudy spent more time with friends showing off their pride and joy, Hanna, Randall's five-year-old granddaughter. Randall adored her, but she hadn't seemed to take much notice of him, perhaps due to the often serious and haunted look on his face. Randall did not consider himself stern exactly; smiling just seemed like a waste of muscle tissue to Randall.

Hitting the slots at the casino located in a suburb of Wichita called Mulvane often provided a brief thrill. Still, sooner or later, Randall allowed mathematical odds to creep into his head that would cause him to gravitate back to his beat-up 1999 Ford F-150. Randall felt lost, unneeded, and irrelevant.

He did love to read, but his Follett novel was now the property of the Reynolds family, and he seriously doubted they would have any interest in giving it back. He dreaded the thought of Follett inevitably being cast aside in the trash mixed with banana peelings and damp coffee grounds. It just seemed sacrilegious to do that to a literary genius.

PEANUT BUTTER PICKLEBALL AND MURDER

Randall analyzed and used deductive reasoning in everything from solving a murder when he was a detective on the police force, to the simplest of life decisions, such as the precise time to turn the coffee pot on.

When it came to matters that might indicate his own shortcomings, Randall was a completely oblivious man. He was just too stubborn and hardheaded to allow his brain to understand that had he not thrown the book at the Reynolds girl, he would still have it in his possession.

Randall had little to no interest in television, but it would now be his only entertainment option. He turned the power button on his television set, feeling as if he had just signed over surrender papers, succumbing to the image of the life of the typical retired American.

He wondered if he might start joining the Wednesday night bingo group. He felt as though he could enjoy a lot of "old man" hobbies. He thought casting a line in the nearest pond while reading Follett could be cool. He was never good at guessing how high to bid when playing pitch, but with enough card sessions with his fellow retired peers, he was sure he could catch on.

But bingo - NO!!! The thought of being surrounded by a bunch of old, bickering ladies trying to shush him and his friends while he talked just so that they could hear Reverend Thomas holler out "B-19! B-19!" was just more than he felt he could ever handle.

Five minutes after turning the television on, he began dozing off. Napping was not his style, but subconsciously his body was adapting to boredom. As Randall started to doze off, he thought, "I truly am succumbing to irrelevance. Perhaps not waking back up at all might not be so bad."

....

It was supposed to be a simple warm-up tournament held on a Friday afternoon. There were only four 5.0 level teams in the Park City Open. Park City is a growing suburb of Wichita. "IT JUST WAS NOT OUR DAY." Those words rang through the tattered mind of The Killer. "Bullshit! How can that punk-ass kid have the nerve to tell me that it just wasn't our day? That punk-ass kid partner of mine couldn't hit a broad side of a barn, let alone a Goddamn pickleball! Second out of four lousy ass teams is absolutely pitiable!"

Driving aimlessly through the streets of Wichita, The Killer scoured the streets, forging forward, seeking his prey. He came across an elderly African American woman sitting on her porch swing, rocking back and forth while knitting. The Killer found her peaceful disposition abhorrent. Life was full of turmoil and chaos. He felt there was no damn good reason she ought to be able to relax and knit on a front porch swing.

His mind raced with elation to have discovered his next move. "She has to die. She must die."

It was 8 p.m. Darkness had not yet fallen upon the sultry May evening. He parked his jet-black Mercedes at a nearby Costless grocery store. Although his car was nice, a Mercedes in 2022 wasn't exactly considered a flamboyant vehicle of luxury. He was confident that it would not stand out.

    The Killer was still wearing the sweaty gym shorts he wore during the day's tournament. He did change shirts and pulled a dark grey sweater over them. He pulled out a pickleball paddle, a jar of peanut butter, and a small crowbar out of his pickleball bag. He was able to tuck all three in a sizeable pouch-like pocket on the front mid-section part of his sweater. The Killer hoped that on this humid 90-degree evening that wearing a sweater would not draw the attention of curious onlookers. He pulled the hood from the sweater over his head. The Killer traveled the two-block distance through alleys. He scampered past some barking canines, hoping not to draw the attention of their owners.

    The Killer approached the backyard of the greenhouse. He thought he had a much larger task at hand, as he assumed he needed to use the crowbar to pry the backdoor open. To his amazement, the back door was not locked. He slowly opened the door further, entering the kitchen. He peeked to the side of the kitchen door and noticed the elderly African American lady in her living room swaying back and forth on her rocker, singing, "Amazing Grace, how sweet the sound, that saved a wretch like me. I once was lost but now am fou…." She suddenly stopped singing in the middle of the verse. "You don't have to be sneaky young man."

He walked into the living room and positioned himself in front of her. "Take that hood off, boy. If you're gonna do something you ought not to, at least be man enough to face me. Even Judas had enough courage to kiss Jesus before he betrayed him." He proceeded to take the hood off.

The Killer spoke. "As you see, I'm not some grandchild, family member, or whoever you were expecting."

"Who said I was expecting a family member or what not? But I was expecting a young boy. That is you. You might hide behind a white, middle-aged man's image, but you are just a young, scared boy, fixing to do something dumb to try and make ya self-feel tough. So, what kinda devious plan you have set for me, mister?"

"I'm going to kill you, Madame. Aren't you afraid?"

"Though I walk through the valley of the shadow of death, I will fear no evil: for thou art with me, thy rod and thy staff they comfort me."

The Killer responded, "Psalm 23:4-6."

"You know your bible, mister, yet you gonna do some killing today?"

"Yes, ma'am, but I am curious to know, why did you say that you were expecting me?"

"Oh, son, I know things. I know a lotta things. The good Lord talks to me in ways that others can't hear, or at least, I should say, choose not to hear."

"Interesting, normally part of the exhilaration of doing what I do, is the enjoyment of watching the trembling fear on the faces of those whose lives I take. You are taking some of the fun out of this."

"Oh, how 'bout I make the situation more rousing for ya, sir?"

"And how might that be?"

"Before you kill me, I'd like you to pray with me."
"Now, why on earth would I want to do that?"
"Think about it, sir, how stimulating it might be for ya to pray with the person that you're about to take the life from in this world. Would that not grant you a sense of power and dominance that you so desire?"
"Great point. Okay, I'll play the game. Let us pray."
The elderly black woman took his left hand. He still held the pickleball paddle in his right hand. She then began her prayer, "Dear Lord, thank you for the gift that you have brought me here today. He is sending me to you, my Lord. I am more than willing to release myself of all burden and sin and be at your side for all eternity. "
She then turns to the killer, facing him in the eye.
"I forgive you for what you are about to do. You will be called upon someday to make up for your transgressions. I will be here for you and message your assignment to you when that day of judgment shall rise. Amen"
"Amen"
"Not sure how you're going to give me an assignment when your seconds away from being buried six feet under."
"Only my body shall turn to dust. The soul shall forever be present."
"Whatever you say, lady!" The Killer then pulled a lever on the handle of the pickleball paddle. Rising from the outer edge of the paddle were several triangle-shaped blades that now surrounded the paddle. He sliced her throat. She slid off the rocking chair to her death.

....

    A half-hour after waking up, Randall heard the Morning News from anchor Julie Kennedy. She announced she had breaking news, and then reported the murder of Elaine Stewart.
    Elaine was an African American woman in her 80s. She lived just a few blocks away. He recognized her face, as her picture was shown on the screen while Julie Kennedy spoke. Randall often saw her sitting on her front porch while he took his morning jog. Well, he used to take jogs, but in the last couple of months, he had replaced running with eating *Doritos*, *Captain Crunch* cereal, *Hershey* bars and whatever sugar-filled pleasure he might sink his teeth into. But back when he did run, he would see her rocking on her porch swing while knitting something or another. He never acknowledged Elaine. But he did admire her. He often thought to himself that at least someone is out being productive at 7:30 in the morning. He thought many of his fellow Wichita citizens wasted their lives away, sleeping past 7 a.m. Well, unless they were up banging harder-than-a-rock Wiffle balls against a garage door with an oversized ping-pong paddle.
    Since Randall did know of her, he quickly jumped up from his sleepy stupor to hear more. Not much information was given on Elaine Stewart, but he perked up more when Julie Kennedy announced that this was the third murder in the mid-west in the past six weeks in which the victim's face was covered in peanut butter. Julie Kennedy further reported that the peanut butter was

painted so smoothly and carefully that it almost looked like the victim was wearing a mask.

"A serial killer with a fascination with peanut butter; this is even odd by serial killer standards," Randall mused.

Elaine was killed on Friday, May the 27th. Of the other two victims, one was killed in St. Louis just less than two weeks ago on Sunday the 15th, and the other was slaughtered in Kansas City six weeks ago to the day on April 16th.

"Peanut Butter Killer? Really? If three had not died, it would almost be laughable. It just didn't fit the mold of a serial killer. The last serial killer in Wichita was BTK; Bind Torture and Kill would be what the coward would sell as his MO. There were labels such as the Green River Killer. You had the Acid Bath Murderer, Doctor Death, and so on and so forth. All had some semblance of toughness, even though without weapons, none of the crazy killing bastards were capable of fighting their way out of a wet paper sack. So, selling him or herself as "The Peanut Butter Killer" was utterly baffling to Randall.

Randall turned off the television to try and distance himself from the situation. He attempted to have no thoughts at all. Randall continuously argued with himself by notifying himself that this was not his problem. He tried unsuccessfully to transfer his thoughts on the matter to one of amusement rather than fear. He told himself that some other homicide detective would have his hands full.

"Better him than me," were the last words in his mind before he set off for a drive down to Home Depot. He convinced himself of the need for a plunger for his toilet in case it clogged up. He, of course, already had a plunger, but he rationalized he probably needed a new one, as it was old. (He had purchased the plunger just five years ago and it had barely ever been used.) Randall could probably count on one hand how many times the toilet was clogged since its purchase. But he needed a mission, a purpose, a reason. Going to Home Depot for a plunger would be that goal for the day. "How pathetic that this is the height of my day," he told himself.

    He knew every employee at the local Home Depot, and they all knew him. And most knew why he was there; to make conversation over household products that are rarely to never needed or used in his home. They humored him by acting amazed by the inquisitive questions that he had. They reminded him often how grateful they were to learn from Mr. Randall Baines, just before Randall purchased whatever product had sparked the discussion. Deep down inside, Randall knew they were making him feel good to maintain customer service. He felt pathetic that he needed this to provide himself with reasons for self-worth. Mr. Baines walked up to his old beat-up F-150. He took the plunger out of the unnecessary Home Depot bag and threw it in the back of the pick-up. Why throw it in the back? He could get it dirty. It could fly out, become damaged, etc. Inside he knew the plunger had no true purpose. It was simply the mission of the day to obtain it.

....

PEANUT BUTTER PICKLEBALL AND MURDER

Grandma Edna was an extraordinary woman. Although she was sixty-seven years old, one would think her possibly in her mid-fifties. Her complexion was clear, dark, and wonderfully alluring. Her eyes were beautifully brown rays of wonder that were further accentuated by eyebrows so perfectly placed that Cleopatra would have been filled with jealousy. Edna was also very athletic. Her figure could be credited to one six-letter word – tennis.

She had played tennis since she was five years old. She was a two-time state champion for Hoisington High - a small town in Central Kansas. Edna had never technically been a citizen of Hoisington. She lived half a block away from a small green sign that said welcome to Hoisington. As many as a hundred people lived that half a block away from that sign, but Hoisington would lay no claim to the black community. Although things had changed over the years and Hoisington had recently extended its borders to include all its true residents, the bitterness and hurt still haunted Edna Reynolds.

Since her childhood was spent growing up in a home that should have been condemned, a hobby of hers had been collecting cardinals. She had cardinal salt and pepper shakers, cardinal figurines, and cardinal bath towels. She had several bird feeders in the backyard, as she hoped to see the cherry-colored bird enjoying a good meal of sunflower seeds, grain, and lettuce. What was her fascination with the little bird? It was Hoisington High's mascot.

Although the pain of the little Kansas town's prejudice stung worse than killer bees, representing the Cardinal tennis team as its number one player symbolized hope. Her white teammates loved her. Although they had grown up hearing N-word jokes and were led to believe that the white race was superior, they couldn't help but be drawn to Edna. Edna was not shy, but she wasn't exactly full of personality, either. It was her tenacity to achieve that won her teammates' hearts. She sought not only her own success, but that of her teammates, as well. She spent endless hours working with even the JV players to help them get better. JV players wouldn't help the varsity team, but they might make better humans by learning to follow instructions. She liked her tennis coach, as he treated her well and appeared to care less about the color of her skin, but he wasn't exactly a tennis instructor. Coach Troy Smith was an excellent science teacher, but he knew little of tennis. The school needed a body, and so he would be that body. Mr. Smith had no problem with his number one player being the real tennis coach.

After high school, Edna received a tennis scholarship to Fort Hays State University. Fort Hays State was a small school at the time, although it is now the third largest college in Kansas and an NCAA Division II college.

Edna would do well playing for Fort Hays, but not exceptional. She was an average varsity player at best, but she proved to be very helpful to her teammates and coach. This allowed her to eventually become the head tennis instructor at Sterling College, as well as a very good business instructor.

Edna eventually met the man of her dreams, Edward Reynolds. He was a moderately successful black man who owned Reynolds Mattress Company. Although his mattress company was doing well and provided him with a fine middle-class income, it boomed once Edna lent her expertise to the business aspect of the mattress world. Reynolds' mattresses went from being sold at one location in Wichita, to being sold in three locations. Edward and Edna would reside in Wichita at the home that Edward had owned and lived in the four years before he had met Edna. He had purchased the house at just twenty-eight years of age.

This home, which was located next to Randall Baines' home, was a nice, comfortable, red Victorian home with four bedrooms and a large two-car garage. It was a nice but modest home for a business-savvy, upper-middle-class couple. They had two children: Andre and Brandon. Andre lived in Connecticut with his wife, Peggy, and their three children. Andre owned his own mattress company there. Brandon worked for his parents, intending to take over their mattress business and possibly even merge with his brother Andre's business eventually. They had thought they might expand the mattress business across America and possibly even further. Everything in Edna's world was good. Well, until that dreadful December day four years earlier.

Brandon and his wife Stephanie had been traveling to drop some mattresses off at the Hutchinson location. Generally, Stephanie did not go along with Brandon, but Edna convinced them to allow her to watch their three kids for them to spend time together, even if it was work-related. Not long after they left, a whitetail doe ran in front of them. Brandon swerved to avoid the deer and nearly went into the ditch. Brandon overcorrected, turning the truck too far left. It slid into a semi-truck, killing Brandon instantly and leaving Stephanie to cling to life for seven days before she passed away. Edna's world crumbled. Stephanie grew up in foster homes and had no siblings or parents to raise the children.

Edward and Edna quickly found themselves filling the roles of parents, as well as grandparents, to the kids. And if the despair felt from losing her son and daughter-in-law was not tragedy enough, her husband Edward passed away just five months later from a massive heart attack. The stress of running the stores, in addition to the heartache of losing his son, was just far too much for Edward to bear, leaving Edna to watch over their grandkids by herself.

Elijah was now 14, Matthew 16, and Keisha 18. Even four years after the loss of her husband, Edna still felt overwhelmed. Edna filled her roles as mother and grandmother well, but guilt prevented her from seeing this. She felt guilt every time any of the children made her smile and feel happy. She thought to herself that the reason both of their parents were dead was because of her suggestion that they take the load of mattresses to Hutchinson. Now their children would never see them on Earth again. She felt that she had no right to feel any sort of happiness at all.

....

"Good morning, Grandma," Keisha lovingly said as she gave her Grandma Edna a kiss on the cheek. Edna, being the general that she was, replied,

"Good morning, Keisha. Now go get your brothers out of bed. They have slept long enough. "

"Ahh, let them sleep in, Grandma. I'll help you prepare Saturday brunch."

Edna argued briefly with her but decided that Keisha was right. They'd just be in the way. Edna instructed Keisha to put up the "cucumber stuff" and get to work. Keisha knew that her grandma was well aware that the equipment she had in her hands was pickleball equipment, but Edna often attempted to make Keisha think that she couldn't remember, to try to display the insignificance of pickleball. Keisha dropped the paddle and the balls from her left armpit in the living room. Her grandma, of course, reminded her to put them up in her room after brunch. In her left hand was the Follett book. Keisha entered the kitchen and dumped it in the trash can near Edna.

"What are you doing, child? "

Keisha explained what old man Baines did to her, describing the book as having "missed her by inches." Edna immediately scolded Keisha for throwing the book away. She demanded that she thank Mr. Baines for the book and read it. Keisha tried to convince her that because of the book's penchant for air flight, its cover was in disarray. Edna simply pointed out that she could recover the book, and the cover has nothing to do with the words inside of it. Edna then made it clear that Keisha *would* read the book. Keisha pouted and grumbled, as she thought what a dread it would be to read a book with over a THOUSAND pages in it by some old white European dude, but she didn't argue much. She knew arguing with Grandma Edna about this was a losing battle.

Throwing any book away was inexcusable to Edna. Books were knowledge, even bad ones, because they were written for a reason. As they prepared the pancake batter, set the table, and placed bacon on the griddle, Edna continuously tried to convince Keisha to give up the "silly cucumber game." Edna felt as though it would hurt Keisha's tennis game. Keisha had graduated from a Catholic School a few days ago yet was still undecided on where she wanted to go to college. Edna wanted her to take one of the few scholarships in tennis and track & field that were still offered to her. Many colleges had rescinded their offers by mid-April to give their scholarships to someone else instead of chancing to leave a vacant spot on their rosters. Keisha took 7th in the state in tennis her senior year, giving her opportunities at Division II colleges. In addition, Keisha was a track and field star. She qualified for the state championships and medaled in several events every year during her four years of high school. Keisha's two best events were the high jump and the long jump. She took 3rd in the state in high jump her junior year and won the state championship in the high jump two weeks ago. Also, she had just successfully defended her state champion status in the long jump. Several NCAA Division 1 colleges offered her full-ride scholarships in track and field. Edna didn't mind if Keisha went to college on a track and field scholarship, but she hoped that Keisha would choose a school to play tennis.

Edna was not rich. Sure, she was living comfortably, but not enough to set her up in life in today's society if she spent her money foolishly. But she did have enough funds to provide Keisha and her two brothers with a good education. Plus, their father, Brandon, had left a modest life insurance policy that Edna had the option to release to the children at her discretion. But handouts were not what Edna or her late husband, Edward, were about. You worked for what you had and lived a conservative lifestyle, as you never know when it all might be taken away from you.

Keisha knew exactly why her grandmother wanted her to do well in tennis. A scholarship in tennis or track and field would be instrumental in getting a great education. Keisha's grades in school were okay but not stellar. If Keisha could pay most of her way, Grandma would help her with the rest. She needed to continue to succeed in tennis. The truth is, she didn't even like tennis, but the feel of that tough, heavy-but-firm pickleball paddle sometimes made her feel invincible.

At times, she felt so angry over the sudden death of her parents that the feeling of smacking the pickleball with her graphite carbon fiber paddle was her only relief from the pain.

Keisha would tell her grandmother not to worry. Keisha continuously tried to convince Edna that pickleball would not hurt her ability to play tennis. Keisha often informed her grandmother how much pickleball helped her net game, gave her a different perspective, etc. But her arguments fell on deaf ears. Edna was set in her tennis ways. Edna did not spend countless hours teaching Keisha the art of tennis just to let her throw a good education away over a silly game named after a dried-out cucumber.

CHAPTER 2

Randall drove to an IHOP. It might be late in the morning, but a good omelet was still on his mind. He looked at the small screen on his iPhone 5 and checked Facebook (now known as Meta) while sipping his coffee. He didn't check his Facebook account much. He wasn't even sure why he had it, but he figured it might have some value to him at some point. He had just seventy-five friends and maybe only truly paid attention to five of them; one being his daughter, of course. He would usually get depressed seeing pictures of his daughter. He saw a picture of Samantha, and his granddaughter, Hanna, in Branson, Missouri. Also, in that same picture was his daughter's mother. This angered him.

He remembered the great times that he, his daughter, and Pam had at Silver Dollar City. Now the trips apparently continued without him. He quickly scrolled past the pic.

He saw a breaking news feed from the Star Action News page that he followed. The site provided information on the so-labeled Peanut Butter Killer. The site reported the names of the other two victims. In St. Louis, it was a white man, forty-five years of age, named Charles Ogafer. He left behind three children and his wife of 25 years. The Kansas City victim, Renee Booker, was just nineteen. She was a white woman in her sophomore year at UMKC. She was on the varsity soccer team. Randall was baffled.
"Three victims of different ages, races, and backgrounds. This will be a tough one for the FBI, Wichita, St. Louis, and Kansas City Police Departments."

Randall began to feel empathetic toward the victims. But he told himself that he was happy it was not his problem. Detective life was in the past. He slammed another cup of coffee in one gulp. Randall often did this when he was nervous. He wondered why he felt so anxious. He tried to convince himself that he was still angry about seeing his daughter, grandchild, and ex-wife living it up in Branson, or that maybe he was just lonely and bored.

Although all of these were true, he knew they weren't the match that sparked the flush of anxiety. Those fretful thoughts derived from one thing and one thing only. "THERE IS A KILLER ON THE LOOSE, AND THE BASTARD JUST MADE HIS LAST KILLING IN MY NEIGHBORHOOD!"

The Killer was not operating in only one area, but in multiple cities. This was something he never had to deal with as a detective with the Wichita PD. All his cases were near. He knew it was not his place to find The Killer, but he also knew it was not in his DNA to let it go. For the first time in two years, Randall Baines was preparing to work on a case, with or without a paycheck.

Tara arrived at his table with his omelet and toast. Tara was a cute girl about eighteen years of age. She was slender, perky, and dark-haired. He liked her because she looked and acted a lot like his own daughter when she was eighteen.

Tara stated that she would be right back as she realized she had forgotten his favorite condiments for his toast. Although he had not asked for them, she knew him well enough that she knew exactly what he wanted.

"Oh, Mr. Baines, I'm so sorry. I forgot the peanut butter and strawberry jelly for your toast."

"Bring the strawberry jelly, but I'll pass on the peanut butter today. Thank you."

………

No, it wasn't a huge crowd. After all, it was pickleball, probably soon to be declared an Olympic sport, but still not something that packed the seats. Nevertheless, it was something he was good at, and he enjoyed the accolades he got for it. An audience of around forty might not sound like much, but considering the sport is pickleball, and the location was a town by a beach on the Gulf of Mexico on a warm sunny day, getting forty people to walk away from the waves to watch the championship was impressive. The enthusiastic crowd watched him and his partner take second in the championship of 5.0 co-ed doubles.

Of course, to The Killer, if he had a better partner who could have selected her kill-and-dink shots correctly, they would have won the whole damn thing easily. But he was okay with going home with a medal. He figured he had something to show for his day-long adventure with the broad, who had nice, tan legs and luscious boobs. Those double D breasts talked to him in a manner that he could not resist, even if he was angry with her. He wanted her. And that night in the hotel, he would have her. The naked intimacy was a temporary pathway to fulfill his desire for exaltation. But in his eyes, he saw her as nothing more than the bitch that lost him the championship. Second place was okay, but to feel complete, he needed more- much more.

After he exited her, the orgasm that she had experienced left her in blissful, erotic peace, thus moving her expeditiously from consciousness to a serene, dreamlike state of tranquility. Her tethered sense of happiness did not allow her to notice The Killer's absence.

He hit the streets in his 2022 Mercedes Benz. He soon found an obscure beach area five miles from the city limits. There, walking barefoot alongside the waves that violently crashed upon the sand, was a man of Asian ethnicity. He was fascinated by the calmness and serene look that the man had.

"It is Friday night. Shouldn't he be at a bar looking for girls?" He was fit and handsome enough. Or, if he had enough conquests in the lady department, wouldn't he want to hang out with his buddies and guzzle down some Buds at one of the many pubs in the area? But no, the bastard chose to walk alone. He deserved to die if this was his idea of life. So, it is time to put him out of his misery. That bitch lost me the championship! How could she continuously dink the ball WAY too fucking high? What the hell was she thinking?"

The Killer swiftly retrieved his pickleball bag and his trusted paddle. He looked at it briefly but then put it back in his bag. He then pulled out a different pickleball paddle that he personally had designed and built. It looked like any other pickleball paddle, except for the triangle blades embedded into the paddle.

He pulled up the lever on the handle to make the triangle blades rise from the outer edge of the paddle. He marveled at the idea that he had invented the world's first switchblade pickleball paddle. The triangle blades nested against each other all around the edge of his paddle. He was proud of his paddle weapon. He thought he could probably sell the product on eBay, but then his murderous hobby would be discovered. So, the only admiration for the switchblade pickleball paddle would have to come from him and him alone. Well, and from his victims, of course.

He snuck up from behind the sand-traveling Asian man and slashed him over the head quickly, fast, and without hesitation. The man didn't know what hit him. He was aware of The Killer's presence behind him for no more than a second before the blades on the paddle struck, slicing through his skull. The young man screamed in agony. Not wanting anyone to see or to draw attention to the area, The Killer's hand swept across the man's mouth, silencing him. He screamed no more. The angry athlete finished him off by snapping the young man's neck.

A jar of peanut butter was taken from the pickleball bag. The Killer decided to change the whole paint-the-face-in-peanut-butter-thing up. The Killer ripped the front of the victim's tank top shirt. The Killer pulled a razor out of his bag and swiftly shaved the victim's chest. He then dipped his finger into the jar and spelled out in peanut butter across the victim's ribs – THE PB KILLER

The Killer now considered the Galveston Island Pro-Am to have been a stunning success. After all, a good, cold-blooded beach murder was a massively larger thrill than the damn tin "gold" medal he missed out on, along with the measly two thousand dollars in prize money. Blood covered his face. As he sat in his Mercedes, he started to drive away. He thought that a shower was a must, but not yet. He looked in his review mirror and admired the dead man's blood covering his face. He shouted to himself, "There's my beloved prize for the day. Who needs a damn medal?"

He got out of the Mercedes, walked back to the water's edge, and tossed the disgusting runner-up medal into the crashing waves as he laughed a most sinister and wicked laugh.

He jumped back into the Mercedes. The Killer pulled an INXS CD out of his pickleball bag and played his favorite song – "Devil Inside." He cranked up the stereo system. He then drove off, as far and fast as he could from the murder scene, back to the hotel.

The Killer walked into the hotel with his hood over his face and his head down. He washed up in the restroom area near the fitness room. He removed his clothes and slipped back into bed, putting his arms around Tasha. Well, to the rest of the world, her name was Tasha, but to him, she was still the bitch that lost him the championship. She grasped his hands. Tasha eagerly whispered, "You are an animal! Ready to go again?"
"Hell, yes!"
He was full of excitement. Sleep was the last thing on his mind. His hormones allowed him to temporarily forgive his lover for her awful dink play on the court. After all, if they had won that championship game, he might not have had the fortitude to immerse himself in another kill. Seconds before entering her for the second time that night, he thought to himself, "Awe pickleball paddle for sport, pickleball weapon for thrill and my peach-colored pickle in the bad-dink bitch."

CHAPTER 3

With Ryan Chang being the fourth victim, the sickening acts by the madman were now portrayed on every news outlet in the nation. CNN, FOX News, MSNBC, CBS Morning News, you name it. Everyone across the nation had at least *heard* of the Peanut Butter Killer. This time The Killer waited just six days to strike his next victim.

The murderer was running on his treadmill. He was surrounded by the most expensive workout equipment that Amazon could possibly sell. The room was filled with dumbbells of every weight, an elliptical, a rowing machine, a pull-up bar, and more. A 70-inch Samsung TV rested high in the middle of a wall behind the exercise equipment.

While working out on Sunday, June the 5th, two days after the beach slaying, The Killer was watching Star Action News. The words – "BREAKING NEWS" – appeared on the screen. The news anchor informed viewers that the Peanut Butter Killer had struck again, this time at a beach on Galveston Island.

The Killer's footsteps on the treadmill increased from 3.5 miles per hour to 8.5. The more that news anchor Julie Kennedy revealed about the case, the faster his feet on the treadmill moved. He felt a sense of intense euphoria.

Obtaining a live audience of forty or more for championship pickleball matches was nice, but the thrill of knowing an entire nation was in fear of him left him experiencing an elation that made him feel immortal. He had the power to take a human life with a personally designed original weapon.

The Killer, however, was bothered by the fact that it took three days from the time of the Galveston killing for it to reach national news status. He was happy that he was finally getting recognition for his bloodthirsty peanut butter accomplishments. But he would need to do more to reach a Ted Bundy status.

Mrs. Kennedy further stated that Ryan Chang was a successful computer software programmer. He had created software programs with his brother, philanthropist Justin Chang. Justin Chang owned several companies with a net worth of around $1.5 billion. Mrs. Kennedy further reported that Justin Chang was offering a $2.5 million reward for anyone with information that led to the capture of the person or persons who killed his brother.

Instead of seeing this as a threat, The Killer was elated. "I thought I nailed a small fish, but I knocked off a shark instead."

The doorbell rang. A feeling of annoyance gripped him. He let it ring a couple of times until finally, he answered the door. How dare any visitor disturb him in his moment of triumph? He looked through the peephole. He saw his co-doubles partner standing there in a short skirt and a skimpy, red blouse. He opened the door and greeted her with displeasure, "What do you want, Tasha?"

She picked up on his anger immediately. "I-I-I-I-I'm sorry. I just thought I'd bring over some wine to celebrate our victory."

He stared at the wine in her hands. "What victory?"

"Our second-place silver, baby "

"Second place is not much of a victory."

She then kissed him on the cheek. "We could create another kind of win!"

The Killer grabbed Tasha and pulled her into his house. Although she was twelve years younger than him, in his mind, he was the youthful and more vibrant person in the so-called relationship.

He threw her on his leather couch. He ripped open her red blouse and placed his lips on her right breast. He roughly licked her tits. The Killer then moved his tongue up to her neck. She smiled. The blond, with her perfect tan body, revealed all of herself to him, taking the rest of what was left of her blouse off. There was nothing left to remove. She was not wearing a bra or panties in anticipation of this moment. She took off his shirt. She ran her finger down the middle of his chest. "I find the perfectly aligned discoloration of your body entrancing, amorously alluring, and sexy as hell."

"At least somebody feels that way about it," he replied.

The killer kicked off his shoes and kept his socks on. After quickly pulling his workout shorts and briefs off, he grasped her breasts and aggressively rubbed them. The Killer thrust himself into her. She moved her mouth up next to his ear as he continued to please her internally. The beautiful blond pickleball player whispered, "Oh, you are my champion!" He smiled and stroked her harder to further confirm her acknowledgment of him as a winner.

....

Randall Baines felt that he had lost his edge. He didn't know where to begin. His lack of confidence in investigating the case of the psychotic peanut butter freak derived from his forced retirement from the Wichita PD.
Mr. Baines had not been keeping up with more advanced methods of investigating, ranging from computer searches on past criminals to attempting to understand and analyze all that DNA stuff. He felt dejected that a twenty-six-year-old kid named Tomas Menzies, fresh out of graduate school from Wichita State, took his place. This kid had no experience other than a two-month internship with the Park City PD. The kid spent those sixty days learning reports, computer stuff, and more computer crap, along with calling numbers to ask questions of people who would skip town the second they got off the phone with him, anyway. Detective Menzies had no hands-on training. It drove Randall crazy knowing the little computer geek had replaced a Vietnam Vet with decades of experience. "What has the world come to?"
These thoughts in his head had multiplied hundreds of times over the past couple of years at any reminders of his forced termination. Sure, he had reached retirement age, but he had considered himself fired all the same. Instincts and experience

meant nothing. Randall viewed Tomas as nothing more than a punk-ass kid who had taken his job as a detective.

After his temporary feel-sorry-for-himself session had played itself out, Randall marched on with his objective. Some freaking nut case with a fascination for peanut butter wasn't going to progress much further with this murderous path, as far as Randall was concerned. But Randall did consider that if he did fail on this find-a-killer quest, it really wouldn't matter. He felt he had nothing to lose. At worst, he would simply go back to his usual mundane, boring existence.

As excited as Randall was at the prospect that he had something worthwhile to do, he did wish that it wasn't necessary. The pain and anguish the victims' families suffered had to be unbearable. At the same time, the empathy that he felt for the victims and their families acted as his motivation.

Randall was disappointed that he was never given a chance to work on the BTK case. He often thought about investigating the case on his own but didn't want to "piss off" the wrong people. Now he had no people to answer to. He was working for himself. More importantly, he was working for the safety and security of the Wichita community and beyond. This was his opportunity to catch a serial killer. Randall was confident that he did have one advantage over the KBI, FBI, and four city police departments, and that was his keen sense for looking at more than the obvious possibilities.

His way of thinking a little outside the box was mostly taking the time to do just that - think. Despite his lack of knowledge of the latest up-and-coming computer techniques, he wasn't computer illiterate. Randall began by googling websites for assistance.

Randall learned that peanut butter contains a plant sterol called beta-sitosterol, which works to fight against stress. If The Killer was a Peanut Butter Freak, he might not realize that his body craved the substance because a person with a desire to kill probably had a higher stress level than others. Randall also thought the peanut butter thing might be tied to a high-stress job.

BTK had killed to fulfill pure, sadistic, bizarre, sick sexual desires, but this type of killer must be tied to anger over some position he held in the peanut butter world. Why else would he make a point of incorporating peanut butter into the murders? Not much to go on, but he figured he had to start somewhere.

Randall googled high-stress positions that lead to violent behavior. He soon learned that often it wasn't the position that led to violent behavior, but the lack of respect that the person might have felt in his work position. Perhaps The Killer felt disrespected by a boss or co-workers. The research pointed to a man who felt very upset, possibly about being passed up for a promotion. The violence usually occurs in the person's place of business or where they live.

The Peanut Butter Killer had murdered people in four different cities. Three cities were relatively close to each other, but the fourth murder, in Galveston, Texas, was six hundred miles or more away from the other cities. Randall reflected further.

At the Wichita PD, he conducted the heaviest part of his thinking while going for a jog, playing racquetball with his buddies, or lifting weights at the academy. But his favorite hobby in retirement was eating popcorn smothered with butter, with honey drizzled over it. Sitting and eating made him feel helpless to the powers of gluttony. His willpower in both mind and body was crumbling. Randall wished he could do something more. He wanted something to help him feel good about himself again. Searching for this killer gave him something he hadn't had in a very long time- HOPE.

CHAPTER 4

Cluck Putoo Puh - Cluck Putoo Puh - Cluck Putoo Puh

Once again, Randall sat with a book on yet another early Saturday morning.

Cluck Putoo Puh - Cluck Putoo Puh - Cluck Putoo Puh

7:03 a.m. – The teenage girl was with her younger brother. The monstrous ping-pong paddles in their hands hit the harder-than-a-rock Wiffle ball back and forth across the driveway to each other. It truly was an indestructible Wiffle ball from hell.

Cluck Putoo Puh - Cluck Putoo Puh - Cluck Putoo Puh

BACK AND FORTH, BACK AND FORTH, BACK AND FORTH. The infuriating sound was maddening to Randall. "Now the girl even has one of her brothers up early making unnecessary noise," he thought.

He knew there was no option A, B, C, or any other letter in the alphabet that might restore the peaceful solitude of reading Follett. Although he wasn't a poor man, he still wasn't well off enough to afford to buy any more Follett books of the same title twice. Therefore, throwing his second copy of *World Without End* was not an option.

Cluck Putoo Puh - Cluck Putoo Puh - Cluck Putoo Puh

7:05 a.m. – Knowing the young kids next door would not stop their silly ping-pong-Wiffle-ball game anytime soon, he decided to go downstairs and pour himself a large bowl of *Fruity Pebbles* and indulge himself in the sugary cereal pleasure. Without the opportunity to envelop himself in the one positive hobby he still retained (reading), his mind raced in several different directions.

His first thought was bewilderment. He couldn't understand the enticement of the weird pong game to the two kids. His mind then floated back to the Peanut Butter Killer. Randall retrieved his lone jar of peanut butter and stared at the container. He read every word on the jar. He looked at all the nutrition facts, from calories to sugar content to preservatives. He tried to imagine how any of it could lead to murders in multiple cities but could think of nothing. He considered working out but instead decided to pour himself another bowl of *Fruity Pebbles*.

Randall felt immensely frustrated, and the frustration grew each time he heard the oversized ping-pong paddle striking the rock-hard Wiffle ball.

Cluck Putoo Puh - Cluck Putoo Puh - Cluck Putoo Puh

7:20 a.m. – Randall rocked in his recliner. The younger brother was evidently not as passionate about the stupid, paddle, toddler ball game because Randall once again heard the banging of the kiddie Wiffle ball against the garage door. Randall closed his eyes, hoping to go back to sleep. But he knew his body and mind. He knew that sleeping wasn't going to happen anymore today. His feelings of annoyance, worthlessness, and loneliness had him begging God to let him sleep, to forget his dismal life, if even for just a little while.

7:25 a.m. – Randall acknowledged the fact that he would not be getting any more sleep. He tried to read his second copy of Follett's *World Without End* once again. The banging doesn't stop. A burning hatred toward Wiffle balls and ping-pong paddles engulfs his mind.

Cluck Putoo Puh - Cluck Putoo Puh - Cluck Putoo Puh

7:33 a.m. – Randall's front door opens, and yet another copy of Follett's classic work takes flight. Luckily for Keisha, her trusted, oversized ping-pong paddle smashes into the book, deflecting Follett from striking her in the head. Once again, Keisha expresses her appreciation for Mr. Baines by telling him he is her number one guy, with her middle finger rising on another weekend morning.

....

Randall Baines was not much for funerals. Funerals were just a reminder of how short life really is. It was not that he did not care about those who passed away. It was more the opposite. He felt the pain of the families who lost their loved ones and, more importantly, the complete agony for those who lost loved ones unexpectedly in car wrecks or due to sudden heart attacks, suicides, or murder.

Murder was the reason Randall attended the somber occasion of Elaine Stewart's funeral. He knew that asking family members and loved ones questions as they searched for solace would be inappropriate, but he paid his respects and listened.

Although the vast majority of those in attendance were African American, there was a fair share of white attendees, as well. Everyone knew Elaine as the loving neighborhood favorite who had visited the doorstep of each of those who lived on her block with a freshly baked cherry pie or batch of her coveted chocolate chip cookies.

Randall blended in well enough that no one paid him much notice. He did not know many of the people who attended the service personally, but he did know most of their faces. He saw his next-door neighbors, the Reynolds family, sitting towards the front. He was most glad that he would not run into his oversized, ping-pong-paddle-loving adversary since he was clear in the back of the very packed church. Odds were one in a thousand that they even knew he was there at all, he told himself.

The flowers for the service were spread throughout the church. Coincidentally, the arrangement of chrysanthemums he had sent was positioned near him, at the back of the church. He was pleased with the local florist's artistic talent. Of course, being Randall's style, the name on the arrangement simply read, caring citizen, leaving his name absent from the tag.

Through Pastor John's eulogy, Randall learned of Elaine's caring nature. She was the mother of three grown daughters and one grown son, all with children of their own. Her husband, Mark, had passed away fifteen years earlier from cancer. She was a retired cook for a local public school, fitting her caring personality. He attended the lunch, listening to conversations that centered mostly on her generous, warm-hearted ways. She tithed consistently, giving 15% of her income to the church, along with the hundred dollars that automatically came out of her checking account monthly to St. Jude Children's Research Hospital.

The information that Randall received from the funeral did not appear to be connected to the serial killer. He still found attending the funeral useful. He was able to pay his respects, which led him to conclude that the Peanut Butter Freak was not choosing his victims with any real rhyme or reason at all. The victims were of different ages, races, and lived in different cities. None could be found to have a dark side, and none of them had anything in common. This might not seem like much to many detectives, but to Randall Baines, it was everything. This was because he could eliminate the tedious time spent trying to find logical answers to senseless actions. Instead, he could work on finding a correlation between time and place between the murders.

When Randall got back home, he studied and read everything he could find out about peanut butter. Of course, the logical place to look would be peanut butter companies, and that would be no different than every FBI, state bureau of investigation, and police department that had a peanut butter murder victim in their jurisdiction, not to mention the private investigators out for the $2.5 million reward.

All agencies had first tried to find a disgruntled employee of one of the factories. They were looking for a worker that had either been fired or was passed over for promotion. Generally, the description of the psycho would be a white male in his late twenties or early thirties looking for a promotion but was passed over for those with much more common sense. The worker was probably socially awkward with very few, if any, friends. This seemed to be the quintessential image of a psychotic freak. The freak would often make the news for walking into his place, or former place, of employment and shooting to kill every harmless being he could find; his warped purpose to feed his thirst for revenge and in his own mind, a misguided need to increase his feelings of masculinity. Without a powerful semi-automatic weapon, this type of coward would hide in a bunker, fearing for his life against a third grader.

What is the difference between the store mass murderers and the Peanut Butter Freak? The store murderers wanted instant and immediate name publicity, not minding at all if it meant instant death, a life behind bars, or an all-expense paid hands-on experience visit to an electric chair. On the other hand, the Peanut Butter Freak wanted recognition and fame, but not at the expense of his freedom or death.

………

Randall began his peanut butter enterprise search with the largest of all, *JIF*. *JIF* was owned by the *J.M. Smucker Company*. It was a company out of Orville, Ohio, with little connection to St. Louis, Kansas City, Galveston Island, or Wichita. Next, Randall studied *Peter Pan,* owned by *Post Holdings* and made in their plant in Sylvester, Georgia. He discovered that peanut butter was primarily served in tin cans until WW II. Then after a metal shortage, *Peter Pan* began selling their peanut butter in glass jars. He moved on to *Skippy*. It has its main plant in Little Rock, Arkansas, along with a plant in China. He found it interesting that *Skippy* was the best-selling peanut butter in China. He even looked at off-brand peanut butter products such as *Kroger*, which is generally sold at *Dillons* grocery stores, and *Great Value*, which is sold at *Walmart* stores.

Randall spent two days researching peanut butter products, and to his dismay, he did not find any connection to the cities where victims of the Peanut Butter were killed. Randall concluded that it wasn't exactly peanut butter that would provide the crucial hint to identify the killer, but something else. Yes, there would be a reason for the use of peanut butter in his killings, but that famously smooth, brown product might not be the key.

Randall noted that all the murders were committed on a Friday, Saturday, or Sunday. This told Randall that The Killer either chose the weekends because he had a job during the week or there was an event that happened on weekends that he enjoyed attending. Randall decided rather quickly that this was not the stereotypical later-twenties-early-thirties-disgruntled-employee that personified whom all the hotshot FBI agents and investigators were looking for, but something very, very different. The guy probably had a very established job that he was highly successful at, or else he wouldn't be able to afford to travel all over the Midwest and even into the Deep South. And traveling was not part of his job, as most companies conduct a major part of their business during weekdays. This was a weekend killer.

Randall used deductive reasoning to further conclude that The Killer was not visiting these cities for pure enjoyment. Yes,

Galveston would be a great tourist hotspot, but the others, unfortunately, not so much. He considered this unfortunate because he knew the treasures that Wichita had to offer, with its new minor league baseball team, the Wichita Wind Surge (a Double-A team), the Mid-America All-Indian Museum, and many other interesting venues. Randall loved Kansas City. Randall's thoughts of Kansas City were of the most beautiful baseball stadium in the country, Kauffman Stadium, which was world-renowned for its fountains behind the right-field fence.

And Arrowhead Stadium is arguably the best place for tailgating in America, as well as housing the football team led by Patrick Mahomes. Also, KC is home to the Negro League Museum and the National WWI Museum and Memorial. It has fantastic jazz music, a NASCAR speedway, Sporting KC (an American men's professional soccer club), and all the shopping venues anyone could want. If a person likes great barbecue, Kansas City is the barbecue capital of the world with Arthur Bryant's Barbeque, Q39, Joe's, and Gates Bar-B-Q, just to name a few.

Randall's mind then turned to St. Louis. His mind immediately flashed to beer. He loved the taste of cold beer that came straight from the brewery at the Anheuser–Busch plant. Of course, nothing could beat visiting the beautiful Gateway Arch, with its newly renovated museum that outlines the rugged terrain and lifestyle of our pioneer ancestors as they traveled west for land, gold, and fur harvesting. Then there are the St. Louis Cardinals and their extremely rich baseball history. Of course, St. Louis was also the home of the NHL hockey team, the St. Louis Blues.

It did bewilder Randall as to why these beautiful places weren't hotspots for most Americans to visit. Nonetheless, they appeared to have become hotspots for one particular visitor, in any case. The Killer did not use guns, meaning that he was probably athletic. To kill someone with a knife, even the evidently very sharp system he had used on his victims, would take a very fit and aggressive human. That thought then sparked the idea that the Peanut Butter Freak might be into athletic events, either as a spectator or participant. Randall first turned to the major sporting events. He had killed in Wichita and Galveston, but both locations were close enough to Kansas City and Houston that The Killer could easily murder someone in those locations and still be in KC in less than three hours and in Houston in less than two hours, to catch a game. But football season was over when the killings started. Baseball season had begun, making it a possibility, but it was too early in the season to entice many to travel to see the games with a 162-game schedule. The NBA Houston Rockets were still playing, but they were not in town the weekend of the Galveston slaying. The St. Louis Blues hockey team was a possibility. They were playing the night of the killing in St. Louis, but there was no connection to the other three murders.

Could the Killer be a participant in some type of sport? Flag football is popular with adults in some areas, but it isn't really a traveling sport. Although there are many tournaments across the country in softball, it was not even close to being amateur softball season. Legion baseball teams might be in full swing, but Randall felt that this killer was probably in his forties or early fifties, aging him out of Legion ball.

As far as "pick-up" tournaments that he could play in, hockey was not played by "average Joe's" in the Midwest. Still, there were plenty of three-on-three basketball tournaments played all year long, making basketball a possibility. He then searched every recreation department and every individual club in all four cities. There were basketball tournaments, but they were not in all four cities at the time of the killings, and most were only for members of the designated fitness club that was hosting the tournament.

This led Randall to look at lesser known but still popular sports that held tournaments, such as his favorite, racquetball. He even considered adult wrestling tournaments. Still, all he found were dead ends, as far as events being held in all four cities during the time of the murders.

He discovered golf, disc golf, and corn hole tournaments in all four cities that anyone in the country would be allowed to participate in, but he doubted that The Killer even knew of some of these tournaments. For example, most corn hole pitchers in Houston might know of their tournament held in a fitness club in a suburb such as Angleton, but anyone living outside the area probably would not. Anyone would know of all these lesser-known tournament sports in their area, but they probably wouldn't know about them in all four cities that had a victim.

Rob MUNDEN

Also, with Randall sticking to his guns that the Peanut Butter Freak is athletic, sports such as golf, disc golf, and corn hole just wouldn't hold enough adrenaline to keep his focus. Randall was getting frustrated but felt he was being productive as he continued to eliminate and add possibilities.

CHAPTER 5

The Killer resented finding himself in Hays, Kansas. Larger and more prestigious pickleball tournaments were generally played in cities with a population of at least 500,000. Hays was a small college town of around 25,000 people. But this was different, as the Hays Recreation Commission had teamed up with Fort Hays State University to sponsor a 5.0 tournament. 5.0 was the highest-level tournament in the game. Pickleball players with a 5.0 ranking were not getting rich but would be able to obtain enough income as professional-level players to make a decent side living at the sport.

The average 5.0 player could make anywhere from five thousand dollars a year up to ninety grand. Most of the 5.0

players were still in college or fresh out of college. Not bad part-time income to play a sport he or she loved. Only the best of the best could win even a single match in a 5.0 tournament. The city of Hays probably only had one or two players that were 5.0, and they were lower-end 5.0's. But the sport had turned so popular that Recreation Commissioner Maverick Cain wanted the people of Hays to see first-class, pro-level players. So, 5.0 players across the mid-west were not only given invites to the tournament but were paid gas, travel, and hotel expenses, along with $500. The top doubles team to win gold would receive a nice check of three thousand dollars, which comes out to eleven hundred each, after taxes. The Peanut Butter Killer looked at the large bracket on the wall. This men's doubles tournament placed The Killer and his partner seeded eighth in the sixteen-team, 5.0, invite-only tournament. The Killer's corrupted and distorted mind was fueled by anger. "Eighth. Really? Eighth? I should be ranked eighth in the nation, if not the whole goddamn world. If I'd get a decent fucking partner for a change, I'd probably be seeded higher. Eighth. Are you fucking serious? Eighth in the Midwest. Hell, that means these pieces- of-shit-ranking people really rank me lower since many of the better Midwest 5.0 players aren't even here today. They're hanging out at the Chicago Invitational. Did I get an invite to the Chicago Invitational this week? Fuck No, cuz my partner has about as much athletic ability as a sloth."

Disrupting his angry thoughts, the very partner who sparked his unfounded anger approached him. "Hello, Killer. Ready to take on these douchebags?"

Rob MUNDEN

   Half of the Peanut Butter Killer felt repulsed by seeing his partner, knowing he was bringing him down. On the other hand, it juiced up his fragile ego, as he liked the nickname "Killer." His partner called him Killer because he played with so much anger, seriousness, and tenacity, that it appeared that he would not only defeat the enemy on the other side of the net but torture and kill them through intimidation and relentlessness. The Killer loved the irony of being given this nickname. "Killer on the court playground and a killer in the playground called life, as well; or in this case, death," he mused.
   "Hello, Rusty," he said. "What brings you to Hays, America? Are you playing today or something?" He then laughed in an almost sadistic manner.
   "Yes, Killer. You know that – playing with my best pickleball friend, of course. The one, the only, Killer... uh, um Killer..." The Peanut Butter Freak replied. "That's right; Killer is the only name I need. Killer sums it all up. Are you going to play worth a shit today or what?"
   "Oh, Killer, I played just fine in Lincoln. We won the whole damn thing."
   "Ya, well Rusty, if you'd start playing like a twenty-one-year-old should and not like your name - Rusty, we'd be playing in Washington, D.C. or New York, instead of Nebraska and Kansas."
   "Nothin' wrong with Nebraska and Kansas, Killer. Maybe if you had less killer in ya and more love, you'd see the beauty in the plains. And, you know, since you're fifty now, and you don't like the way I play, you can find a fine enough senior

partner, get in all those fifty-and-older tournaments, and mop up on those distinguished fellas."

"Listen, shithead; I am not entering the senior pickleball open just yet. I may not have found the fountain of youth, but I still got skills enough to avoid the old man shit."

"Okay then, Killer. Shut the hell up, dogging on my play, then. Cuz if you didn't have me, you'd be stuck playing in the grandpa league." The Killer laughed and smiled. He then patted Rusty on the back,

"Fair enough, Rusty. See ya at warm-ups tonight."

"Later, dude, or uh, I mean, Killer."

"About the Killer nickname, I like it, but perhaps it needs to be dropped from here on out. Some people might get the wrong idea and think I'm a real killer or something. "The Killer then laughed.

"You got it. I'll lay off the aggressive nicknames." Rusty then bumped the Peanut Butter Killer in the arm with his fist and walked away.

....

Randall Baines eventually strayed entirely away from thoughts of peanut butter and focused solely on athletic events. It's not that he didn't think that The Killer might not have a strong connection to peanut butter, which he likely did. But Randall knew Tomas Menzies, along with the rest of the Wichita PD and the police departments of the three other cities involved, the KBI, the FBI, all those private investigators, and every damn person that ever attended one of those damn murder-mystery dinner theatre things would be searching for a peanut butter connection.

So, why cover an area already being covered ten-fold by everyone including himself early on? He was just damn tired of the whole peanut butter crap and ready to move on. He thought to himself, "The only way I'm going to think about peanut butter in this case is if it's related to some kind of damn sport." Since his obsession with catching the Peanut Butter Freak began, he generally sat in his recliner with the TV off and his book, the third copy of Ken Follett's *World Without End* closed with the bookmark sitting on page one ninety-two for the seventh day in a row. Randall would just sit and think and think and obsess about the peanut butter murderer.

Sometimes he looked up information on his iPhone 5 that he thought might relate to the murders, but generally, he would just think. He would think until he drifted off to sleep for a fast catnap. Then he would wake up and think some more. Much of the thinking was geared towards his obsession with connecting a wealthy, middle-aged athlete to the four murders.

....

As much as The Killer was annoyed with playing in Hays instead of the bright lights of Chicago, he was mesmerized by the passion that the people of Hays had for this tournament. Tickets at Fort Hays State's Gross Memorial Coliseum were fifteen dollars apiece, and the six-thousand-seat coliseum was over one-third full. Two thousand three hundred people may not sound like a remarkable number, but they were paying fifteen bucks to watch pickleball!

"Hell. Chicago, a city two hundred times the size of Hays, might get a thousand paying just ten bucks," he thought with a smile.

This was because there were a ton of things to do in Chicago, but in little Hays, Kansas, top-ranked pickleball action is the only show in town. Hell, it was the only show within a three-hour radius. He had ten people ask for his autograph. Before today, he had not had one person ask for his John Hancock in his life. This stroked his ego beyond comprehension.

Although there were three other courts with matches playing at the same time, there were more spectators surrounding his match than the other three. He thought, "People actually know my name now. People know me. I'm getting my name out there. They love me. I'm a total stud."

Of course, this narcissistic thinking would not allow his corrupted mind to conceive the truth. And the truth was that as the eighth seed, they were playing the number nine seed with the right to play the number one seed. The number one-seeded team had already crushed their number sixteen-seeded opponents in straight sets 11-0 and 11-1.

The citizens of Hays wanted to see the team that would next take on the number-one seed. Also, some of the younger women and girls were there to see Rusty. Rusty was a handsome 6'3" black man with a smooth baby face and muscles that would make Dwayne "The Rock" Johnson sour with envy. Some of these girls followed him like groupies back in the 80s who would follow Mötley Crüe to whatever concert they played next.

One group of eight girls drove together, crammed in a beat-up 1967 Volkswagen van. They went to all of Rusty's matches that were anywhere close to Wichita. Rusty enjoyed the attention, although he did worry about high school kids traveling together in such an old load of tin. He lived in Wichita as well. This was how they had gotten to know him, as he held pickleball camps at the Gabrielle Pickleball Club three times a year.

Sometimes those same eight girls would be the only attendees of his camp. At fifty-five dollars apiece, this was still four hundred and forty tax-free dollars. He didn't even have to pay the owner, Mia, for use of the courts, as she just wanted him to play there as often as possible to draw others to the club. In fact, he didn't even have to pay membership dues. He also made money by having Mia sponsor him. She would pay his air flights and cheaper hotels, plus three hundred bucks in spending cash, to travel anywhere in the Midwest. And all he had to do was wear Gabrielle Pickleball Club shorts and t-shirts during his matches. Mia would also give him about twenty or so shirts to hand out to whomever he wished, adding to his fan-favorite status. This continuously upset The Killer, because he was not given the same opportunity.

The Killer didn't need the money. The Killer was worth millions, but he wanted the sponsorship to feed his own ego. He wanted acknowledgement that he was a pro. Mia liked The

Killer but did not see any drawing power in a guy that did not have youth and charisma like Rusty. This drove The Killer crazy, watching all the other 5.0 teams with matching outfits and sponsors.

Rusty wore a classy green, collared shirt with the words *Gabrielle Pickleball Club* on the front with *Collins* (Rusty's last name) across the top of the back. The number 23 filled the rest of the back of the shirt. Rusty chose the number 23 in honor of the number that Michael Jordan wore throughout most of his career. On the other hand, The Killer wore a red Coca-Cola shirt. He hoped those around him thought he was sponsored by Coca-Cola, to soothe his pride for having no one to promote him.

Rusty gave private lessons to the Pickleball Eight as well. During these camps and private lessons, seven of the eight didn't really care about pickleball; they just wanted to be near him. Their fascination with Rusty went beyond his good looks; his charm was enduring. Rusty was quite aware of their teenage crushes and their true reasons for seeing him on the court. Many twenty-one-year-old hunks might have allowed their hormones to go places they shouldn't with the cute teenagers, but not Rusty. He was a true professional. He knew that he was there to provide a service and that service was pickleball. Sure, he would flirt at times. But the flirtation would be just enough to keep ahold of his clientele. After all, he was a junior at Wichita State, majoring in law. Even with scholarships, an education wasn't exactly cheap. Rusty did wish that they would take the game more seriously, but he still did everything he could to improve their games.

"Alright, Killer, let's kick some ass, dude."

"You do your job and don't turn into a rust bucket, Rusty, and we will be just fine."

"Don't worry 'bout me, Killer... uh, sorry. Not supposed to call you that. Anyhow, I got my game face on."

And game face he did have. The Killer and Rusty were playing two guys named Topper Barton and Jeff Helton. They were both in the Army National Guard from Kansas City. Of course, the Army National Guard was their sponsor. They wore camouflage shirts and shorts with the words, "Army National Guard" on both.

The players stuck their paddles out towards each other. The two National Guardsmen were sure to be the mightier warriors in a real military war zone, but on the battlefield of Pickleball, they were no match for Rusty and The Killer.

From start to finish, the military guys were taken to the woodshed, with the Pickleball Eight fan club cheering on. Seven of the eight had made signs that said things like "Rusty Rocks." and "Roundhouse Rusty." These signs and cheers for Rusty drove The Killer crazy.

"If it weren't so obvious who had committed the murder, Rusty would be deader than a pile of old RUSTY nails," The Killer thought.

The girls would scream and cheer after every great play Rusty made, driving The Killer mad. The Killer was; however, especially drawn to one of the Pickleball Eight. Why? Because she never cheered Rusty on. She instead shouted out commands, pointing out things that Rusty did wrong. She screamed out universal racket-sports terms such as "Keep the ball low, Rusty," and more complicated commands regarding his foot placement while he was serving.

The Killer could not see that this was her way of cheering on Rusty. The Killer only saw it as her pointing out many of Rusty's flaws. "How ironic that the girl receiving private lessons from Rusty, was the one trying to teach him basic fucking pickleball techniques." The Killer humorously smiled at that thought.

After the match, Rusty was given a smothering bunch of hugs from the vast majority of the Pickleball Eight. With some COVID-19 restrictions still in place, the hugs could have been deemed unwise. Of course, the one girl in the group not handing out a hug to Rusty was the very girl hollering out coaching orders to Rusty. She simply slapped him on the back and congratulated him. The Killer was fond of the girl because she was the only one of the groupies that also congratulated him. She winked at The Killer and said, "Pretty damn athletic for an old man there, dude. Way to make us Gabrielle Club members proud."

The Killer responded, "Thanks, that means a lot to me, Keisha."

....

It was slightly chilly for a day in late May. Generally, not what one might call perfect grilling weather, but Mathew was craving T-Bone steaks. Mathew and Elijah both seemed to have holes in their stomachs. Mathew had already thawed the T-bones and was ready to barbecue. In the past, Edna had left the grilling up to her husband. Since his untimely death, the grilling captain's duties had been passed on to Mathew.

The back patio area was Mathew's domain. The patio was well-manicured and breathtaking. In the middle of the lawn was a ten-foot-wide pond that held six beautiful goldfish. The pond had a waterfall that flowed down majestically placed rocks. In the Northwest corner of the yard was a hand-made swing set equipped with monkey bars, a steel slipper slide, and a mini playhouse under the slide for the grandchildren. Edna had thought of getting rid of it since the grandchildren she was now raising never used it anymore, but it reminded her of a gentler and less volatile time.

The back sliding doors connected to a large patio. On that patio sat the five-burner Weber grill with the side smoker. For years, Edward had a much smaller, three-burner grill. He liked his cheaper three-burner grill, although he had wanted a larger one. He and Edna made a commitment to each other, though, that they would only purchase what the good Lord felt was needed. He often discussed a larger grill with Edna while sitting on the back porch as he slugged down a nice cold beer and Edna sipped on a glass of wine. She gave him permission to pick one out, but he always talked himself out of it. This made it even more bizarre that after the funeral of their son and daughter-in-law, a beautiful five-burner Weber grill with the side smoker attachment to it showed up on their patio.

Although they didn't know for sure who gave it to them, they concluded that it was Edward's Uncle Bob. He was an elderly man that would not have made the trip from Alabama. Uncle Bob was known for his Southern barbecuing talent. He had taught Edward many of his special grilling techniques in the seventies when Bob would visit him, and once every couple of years, Uncle Bob would make his way to Kansas as well.

Edward and Edna assumed Bob had arranged for a place in Wichita to send it over with a phone call and a credit card number. When Edward called Uncle Bob to thank him, Uncle Bob denied it, but that's how good ole Uncle Bob was. He certainly didn't want anyone to make a fuss over him when he knew the attention should be on the mourning parents themselves.

Edna asked Mathew to run out and check on the steaks. Although she did most of the preparation, she had taught Mathew a thing or two about grilling. He was starting to know the ends and outs. He would have done most of the prep marinating work on the steaks, but she had commanded him to spend the afternoon reading the second tossed copy of *World Without End*. Thanks to the anger of a grumpy, disgruntled, retired Wichita detective, Mathew and Keisha were both stuck reading Follett. As Mathew opened the smoker to check on the steaks, he did so by holding Follett in his left hand and opening the smoker with his right. He glanced at the T-bones while focusing much of his attention on the book.

"Mathew, you know I told you that you've read on Mr. Baines's book enough for the evening. You can relax and focus on the steaks."

"That's okay, Grandma. I don't mind. I'm trying to get through this and get it done so I don't have to mess with European white man crap anymore."

"Bite your tongue. We will not use that language in our Christian, God-fearing home. "

"But Grandma, the word cra…"

Edna interrupted, "Ah ah ah, young man. Don't say it again unless you want to be reading Mr. Baines's book til three a.m."

"Yes, Ma'am."

"Oh, just so you know, it will just be you, Elijah, and I for dinner. It turns out Keisha is going to have to babysit for the Wilsons longer than she planned."

"YES!!!!" Mathew shouted with excitement. "Uh, uh umm, I mean that's unfortunate." He stated quickly as a cover.

"Now, you may not get along with your sister at times, but that's no way to act about her missing a good steak. She is working hard to save money for college, babysitting those two Wilson kids."

"Yes, Ma'am. Sorry." The truth was, he hadn't shouted with excitement because of the no-dinner-for-Keisha news. He was super happy knowing that if she would not be home soon, it meant that the Hays men's doubles-only tournament was down to the championship match. And the only reason that Keisha would stay for the tournament throughout its entirety was if Rusty and the old dude made the championship. He wanted

Keisha to give him updates, but he almost didn't want to know for fear of the worst. Mathew had come to look up to Rusty. Rusty spent time giving Mathew tips at pickleball and coaching him some on the side. He didn't even do it for money.

   Why he would charge his sister and not him was bewildering. He guessed that Rusty knew that Keisha had some cash from babysitting. Mathew had been mowing yards for about a month but would not obtain steady cash flow until the lawn mowing season was in full swing. Rusty probably felt sorry for him. He even found a way to convince Mia to give Mathew a free membership to the pickleball club. He prayed Mia would not discover that the Reynolds family was well-to-do. If Mia associated the Reynolds Mattress Company with Mathew, his membership would be doomed. The money would do no good if Mathew didn't have any himself, and Grandma Edna would never allow, nor pay for, anyone in her family to be a member of a pickleball/fitness center. Matthew didn't do well in school and was too rebellious to get on the good side of any teacher. He had no father, no male figure to look up to at all, except for Rusty.

   Mathew did feel some concern for his sister. He hoped that she wouldn't get caught. Edna was strict but not so strict that she would not have allowed Keisha to be the young woman she was. But if Keisha told her grandmother the truth, she would have never been allowed to go to the tournament in Hays, which was nearly three hours away in a beat-up 1967 Volkswagen van, so long as Keisha was living under her roof. And she also would not have been happy that Keisha remained more fascinated with pickleball than the scholarship-driven sports of tennis and track & field.

"Is it done or not?"

"Umm, uh, about twenty more minutes, grandma."

He figured the steaks were finished even though he didn't really get a good look at them due to reading Follett. He took the steaks off the smoker and moved them to a side burner separate from the smoker that was meant to keep them warm but not cook them further. But he wanted to see how the championship was going, so he texted Keisha. As he waited for the text, he picked the Follett book back up. He found himself slowly being drawn into a novel about building a bridge. He could not wait to see just how that bridge would be built. Mathew loved to build things and put things together. As a child, he owned *Erector* sets, *Lego* sets, and car models. He still made some advanced *Lego* sets and models. He wanted to take woodshop and welding, but all the upperclassmen took those spots. He hoped to enroll in one next fall. Other than building things, his only hobby was the pickleball sessions with Rusty.

Edna walked back out on the patio. "Now, Mathew, I told you that it is okay to put that book down. Take a break from reading and come watch the news with your grandma until the steaks are done. It's important to know what's going on in the world."

He grumbled, closed the book, and began watching the news. Edna yelled up to Elijah's room, telling him to get downstairs to listen to the rest of the news as well. Elijah whined, but he closed his game of Fortnite on his PlayStation and walked downstairs to join them. Before sitting down on the couch beside Mathew, Elijah looked down at the book that was beside Mathew on the coffee table, and Elijah thought,

"My poor brother, having to read that boring-ass book Mr. Baines suckered him and Keisha into reading"

Dallas Richardson from Star News came on to report the weather. Mathew yawned, trying to stay focused, knowing that in Kansas, nobody really knows what's happening with the weather. After reporting a thunderstorm approaching Sedgwick County, Edna panicked, got up off her couch, and said,

"I've got to get Keisha home. I'm calling the Wilsons to get them back to the house early. I don't want Keisha to walk back here, slipping on her behind. With the Wilsons only two blocks away, I figured she would be okay to walk, but she has no business walking in some monsoon. She will lose her tennis and track scholarship opportunities if she gets hurt. I left my phone in my bedroom. "

Mathew immediately flew up off the couch. "Now, now, grandma, leave her to her work. You wouldn't want her to come flying into one of the mattress companies and try to tell you how to sell a mattress, would you?"

"Well, no, but this is different. This is dangerous weather."

"Grandma, weather lady Richardson reported that the thunderstorm will arrive overnight. The Wilsons only live a couple of blocks away. Keisha will be fine. Relax."

"Well, okay, I suppose you're right. Just not sure why she didn't take her car; she walks everywhere. Not only should she be concerned about walking in such bad weather, but there's also some kind of crazy killer on the loose that done killed good ole Elaine. I'm going to the bathroom, sitting back down, and finishing the news. Then surely it'll be steak time."

Mathew let out a sigh of relief. After the commercials, sports news came on with Tanner Johnson reporting. He discussed the Chiefs' off-season moves. He reported that the Royals were close to a trade with the Yankees for a minor league up-and-coming pitcher. Tanner was thrilled to report that Fort Hays State Women's Basketball was in action against Kearney. He further stated that it was just half-time, but Fort Hays was up fifty-one to thirty-nine, and star player and All-American Lesley Gomez had already scored twenty-seven points as Star News showed a highlight of her throwing down a three-sixty dunk.

And then, unexpectedly, Tanner reported, "And we close with this exciting news! Wichita's very own took second place in the Hays 5.0 Professional Pickleball Invitational." Star Action News then showed footage of Rusty and the old guy shaking hands with the winners. Also on camera was Keisha and her pickleball groupies, going up to congratulate the pair. Reporter Tanner Johnson then proudly proclaimed, "Yes, Rusty Collins and..." Just then, Mathew would see his grandma walk out of the bathroom. He quickly shut the TV off, preventing her from seeing Keisha inside the TV and not inside the home of the Wilsons.

"You know I was watching the news. Why did you turn it off?"

"Sorry, Grandma. They were talking local sports gibberish."

Grandma replied, "But that's what I wanted to see. I wanted an update on Lesley Gomez numbers."

PEANUT BUTTER PICKLEBALL AND MURDER

"Twenty-seven points and a three-sixty dunk, Grandma! And it's only halftime!"

"Impressive for a white kid from little La Crosse, KS, eh?" Grandma stated with excitement.

Mathew then proclaimed, "Those steaks should be done by now, Grandma. Let's eat."

Elijah and Grandma cheered.

....

Randall had nightmares of peanut butter and death. He heard the victims scream in his mind. The nightmares were one thing he did not enjoy nor miss from back in his days as a detective for the Wichita PD. Eventually, he woke up. He turned the TV on. The channel was on Channel 22, Star Action News, with sports reporter Tanner Johnson. He heard Tanner report on some Royals trade with the Yankees and caught some large half-time numbers by the La Crosse girl playing for Fort Hays. He then saw footage of that Wiffle ball game with the oversized ping-pong paddle. He was still waking up but caught something about it being called pickleball, and two local guys did well. He quickly rose in his recliner and glued his eyes to the TV, as what really woke him up was the sight of the next-door girl Keisha in the background.

"So that's the damn game that's cost me two freaking copies of Follett's book. Pickleball, huh? Interesting." He then caught something about the two Wichita locals getting some prize money for taking second. His mind quickly raced as the pieces were coming to him. He thought, "This is a legitimate athletic sport, with not enough prestige to be household news, yet the sport causes enough excitement to make Channel 22 news." This was just what Randall was looking for. He quickly fumbled around his recliner, looking for a pen. He remembered he had one in his pocket. He quickly wrote down on his hand the word – "pickleball." It then dawned on him that there was no reason to jot down the word pickleball. Just start typing it into the iPhone and get to work. And phone googling is just what he did.

………

Mathew enjoyed the steak and felt great that Elijah and his grandma were also enjoying the meal. He giggled in his head, thinking, "A good day; just grilled some mighty fine medium-rare steaks, and Rusty got himself in the championship of a 5.0 tournament. I wish he and his partner could have won it, but still cool." Mathew just hoped that Keisha would get home before Grandma Edna found out that she never actually babysat for the Wilsons.

Grandma Edna soon shouted out, "MMM, MMM! You sure know how to grill some steaks, Mathew. You sure learned a thing or two from your grandpa, that's for sure."

"Thanks, Grandma. And yes, you and Grandpa taught me well."

Elijah snapped back, "Yeah. I knew you had to be good for something, Mathew."

"Ha Ha," Mathew responded sarcastically.

Edna then stated, "Well, Elijah, you contributed as well."

"I did, Grandma?" Elijah said with surprise.

"Yes, because you're cleaning the table and doing the dishes."

"Damn it!" Elijah snapped back, and Mathew laughed.

"You had better apologize to your grandma and the good Lord above for using such language, boy."

"Sorry, Grandma. And you too, Lord," he said, looking to the ceiling.

"Okay. Before you wash the dishes, you and your brother owe me fifty push-ups for such language. "

"But I didn't say it."

"But you laughed, didn't you, Mathew? That's supporting negative behavior."

"Yes, Grandma."

Mathew and Elijah fell to the kitchen floor and did their push-up penance. Mathew was giving Elijah dirty looks the entire time.

CHAPTER 6

Randall Baines found it harder to find pickleball information than he expected. Pickleball still wasn't a sport that made headline news or even page seven of a Monday Kansas City Star or Wichita Eagle. He did learn that of the peanut butter murder victims, there was at least one pickleball tournament in every one of the cities of some kind within a twenty-four-hour period of the times the victims were murdered. He felt excitement at the thought that he might be onto something, but at the same time, he was leery that he might be pushing himself *into* finding something. He compared these feelings to those of people who claimed they had seen ghosts in their lives. People who want to see ghosts see ghosts. They will turn every little shadow, cup falling off a table, or door being blown open into a major poltergeist jam session.

He also knew he had no explanation for the peanut butter being tied to the murders. It must have some meaning, or The Killer wouldn't have been so adamant about including it. And then he thought, "What would peanut butter have to do with pickleball?" It quickly dawned on him that saying peanut butter and pickleball sounded remarkably the same.

"Hmm," he thought, "Perhaps the peanut butter tie-in is simply nothing more than its initials; PB. Peanut Butter – Pickleball."

………..

Grandma Edna was getting nervous. She paced back and forth in the living room. It was very elegant, with an antique lamp dating from the 19th century, a crystal chandelier valued at two thousand dollars, and furniture only three years old from the finest shops in Wichita. She often had to get after Mathew and Elijah for wrestling and horse playing in the living room as she worried about her treasured home. Edna had just as many issues with Keisha. She had to get after Keisha for constantly taking "that cucumber-paddle-thingy and bouncing the ball thing up and down with it." She was completely convinced that Keisha would lose her balance and break something. And that fear was from experience. Grandma Edna had witnessed Keisha run up to hit the ball in the air before it hit the ground, and instead run into a seven-hundred-dollar, oak wood coffee table, smashing it into three pieces two years ago.

Of course, Edna's first concern had been to make sure that Keisha was okay. But soon after Edna realized that Keisha's health was not in question, Keisha found herself doing three hundred push-ups. Not just that one time, but three hundred push-ups daily from January to April. This punishment no longer worked. Keisha became so used to doing the push-ups that she continued to do them daily. The only difference was that the push-ups increased from three hundred to five hundred.

Elijah went back upstairs to continue his obsession with his computers while Mathew sat on the couch and attempted to get his grandma to relax. Edna picked up the phone five times, and Mathew stopped Edna from calling all five times. He told her to let Keisha live her life. She was okay, babysitting was her job, and calling the Wilsons would just scare them away from using Keisha's services again. He also reminded her how inaccurate Dallas Richardson often was with her weather predictions. Mathew reminded her that Dallas once predicted 12-degree weather with a chance of snow, and it ended up 80 degrees and sunny. Edna laughed at that reminder. They both loved to make fun of Dallas and her horrible weather-predicting skills. During this entire time, Mathew repeatedly texted Keisha, warning her to get home quickly before Grandma Edna found out that the Wilsons were not in need of Keisha's babysitting services. Keisha repeatedly texted back, saying things like, "Doing what we can, the old beat-up Volkswagen van has two paces – slow and slower."

She didn't respond to all of Mathew's texts simply because she was keeping an eye on her friend Robin Lebbin. Robin was a good friend to Keisha, but she was a little bit wild. It was Robin's van, and even though Robin had not had anything to drink, Keisha still felt that Robin was too intoxicated by high spirits, laughter, and giddiness. She was singing at the top of her lungs to an old Sammy Hagar song, "I CAN'T DRIVE FIFTY-FIVE!" She sang, adding her own lyrics, "Cuz the car won't go that fast." Keisha loved Robin's energy, but she just wished that she would concentrate on the road. The two friends were complete opposites. Robin was a blonde-haired white girl with a bubbly personality. She was carefree and lived life for the moment. Robin made C's and D's with an occasional F. Keisha generally made A's and B's with a rare C. Keisha was a rather serious person and typically played by the rules. Robin would often play devil's advocate and sway Keisha to do things that, without Robin, she'd never consider. Telling Grandma Edna that she was babysitting all day and into the evening for the Wilsons was not in her character. Keisha was beginning to regret the lie. She felt guilty for deceiving her grandmother, although if Keisha had told the truth, Grandma Edna probably would not have allowed her to go to the tournament. On the other hand, if her grandmother had allowed her to go, she certainly would have let Keisha take her car instead of riding in the beat-up Volkswagen van. Sure, all eight of the girls in the van would not have fit in Keisha's 2005 Impala, but her true friends, Katy, Debbie, and Robin, would have been seated, and they would have been dramatically safer. Keisha and Robin's other two close friends, Debbie Meels and Katy Anderson, had much more in common with Robin than Keisha, yet Robin considered Keisha her very best friend. Somehow their polar opposite relationship worked. Keisha's serious attitude helped keep Robin out of jail. In turn, Robin occasionally drew Keisha into her mischievous lifestyle, which helped her learn to live a little. Time ticked by. Mathew continuously texted Keisha to get home. Keisha finally responded. She assured him that they were two miles outside of Wichita. Mathew texted back, making it known how much Keisha owed him for keeping Grandma Edna from calling the Wilsons. Keisha watched the old Volkswagen van putt slower and slower. Smoke billowed out from under the hood. Most would immediately pull over after such a fright, but not adventurous Robin. Even if she could barely see with all the smoke filtering in front of the windshield, she was determined to get the van home. Normally, logical-minded Keisha would have had her pull over, not only for the sake of the van but for their safety. But in this case, she decided to let Robin see it through. Keisha figured the wrath of an angry

Grandma Edna might be worse for her health than a possible van wreck.

Debbie and Katy, along with the other girls in the van, just laughed and made the usual texting teenage comments verbal, such as OMG or LOL. Keisha looked at the girls and thought about how invincible they all thought they were. Keisha aspired to have those same teenage feelings, but the horror of her parents' death provided her with a true understanding of how fragile life is. With mortality comes the end. She just prayed that the beat-up van, blanketed by smoke, would not allow that end to come sooner than she would like.

·········

Randall became obsessed with his theory that the serial killer was not a Peanut Butter Freak but a pickleball murdering madman. He knew that there was not much he could do with his thoughts at 11:00 at night, so he took an Ambien to try and get to sleep. Ambien was a strong enough drug that it would normally contribute its part to helping Randall reach a happy, comforting, unconscious bliss, but not this night. Not even a doctor-prescribed potion could budge his newfound fixation with a sport that oddly required an oversized ping-pong paddle and tough-as-nails wiffle ball. Nothing – nothing at all. He had his sights on a killer. And he just knew that killer had a hobby. And that hobby wasn't eating peanut butter.

Edna continued to pace back and forth throughout the house. Some part of her nervousness was a genuine concern for Keisha not being home with the bad weather coming in, but the truth was, even if the weather weren't a concern, Edna would have been a nervous wreck. She didn't use to be this way, but losing her son and daughter-in-law due to a tragic accident and unexpectedly losing her husband made her more distrustful. Now, knowing that a serial killer had just taken someone's life a mere two blocks away created an overly paranoid grandmother. There were very few moments in the day that she wasn't concerned about losing one of her grandkids. After all, they were all she felt she had left in her life. Beauty-wise, she was incredibly gorgeous. But all that she had been through revealed her age, more through her lack of smile and look of dreadful anxiety than through an actual physical transformation. Most guardians or parents would want their children to live active lives, but Edna would prefer they stay home within her eyesight.

    She wished they would all be more like Elijah. He had few friends. He generally stayed in his room, attached like a magnet to his computers. Yes, she understood that it was not completely good for his well-being, but at least she knew where he was and that he was safe. Mathew and Keisha were just too damn active, she thought. She then felt guilty for thinking the word "damn" and said several Catholic prayers in her head that included more "Hail, Mary, full of grace, the Lord is with thee's" than filled an entire rosary. She had finally had enough. She took the phone out of her pocket and dialed the Wilsons. Mathew, of course, tried to get her to stop. But not even knowing that Keisha might be mad at her for checking on her would stop Edna this time.

Mathew put his hand on his forehead as he thought, "Oh hell! Keisha's in deep, deep shit!"

Just then, Keisha rushed through the door as Mr. Wilson answered Edna's call. "This is Rodney. Can I help you?"

"Oh, I'm sorry, this is Edna. I must have accidentally butt-dialed you." Edna then blushed, knowing she had used the word "butt." She then figured she wouldn't be going to sleep anytime soon, as she gave herself a penance of praying the entire rosary before getting some shuteye.

Mr. Wilson then replied, "Oh, that's okay, Edna. I was going to call in the morning anyway to see if Keisha could watch the children Wednesday night."

Bewildered, Edna said, "That's fine, Rodney, but why didn't you just ask her when she was over there?"

Mr. Wilson replied, "Well, I didn't know that I was going to need her when she was over here last week."

"But you didn't know that ten minutes ago?"

"I'll take that," Keisha said in desperation. She grabbed Edna's phone from her and pronounced, "Hi, this is Keisha. Sure, sure. I'll be happy to watch them. 6:00 p.m.? Great thanks. Bye, Mr. Wilson."

Edna then stated with concern, "Is Mr. Wilson feeling all right? He felt he needed to talk on the phone to ask you to babysit when he could have just asked you himself. Very strange!"

Keisha then paused, thinking about how to cover up the situation, "Yaa um, um... he's been through a lot lately. Sales have been down, and Mrs. Wilson says the commission cash isn't flowing."

Concerned, Edna replied, "Oh dear, the car sales business is tough to get into. Well, any sales work is for that matter. Selling mattresses probably contributed to the death of your grandfather. I had better pray the rosary for him. I have a lot of praying to do. So, I better get to the peace of my bedroom and get to it. Goodnight, Mathew and Keisha."

"Goodnight, Grandma," they both lovingly replied.

Edna slowly walked upstairs, knowing it would be a long night, as she had burdened herself with a rosary for Mr. Wilson and a rosary for thinking the word "damn."

"That was a close one!" proclaimed Mathew.

"That it was. Thank you for covering for me, Mathew."

"Tell me about the tournament. Second place in a 5.0, and a recent big-time tournament Gold in Nebraska. They are rolling!"

Mathew and Keisha then talked pickleball for the next couple of hours. Some serious talk; some talk with laughter. Their passion for pickleball bonded the two siblings together. Through the tragic loss of their parents and the sudden loss of their grandfather, they had found the one thing that kept them grounded and sane. God had written them a prescription, and that heavenly prescription was pickleball.

Instruction for usage –
> Take a two-hour practice session a minimum of once a day,

> Observe a 5.0 tournament with their favorite player and instructor – Rusty
> Follow up with an occasional chit-chat session on the finer points of the game
> Call God in the morning, thanking him for blessing them with such a brilliant sport.

CHAPTER 7

The Killer was devastated. He didn't look at a second-place finish as a great showing in a 5.0 tournament. To him, the old cliché, "Second place is the first-place loser," couldn't have fit any better. The Killer went straight to his hotel located just off I-70.

The Hays Hotel, simply named after the town, was a nice hotel by most standards, but not to Killer. According to The Killer's high-class standards, the room was nothing more than a simple, sub-standard place to lay his head for the night. He wanted some type of distilled spirit to drink, but nothing was stocked in the mini-fridge. He did crave a shot of Crown, but at the moment, he would have been happy with anything that might carry his mind from the championship loss. He could have simply jumped into his Mercedes and been home by 11 p.m. at the latest, but he wanted a shower and wasn't up to jumping into a car and driving just then. After taking a shower, he hopped into the Mercedes and went straight to the nearest liquor store. The Killer grabbed a pint of Crown, drove right back to the hotel to change into his swimming gear, and scampered down to the swimming pool area.

His immediate thought was that the swimming pool was not nearly large enough for him to swim his laps in the morning. He was, however, impressed with the hot tub. It could easily fit a party of twenty in the massive bowl of bubbling pleasure. The Jacuzzi was abandoned. Most of the hotel guests were there to see NCAA Division II Fort Hays State Tigers basketball. Most were at the game to see the Fort Hays State Women's team's star player, Lesley Gomez. She was a 6'7" gem who could dunk a basketball with more conviction than most Division I men's players.

The Killer was aware of the Lesley Gomez hype. He loved all sports and followed all levels of sports, including Division II ball. The Killer was also aware that little Fort Hays landed the girl when she was a senior out of nearby La Crosse, a city so small that if you blinked while driving through, you might miss entirely. At the time she was recruited, she was only 6'2", which is tall for a girl but not a giant in terms of the basketball world. Lesley had special basketball skills, but she was a socially awkward kid that had yet to grow into her body. Of course, a late growth spurt, and the coordination that was delivered with it, made her the most watched basketball player in the nation by professional sports scouts. The WNBA salivated at the chance to get a 6'7" dunking, blond bombshell who could even hit sixty percent of the threes she tossed up.

  If The Killer had won the championship, a front-row seat to witness the legend would have been in the works; but liquor and soothing, steaming hot water was his only comfort now. The Killer had a small duffle bag with him. Before entering the Jacuzzi, he took a soup spoon, a jar of peanut butter, and the bottle of Crown out of the bag. He placed the three items beside him in the hot tub. He jumped in. The Killer then grabbed the jar of peanut butter, opened it, and spooned out a chunk of peanut butter so huge that it barely fit into his mouth. After swallowing the peanut butter, he chased it with a quick swig of Crown and let out a sigh of relief. The Killer believed that the Lesley Gomez craze would allow him to have the hot tub to himself, but just after his third spoonful of peanut butter and about five swigs of Crown, a red-haired, middle-aged woman entered. She knew she had aged well, and her figure was one that she could still be proud of. Her long legs fit well into the bottom section of her bikini, as the top part accentuated her double D breasts. Her figure was not the tight, slender, twenty-something-year-old body she'd once had, but she had nothing to be ashamed of. She soon entered the hot tub.

  "Mind if I join you there, handsome?"

  "Suit yourself."

  "Hmm, not the most welcoming invitation I've ever received," the red-haired beauty responded.

"Who said this was an invitation?"

"Rough day at the office Mr.... uh um?" She paused slightly. "Okay, I reckon I won't introduce myself either. She then scrunched down in the bubbling water, absorbing the steaming heat that could be seen flowing through her strawberry hair. She did not sit on the other side of the large hot tub but instead remained relatively close to The Killer, just five feet away. She crouched down and slowly lifted her long milky white legs from the steam. "You seem tense, sir. Anything I can do to help you relax?"

He had no reaction. He took another spoonful of peanut butter, followed by yet another swig of Crown. She scooted closer to The Killer, ever so slowly. Eventually, she was right next to him.

She soon thrust her hand underneath the water and up his thigh until it crept under his swimwear and onto his penis. The Killer's long, hard cock rose to the occasion.

"I see there's one part of you that's alive."

"You don't even know me, lady. What is this all about?"

"I simply don't care about sports," she replied while continuing to stroke him.

"And what does sports have to do with me?"

She quickly responded, "My unattractive, bald, overweight husband is getting his jollies off with one of his buddies, drooling over a voluptuous, twenty-year-old, dunking blonde. What's the harm in me doing some dunking myself?" She then dunked her head under the water, pulled down his swimsuit, and wrapped her mouth around his penis. She sucked him hard underwater while holding her breath and not sucking any water into her mouth. It was obviously a talent that she had obtained and mastered from other hotel ballgame excursions. She temporarily stopped to come up for air. She tried to kiss him, but he turned away.

"Sorry, Miss, but kissing's way too intimate for such a spontaneous occasion. He then took another spoonful of peanut butter, followed by another swig of Crown. She then took off the top of her cherry red bikini and grabbed the peanut butter jar. She took a scoop of peanut butter and rubbed it on her large, tight tits. He immediately licked the peanut butter off of them.

"I see you like peanut butter. Hope you're not the so-called Peanut Butter Killer."

"Maybe I am!" he shot back. He then turned her around and ripped the bottom of her swimsuit off, and watched as it floated to the water's top.

"Hey! Now, how am I going to get back to my room Mr.?" she shouted with alarm.

"Worry about that later, Reddie."

"The name's Donna."

"Whatever," he replied.

The Killer then grabbed her ass with both hands and thrust his penis into her. He stroked her hard as she moaned in gratifying pleasure. He then grabbed her hair with his right hand as his left hand kept roughly squeezing her ass. He pulled her hair tight to the point that it hurt her somewhat. This seemed to turn her on even more. "Oh, you like it rough, baby. Yes, yes. Harder, baby, harder!" He then came inside of her.

After finishing, with her still on top of him, he took both of his hands and shoved her head under the water. She struggled to fight him off, but his strength was too much. It took less than a minute for her to turn blue and lose consciousness. He then whispered in a soft but firm voice, "Guess you won't have to worry about making it back to your room naked now, huh?" He then laughed his most sinister laugh. "Oh yes, Reddie, congratulations on your fine detective skills. Turns out you were correct. I am the fucking Peanut Butter Killer."

The Killer checked for any cameras he might need to destroy in the old Hays Hotel, both in the pool areas and the hallway. He had checked into the hotel with his false ID, but he wanted to ensure with extra precautions that he did not overlook anything. He also grabbed the jar of peanut butter and quickly threw it in the trash. He generally relished the opportunity to add to the media's obsession with the Peanut Butter Killer, but a killing in little Hays, Kansas could more easily be tracked back to a pickleball tournament than it could in a metropolitan area. He did everything in his power to make sure that the authorities would not trace this killing to peanut butter.

The Killer grabbed the small trash bag out of the trash can and took it with him, along with his duffle bag and crown. He then returned to his room for another shower, got dressed, and left the hotel before any guests might be questioned. He dumped the trash bag with the peanut butter in it along the way. After getting into the Mercedes, he took off the mustache and wig that fit his fake ID and headed back to Wichita.

....

Randall managed just four hours of sleep. If not for the assistance of his friend, Mr. Ambien, Randall would not have had that much. Although a little groggy from lack of sleep, he forced himself to jump out of bed. He wanted to get back to work on his pickleball killer theory as soon as possible. What he found was confirmation of his theory, much faster than he would have ever expected, for he turned on the news while making a pot of coffee.

Immediately, he would see the words BREAKING NEWS blast across his television screen. News reporter Julie Kennedy was live from Hays reporting the murder of a lady in a hot tub at one of its local hotels. Pure panic set in. He tried to pour a cup of coffee, but it spilled all over his left arm. "Shit, Shit, Shit."

Although the coffee burned like hell, it was not the hot beverage that propelled the profanity from his mouth, but fear for his neighbor's life. He was certain that the incident was connected to last night's pickleball tournament, and he knew that Keisha had been there. As he ran cold water across his arm, he began sweating profusely. He kept telling himself not to panic. He started to relax as Julie Kennedy reported further about the woman that was killed. Mrs. Kennedy stated that due to the family needing to be notified, the name of the victim would not be released at this time. Surely, she would say a girl if it was the Reynolds kid. But then again, he thought, Keisha could easily pass for a woman. Randall then remembered the graduation party he had observed at the Reynolds house. That meant she was eighteen and graduated from high school, making her completely a young woman now.

Oh, how he dreaded her early morning banging of the hardened Wiffle ball against the garage sessions. Now, he would do anything to hear the sweet sound of his neighbor foe slamming that damn ball and making him wonderfully miserable this morning. Agonizing annoyance at least demonstrated obvious signs of life. He quickly ran out the door to investigate his neighbor's driveway.

He was thrilled to see that it was a nice day. It was not supposed to be, but Kansas weather will dramatically change faster than a shooting star flying through the night sky. Not to mention, Star Action News employed the world's worst meteorologist. Randall figured an insect could predict the weather better than Dallas Richardson. Why did he care so much about it being a nice day? The answer was simple. His neighbors headed to Sunday mass at St. Joseph, but not until 10:00 AM, meaning Keisha would be up early to get her garage door pickleball session in.

7:30 a.m. – Randall frantically rocked in his recliner upstairs by the window while trying to read his third copy of Follett's *World Without End*.

7:45 a.m.– Randall looked out the window for the tenth time in fifteen minutes, anxiously waiting for the ritual banging of the Wiffle ball against the unforgiving garage. To his dismay, nothing but peace and agonizing tranquility could be heard.

8:15 AM- Randall contemplated grabbing his pellet gun out of the closet to blow the hell out of the annoying, chirping sparrows. He just knew the sparrows were laughing at him as they conversed about the irony of Randall's sudden craving to hear pickleball madness from his neighbor.

8:30 a.m. – It had been an hour, and Randall had read three pages, none of which he had actually read with any comprehension. "Where the hell is she?"

9:00 a.m. – Randall closed the book and trampled down the stairs and out the door.

9:03 a.m. – Randall rang his neighbors' doorbell.

9:03 a.m. and fifteen seconds – Randall opened the unlocked front door and stepped in.

9:04 a.m. – Randall shouted in anger as the family was startled. Mathew dropped his copy of Follett's book on the ground. Keisha also lost the page she was on, and her copy of the Follett novel fell into her lap. Elijah started to drop his laptop but caught his prized possession just before it fell to the floor.

9:04 a.m. and twenty-four seconds: Edna screamed, "What in the hell are you doing, Mr. Randall?" She then looked up to the ceiling and said, "Sorry, God, but I don't think I should have to say a rosary for that one."

9:05 a.m. – Mr. Randall turned to Keisha. "Why aren't you banging that stupid wiffle ball against the garage this morning?"

9:05 a.m. and twenty-one seconds – Edna took an umbrella and whacked Randall in the back, threatening to call the police and letting him know how insane and crazy he his.

9:06 a.m. – Another copy of Follett's *World Without End* flies from Randall's hands across the room. Elijah yells, "Ahh, shit! Now I gotta read that shit too."
 Edna responded, "Yes, you do. And that will be three hundred push-ups, as well, for cussing."
 "Damn it," Elijah exclaims.
 "Make that seven hundred now! And two hundred Hail Mary's," Edna spits back.

9:07 a.m. – Randall left with yet another copy of Follett's book in the hands of his neighbors.

"I'm calling the police," Edna informs her grandchildren.
"Not a good idea," Keisha responded.
"And why is that?"

Keisha pointed out to Grandma Edna that Randall had never been particularly friendly to them, but on the other hand, he hadn't necessarily been a bad neighbor, either; at least, until recently, with a few flights of his book and an apparent flair for the dramatic this morning. She further stated that overall, he had been harmless over a great many years. Keisha pointed out that Mr. Baines did appear to have had some friendly conversations with Grandpa Edward. (Keisha suspected that he just didn't relate to young people and women so much.) Keisha reminded the family that his daughter, Samantha, was super friendly and always made a point to say "hello" during the few visits she had had over the past couple of years. Finally, Keisha pointed out that he had not done anything that would cause him to be put in jail, and they would still have to deal with him as their next-door neighbor.

Edna was frustrated with Keisha's insistence on not allowing the authorities to be contacted but admitted that she had valid points. As a family, Mathew, Keisha, Edna, and Elijah mutually agreed not to contact law enforcement but to keep a very close eye on Mr. Baines. They all agreed that if there were any more absurd and outrageously unhinged behavior by Mr. Baines, 911 would be on speed dial, ready to go.

Discussing the incident further, Keisha admitted to her family that she was bewildered by the strangeness of it all. He attempted to assault her with a Follett book on two occasions because of the noise from the pickleball, but then he became enraged when she wasn't playing. Edna concluded it was obvious that he is just flat-out crazy. Keisha rejected that notion. She stated that she was convinced it was something more, something deeper than simply being crazy. Keisha insisted that she wanted to get to the bottom of it. She had an intuitive mind, the mind of a detective, you might say. Perhaps she had more in common with Mr. Baines than she might have imagined. Edna tried to convince Keisha not to bother with the situation, and to stay away from the old, crazy, white man, even though, deep down inside, Edna knew that Keisha was not the type of person who would let it go. Edna's blood pressure began to rise, and she handled it the only way she knew how to - prayer.

"All right, kids, put up the Follett books and get ready for church. We all need to do a lot of praying, especially for crazy madman Baines. "

CHAPTER 8

It was early Monday morning. Keisha had already put in a good workout, eaten a light breakfast, and showered. Mathew and Elijah got up around 9:30 a.m. The three of them eventually found themselves sitting in the living room, reading Follett's *World Without End*. Keisha was not about to admit that she was entranced with the book. It fascinated her that even in the 1300's, there were brave women who wanted to prove themselves equal to men. She was totally enamored with Caris, a lady who desired to be a doctor. Keisha loved her tenacity and perseverance in her quest to achieve such a lofty goal, especially as a woman in 1321. Keisha also enjoyed the book because she was infatuated with the chemistry between Caris and Merthin. Romance wasn't something she thought much about, as most teenage girls do. Keisha always felt her will to succeed was too strong to have her goals interrupted by some guy. Her vicarious feelings of passionate love from reading Follett's novel were the first such feelings that she had ever experienced about romantic love. Mathew was wholly absorbed in the book, as well. He rarely had any roundtable discussions with Keisha on their new, shared interest in Follett's work. Every time the book was brought up, Mathew became rapidly bored with the romance and liberated woman talk. He wanted to discuss strategies Merthin might use to build the new town bridge, which in turn bored Keisha to tears.

Edna had ordered all three to read their own personal copies of *World Without End*, thanks to the unintentional book donations of Mr. Baines. But Keisha and Mathew were no longer reading the book because they had to. They were completely enamored with Follett's work.

On the other hand, Elijah was reading under the strict command of General Grandma Edna. Computers were his vice, and computers obviously weren't going to be found in a 1300s historical fiction read. He used his computer skills to capture footnotes and summaries to pass any verbal quiz Grandma Edna might infringe upon him, but he skimmed over some of the actual book, just to be safe. He also dared not get too far away from the book, as Grandma Edna stated before she left that it was either read the book or there would be a ton of chores for the three to do. She gave this command just before walking out to check on one of the mattress stores. All three knew that she could unexpectedly walk in at any moment to check on them.

Keisha suddenly put the book down and paced back and forth across the room. Elijah told her to chill out, and Mathew just wanted to know what the problem was. Keisha continued to pace back and forth, exclaiming, "I gotta know. I gotta know."

Of course, Mathew replied, "Know what?"

After five or six repetitions of this exchange, Keisha finally shouted, "I'm heading next door. I must find out what Mr. Baines' problem is."

Mathew replied, "He is a crazy, bitter, old, white man. That's his only problem."

"No, No. I think there is something much deeper going on. And I'm determined to get to the bottom of it."

"Good luck with that," Elijah sarcastically remarked.

"Are you sure that's a good idea?" Mathew interjected.

"No, I don't, Mathew. But you know the old saying. – 'Curiosity killed the cat.'"

Mathew put his head down in worry and replied, "That doesn't make me feel better at all. Please be careful."

Keisha exited the home. Mathew looked out the window, watching her walk over to the home of grouchy, old Mr. Baines. He worried to the point that butterflies invaded his stomach.

Usually, if there are two teenage boys in a house and one teenage girl, it is customary for the two boys to hang out and the girl to be left to herself. But in this case, Mathew and Keisha were very close. They had a lot in common with their interest in sports.

Elijah cared little for physical competition. His preferred type of competition was games of thought and strategy such as chess or Risk. These two games he often played with his computer geek friends online. He, too, was concerned with Keisha's decision to invade the Baines home, but he would not show his concern. "Any show of emotion is a sign of weakness," he thought. Feelings and emotions had their place, but since the death of his parents and grandfather, he needed to censor his. The pain of getting too close to anyone seemed like an unnecessary move toward personal torture for Elijah. Fall in love with a laptop and a cup of coffee, and leave human companionship to the weak, was the philosophy that made Elijah feel safe.

Keisha took a step onto the porch of Mr. Baines. She turned away from the home and started heading back to her own home, but then she turned around again. Keisha was nervous but determined. She would not allow her fear of Mr. Baines to hide the truth. After a slight hesitation, Keisha rang the doorbell of her bitter adversary. After a few seconds, she rang it again. She felt her knees shake. Her heartbeat felt like it thumped louder than ACDC blaring Thunderstruck from a loudspeaker at a rock concert.

Randall suddenly opened the door. "What do you want, Keisha?"

"I am impressed that you know my name, Mr. Baines."

"Well, obviously, you don't know mine, Keisha. Call me Randall."

"First of all, I'd like to point out that this is a doorbell, Randall. Something you clearly do not understand the use of since you invaded our home Monday."

Embarrassed, Randall replied, "Well, I did ring the doorbell, but not waiting for someone to open the door was improper, scary, and criminal behavior. I am very sorry. I'm thankful that you didn't call the authorities on me. What is it that you need, Keisha?"

"Well, apologizing was a start. I really only have one question for you, Randall. Why are you so weird?"

After a long pause, Randall replied, "Honestly, I don't know. I guess it has something to do with finding a sense of purpose. Please come in."

Keisha then took a step back and replied, "Sorry, but I'm not so sure that's a real good idea, Mr. Baines."

"Again, Randall is the name. Simply call me Randall. I understand your reservation after my deplorable break-in Sunday morning. But remember, I spent a lifetime with the Wichita PD as a detective, so being on the wrong side of the law for three minutes of my life is just an anomaly."

"Fair enough," Keisha responded as she entered the home of her bizarre next-door neighbor for the first time in her eighteen years of life.

Randall offered Keisha a cup of coffee, which she initially turned down. But after smelling the freshly brewed aroma, she relented and happily accepted the offer. Randall asked Keisha how her grandmother was doing and revealed that he had been concerned about the family since the death of Keisha's parents and her grandfather. This surprised Keisha, as it appeared that he genuinely cared about them. She then thought that if he really cared, he would have at least made a consolatory appearance or even sent a card upon their deaths. She was also taken aback by his apparent concern since she had truly thought that he hated them. She wasn't sure that it was necessarily a racist thing, but perhaps anger that a bunch of kids lived next door and he had no patience for them.

After more fruitless small talk, she went back to her original question. "Randall, thank you for the coffee, and the chit-chat has just been dandy, but I need to refer back to my original question at your doorstep, "Why are you so weird?"

"I'm probably not as weird as you might think," Randall said quietly.

She then pointed out his history with the family, which included trivial annoyances, such as yelling out the window for the kids to settle down, as well as more extraordinary measures like hiding skateboards for days to keep them from making noise in the driveway. The skateboard incident bewildered him because he didn't understand how she could know that it had been him. She explained that simple, common-sense logic told her it was him, for why else would the skateboards be returned in a couple of days rather than permanently stolen? He shook his head "yes" in admiration of her deductive powers.

"Ahh, she has the mind of a detective," he thought.

Keisha eventually turned to the most recent incidents that included throwing Follett at her two weeks in a row for playing garage-style pickleball, and then turning around and breaking into their home to throw another at them because she *wasn't* playing pickleball. He shook his head "yes" again, acknowledging the bizarre behavior. Then, after another long pause, he proclaimed, "I want you to teach me your oversized-ping-pong-paddle, super-tough-as-nails Wiffle ball game."

"Why? You throw a temper tantrum when I do play it outside, and now you want me to teach it to you? And just like my grandmother, you don't even respect the sport enough to call it by its name, which is pickleball, not oversized-ping-pong-paddle, super-tough-as-nails Wiffle ball game."

Randall laughed and asked, "What does Edna call it then?"
She replied angrily, "That cucumber game thing."
Randall once again burst out laughing, "Now that is funny."
"No, it's not," Keisha spat back.
"Oh, yes, it is. You gotta admit; that's a little bit funny."
"No, it's not."
"Yes, it is."
Keisha then slightly paused and laughed, "Okay, I guess that *is* kind of funny."
"So, are you going to teach me the cucumber game?"
"Ha ha, Mr. Baines. Why on earth do you suddenly have an interest in pickleball?"
"I'm a lonely old man who was forced into retirement, and it seems to be a great way to get to know people."
"I believe you are a lonely old man trying to find his place in life, but I highly doubt that's why you want to play pickleball. Is it?"
"Oh, you're an observant young lady, aren't you? Will fifty bucks an hour do the trick?"
She reluctantly replied, "Sorry, that is quite a generous offer. However, I don't think I'm qualified. I get private lessons myself by a professional that I only pay twenty dollars an hour."
"Okay, that's even better. Give me his number, and I will only have to pay him twenty bucks."
"No, Randall, I cannot do that."
"Why not?"
"Because I don't want to be responsible for your weirdness. Your brain is quite left of center right now, and I don't know

what it is but the reason you want to learn pickleball has nothing to do with bonding with your fellow man."

"Oh well, I really only wanted you to teach me the game anyway," he replied.

Startled, Keisha stated, "Mr. Baines, do you know how creepy that sounds?"

"Uh um, I guess I can see that. But it's your observation skills and intelligence that I need more so than your knowledge of pickleball."

"So, it doesn't have anything to do with loneliness, does it, Mr. Baine... um, Randall?"

"It's fifty dollars an hour, Keisha. Take it or leave it."

"If you won't tell me what's going on, I'll leave it."

She put her coffee down and started to head out the door.

"Please, don't go. I'm desperate."

"That's an awfully freaky remark there, Randall!"

Randall then blurted out, "I-I-I-I'm working on a case."

Keisha turned toward him in bewilderment and pointed out to Randall that he was retired.

He explained to her that he had been working on his own as a free agent, so to speak. She then proceeded to ask him what the case was about. He told her that it was none of her business. She again started to make her way to the door, making it clear that she would not teach him anything about pickleball if he didn't tell her the truth.

After a long pause, he stated, "Keisha, I could tell you, but you would think me even stranger and twisted than you did before you entered my home today."

She replied with a slight smile, "I highly doubt that's possible."

"Oh, it is, Keisha. It is."

"Try me, Randall."

"Okay, I still want you to teach me your cucumber game, but I won't be paying you fifty bucks."

She then stated, "You can't go back and tell me you'll pay the twenty an hour because that's what I pay my coach. That wouldn't be fair after you told me you'd pay fifty."

"I'm not going to pay you a damn dime until the work is done because if you are all-in on what I'm doing, you'll be doing much more work than just tutoring pickleball. Ms. Keisha, I won't be paying you fifty bucks but instead your share of the $2.5 million in reward money for solving the mystery."

"And what mystery would that be, Randall?"

"There was a murder last night in Hays. Have you heard?"

She then stated with fright, "Oh yes. It really shook me up since I was in Hays on Saturday, watching a professional pickleball tournament. Glad I wasn't at the hotel."

"Yes, yes, I know that. I saw you in the background of the television coverage of the tournament."

"Yes, my brother said that he saw me as well. Good thing my grandma didn't see me, as I was not supposed to be there."

"Keisha, I barged into your home because I freaked out. I was scared it was you."

"Randall, I am quite touched that you were so concerned about me, but just because I was in Hays that day, the odds would be slim-to-none that it could have been me."

Randall then stated, "Your life might have been on the line more than you think, Keisha."

"And why is that?" she asked with alarm.

"The authorities probably have no idea that it's connected to the Peanut Butter Killer since no peanut butter was involved this time."

"And why do you think the Hays murder was connected to the Peanut Butter Killer Randall?

"Because I believe it's not peanut butter that the murdering bastard is truly into, but his obsession lies in the cucumber, giant-ping-pong-paddle, hard-as-a-rock Wiffle ball game that you call – PICKLEBALL!"

CHAPTER 9

The Killer went back to his three-story home. He was still feeling upset about not winning the 5.0 tournament. Usually, a good killing would fulfill his sick desire for an adrenaline rush, but he had not gotten the attention that he so needed from the murder of what he thought of as the red-headed-spouse-cheater. After the family had been notified, the victim's name was revealed as Donna Prescott. But the name was pointless to him. He knew why this murder bothered him. He wanted the Peanut Butter Killer to get the notoriety that he felt he deserved. He had not been ready to kill at that moment, but the unexpected seduction of the redhead was too exhilarating to pass up. He wasn't stupid. He was a Harvard graduate with a Master's in engineering. Hays, Kansas was just too damn small a place to risk having the law associate The Peanut Butter Killer with a major pickleball tournament in the small college town. Sure, he wanted the authorities to eventually figure out that it was pickleball and not peanut butter. If he didn't, he wouldn't have left that clue. But he sure in hell didn't want them to find out yet. He was having too much damn fun. His plan was to run off to a resort in Ecuador, Honduras, or somewhere remote when he sensed that they were getting closer to associating peanut butter with pickleball. He knew he would eventually want the credit for the supposed Peanut Butter killings, but he intended to be safely out of the country with his millions before he was discovered.

It just wasn't fair that his hotter-than-hell co-ed doubles partner got all the attention for her great looks, and his men's doubles partner got all the attention because of his youth, style, and personality. The peanut butter murders were his own. No blonde bimbo or studly, cool, athletic guy could take that from him. As he worked out in his fitness room, he suddenly heard the doorbell ring. He reluctantly quit working out and answered the door. When he looked out, he saw the delivery man getting into his truck and driving off. On his porch lay a package.

PEANUT BUTTER PICKLEBALL AND MURDER

The Killer picked up the package and looked at the box with his name and address in the middle. Then he thought with dismay, "Oh, God. Perhaps I went WAY too far with the peanut butter thing? Why did this package even have my middle name on it?"
The name that he read on the label of the package –

Peter Branton Weatherford.

. . . .

Keisha did not want her grandmother to have even a hint of her communication with Mr. Baines. She knew that Edna thought Randall was crazy. And quite frankly, Grandmother was probably right in that assumption. She now felt that he was crazy in a weird, bizarre way, not crazy in a violent, psychotic way. After all, even she would have broken into any of her neighbors' houses if she thought they might have been endangered or killed. Of course, she couldn't explain this to her grandmother, as Edna would then know that she wasn't at the Wilson's house babysitting that night.
 Keisha carefully knocked on the backdoor of Randall's home Tuesday after school. She was overwhelmed by the thought that the Peanut Butter Killer could be connected to pickleball. Just yesterday, she had told Randall he was a crazy, old man with too much time on his hands if he was coming up with such bizarre ideas. And she had walked out. But her restless thoughts began to take a toll on her. She knew it was probably

best to leave the matter alone, but in the end, her inquisitiveness got the best of her. It took Randall some time to open the back door. He thought it intrusive that someone had walked through the gate of his fenced-in backyard rather than arrive at the front. When he opened the door and saw that it was Keisha, she didn't have to explain. He already understood her reasons for being sneaky.

After he let her in, she simply said, "Okay. I'm all ears. Why do you think the Peanut Butter Killer is a pickleball player?" They sat down at Randall's table with fresh cups of coffee. Keisha wasn't much of an afternoon coffee drinker, but she gladly accepted a cup this time to calm her nerves. He proceeded to show her that there were advanced-level pickleball tournaments in every city that hosted a murder. He pointed out the PB initial connection and gave her his reasons for thinking that The Killer was likely a middle-aged rich guy. Keisha pointed out to Randall that his "evidence" was not much to go on.

He put his head down dejectedly and stated emphatically, "I know you think I'm insane, but I know I'm right on this; I just know it!"

Keisha replied, "Mr. Baines… um, um…I mean, Randall, you didn't let me finish. I was going to say, this "evidence" is not much to go on. However, it is enough that your idea is worth further investigation."

Randall then exclaimed with excitement, "Yes, yes! So, you'll help me?"

"Yes, Randall, I will help."

Randall then remarked, "But Keisha, you must know that getting involved could put you in danger."

"Sir, if The Killer is a higher-level pickleball player, or "one of my kind," I could be in even more danger if I don't get involved."

Nodding slowly, Randall replied, "That was my concern as well."

"Well, what are we waiting for? No time to waste. We have a serial killer to find. Where do we start?"

Randall reminded her that he wanted her to coach him because he would need to get really good, really fast, to engage with upper echelon pickleball players. He had done his homework on the game and understood that the levels of proficiency ranged from 2.0 to 5.0. He knew that 2.0 players were not only beginners but those who had probably never played a racket sport before in their lives. 2.5 players were beginners with some tennis or racket ball experience. 3.0 were average players. 3.5 players were good. 4.0 players were not only good but borderline great. 4.5 were excellent, and 5.0 players were playing pro tournaments for cash, and many even had sponsors. Randall told Keisha that he had once taken 4th in the nation at a National Army base racquetball tournament for those in the armed forces. He also told her that he had taken third in the state in tennis his Senior year of high school and that he still played tennis and racquetball regularly (he knew this was a bit of an exaggeration, as he had been less diligent about his usual physical activities in recent months). Randall noted that he had read that many new pickleball players could get very, very good very, very quickly if they had previous racket-sports experience.

Randall told Keisha that to be around or near The Killer, he would need to be a 5.0 player within a month or so, if not sooner.

Keisha responded not with words, but with laughter. After laughing for what seemed like a humiliating eternity, Randall asked her why this would not be possible. She let him know that most of the players that became 5.0 level players that quickly were college kids who had played tennis throughout high school and college and were still young. She then asked him his age. After finding out he was in his 70s, she started laughing again.

He just looked at her with a cold, hard stare and said, "Damn it, Keisha, there's a sick f'ing prick out there that could kill someone again at any moment. If you don't like my plan but want to be a part of this, don't laugh. Come up with your own idea. And when you present it to me, no matter how out-of-the-box or weird it sounds, I guarantee you; I won't laugh!"

After a long pause, she responded. "I'm sorry, Randall. You're right. And although I don't have a solution off the top of my head, you are correct that you will need to know more about the game. So, let's get started. Let's get to Gabrielle Courts. I'll drive us there. I refuse to give you the chance to drive home and escape because we aren't ending this pickleball session anytime soon. I just hope Grandma doesn't find out I'm not actually at the Wilsons' babysitting. I texted her that they needed me tonight and tomorrow night. Somewhere down the line, that lie is going to get me burnt. Meet me down the block in ten minutes, so Grandma doesn't see you get in my car."

"Done," Randall stated with a smile.

After Keisha picked Randall up, the two headed straight to the Gabrielle Pickleball Club. She explained some of the basics of the game. Some he already knew through his research, but she reiterated the information. Keisha let it be known that the sport is getting so incredibly popular because there is less ground for each player to cover. The sport gives those who are less able to cover an entire tennis court due to age, injury, etc. a new lease on racket life. She went on to explain that this is because the court is half the size of a tennis court. Keisha told him that, like tennis, players still serve the ball to the opponent diagonally and switch to the other opponent diagonally across. The biggest difference is that when serving in pickleball versus tennis, a player only gets one serve. There are no double-faults. Also, players must serve underhand otherwise; in a small court, players could just smash the serve, easily keeping their opponent from returning the ball. Unlike tennis, where players must get the ball to hit the court in a square diagonally, pickleball players just need to get the ball anywhere on the opposite side of the court. It just has to get past the kitchen.

"Kitchen...?" Randall pondered.

"I'll get to the whole kitchen thing later," Keisha responded. She then further explained that you can only win a point on a serve. Aside from the beginning of the game, when a player loses their serve, their doubles partner gets a serve until they lose it. To make things fair, when the game begins, only one server on the beginning team's side gets to serve, and the opponents both get to serve until they lose their serves. Then both members of the beginning team serve until they lose theirs until the game ends. Keisha explained that scoring is more similar to how ping-pong or racquetball is scored than it is to tennis. Each time a player wins a point when they serve, it is a whole point, unlike tennis with the 15-love, 30-love stuff. The official rules state the score goes to eleven, and a team must win by two points to win the game. The team that wins two out of three games wins the match. Keisha patted Randall on the back and let him know that the rules seem a little overwhelming at first, but after playing the game a couple of times, he would catch on fast. She then proclaimed that one word described why she thought pickleball was the "granddaddy" of all racket sports. She turned to him and said, "That word is the most special four-letter word in the history of language."

"And what word would that be, Keisha?" Randall asked.

With a wide, beautiful smile, she turned to him and said enthusiastically, "DINK!"

"Huh? Dink? Not exactly a manly sort of word, Keisha."

Without hesitation, she replied, "Yes, well, if you don't embrace the dink, Randall, the game will most certainly take your manhood."

He laughed and said, "I'll take your word for it."

She pointed out to him the lines in the middle of the court surrounding the net. She stated that this was the "kitchen."

He laughed and sarcastically said, "Oh, man. The main word to know to win the game is 'dink,' and the game involves a 'kitchen'. What kind of kiddy-girly game is this?"

She hastily responded, "Close your eyes."

"What?"

"I said, close your eyes!"

"Okay, okay, I'm closing my eyes."

"Picture your mother on Thanksgiving Day. You smell the stuffing, the sweet aroma of cranberry sauce. Oh, oh, oh, the mashed potatoes and gravy. You *love* the taste of your momma's homemade special gravy."

"OH, yes, I do. Man, did I love mom's cooking back in the day. God Bless her soul."

Keisha continued, "You peek through a crack in the kitchen door connected to the living room. You see the lid. The lid is the crown placed upon the golden jewel of all foods. Your momma struts up and takes her place before the treasure chest she calls a roaster and lifts the crown off. You see the steam gracefully float up to the ceiling. The hypnotizing aroma of that quintessential, glorious roast enters your nose. You see the steam dissipate, and that beautiful, golden-brown bird peacefully fills your vision. Momma's ultimate culinary masterpiece is carefully pulled out of the roaster and placed in the middle of the dining room table. And then she gets out the desserts - cherry pie, peach cobbler, and your favorite, your all-time favorite dessert in the world – your momma's very own, specialized, secret recipe pumpkin pie. Like all kids, you fantasize about putting a nice, large spoonful of whipped topping on that pumpkin pie."

"I'm starving now, Keisha. You're killing me."

But Keisha continued, "Momma then places some of her hot and fresh chocolate chip cookies on the table. She sets them close to you on a small coffee table set up for the occasion, still in the kitchen but just a few feet away. As you're still outside the kitchen peaking in, you feel your stomach roaring like a lion in his den. You decide to sneak in, grab a cookie, and run out before she catches you. You pause slightly to contemplate the consequences of the cookie crime, but you don't think about it long. The smell and the sight of the food kingdom are too much for you to bear. It's time for you to go in and get that cookie!"

With his eyes still closed, Randall said with conviction, "Good idea! I'm going in."

"Are you there? Are you grabbing the cookie, Randall?"
He stated with excitement, "Yes, yes! I got the cookie."

Just then, without hesitation, Keisha walked behind him and smacked him in the back of the head.

He opened his eyes and shouted in pain, "HEY! WHAT WAS THAT FOR?!"

Keisha then got right in Randall's face, staring into his eyes, and shouted, "MOMMA SAYS STAY OUT OF THE KITCHEN!"

Randall angrily replied, "OWW, MAN. WHAT A STRONG, PAINFUL WAY TO MAKE YOUR POINT!"

"I bet that's what happened to you, Randall, just like all the rest of us, every Thanksgiving. Am I right?"

Randall lowered his head in agreement, "Yep, every year."

Keisha responded, "I bet you don't think of the kitchen as some girly, kiddy place now, do you?"

Randall laughed uncomfortably and replied, "Nope. We all hold onto those precious memories of finally eating that Thanksgiving meal but tend to forget the pain we suffered when we got in mom's way as she was preparing it."

Keisha then pointed out to Randall that the kitchen lines mark a place as forbidden in preparing for a win as momma's kitchen was while momma was cooking. She told Randall that there was an exception to this, of course. If the ball bounces in the kitchen, then you can enter it to hit it. She explained that, unlike in tennis, players can't set foot in the kitchen area or hit the ball while it is in flight unless it touches the ground of the forbidden area. Only then is it fair game. She further explained why the dink was so important.

"Just as your momma's hand across the back of your head was her way of protecting her kitchen kingdom, the dink is your way of protecting the kitchen. Want a make a great meal of your opponent and serve a dish of pickleball victory? Embrace the DINK!"

She then pointed out that dinking the ball means to hit the ball lightly over the net, so it barely drops over into the kitchen. Since the opponent can't step over the kitchen and smash it, they must either let it drop or hit it low in the air without their feet crossing the kitchen line.

Keisha pointed out that this is what makes the game so special. In tennis, points are fast, and there is a lot of area to cover on the large court. Pickleball requires much more finesse and patience.

She told Randall that to be a great pickleball player; you must hit low. Hit high, and the opponent can smash the ball, as there would be plenty of room to slam it down an opponent's throat. Lobbing the ball can work, but if an opponent is tall, it is hard to find the space on the small pickleball court to get the ball over him or her and keep it in play.

It sounds simple, but continuously hitting a ball an inch or two over a net is a science. Keisha let Randall know that when he played good players, he might get bored and decide to take a chance by hitting the ball harder. Then it would likely fly out of bounds across the court, or the opponent would see it while it was still high enough to completely shove the ball down his throat. Choking on a huge cube of ice would be more comfortable than the misery of humiliation Randall or his partner would suffer from the rotten, selfish lack of patience.

Keisha then started an official practice with Randall. The two-hour practice consisted of nothing but net play. DINK, DINK, AND MORE DINK! And every time that he would hit the ball too high, she would show no mercy to him from the other side of the net. Keisha was so accurate that she could purposely smash the ball into both of his exposed arms with all her strength, at will. About every fourth ball that Randall hit would either meet the net, for which he was ordered to do twenty push-ups, or would soar too high, resulting in yet another hundred-and-ten-mile-per-hour hardened Wiffle ball reddening either his left or right arm, leaving yet another bruise.

This carried on for over two hours. The whole time, Randall complained. He complained to Keisha that he found this game monotonous, boring, and painful. He pointed out that most instructors introduced the fun aspects of a game by playing it nicely, the instructor lightly hitting the ball back so the player could get used to the motions.

But she ignored all his requests for her to change her coaching style. When the session was over, she told him she would see him back on the court when the club opened at 8 a.m. He protested. She ignored his protest. She let him know that she was his coach and that every word would be obeyed. He shook his head as if to say, "okay."

"I suppose after you give me a ride back home, I'll see you tomorrow at 8 a.m.," Randall replied.

"No, you will see me tonight at 9 p.m. at the Wilson's house, where I'm babysitting. I told Grandma Edna a small white lie by making her think I'm there now, but I really do have to babysit there tonight.

"Their young kids of five and three should be asleep by then, and the Wilsons won't be in until midnight. I'm not just your pickleball coach; I'm your fellow private eye, co-worker, detective, colleague, whatever the hell you want to call it, Randall. There's research to be done. We got a killer to catch!"

"I know where the Wilsons live. They have a fancy-schmancy Wichita State Foundation banquet to attend tonight. They're both alumni and high-end donors. They told me about it when I stopped to say "hi" on my morning walk today," he confirmed.

"There's always a fancy-schmancy something-or-another they are involved in with the college. It's how I make my living babysitting only their kids!" she remarked with a grin. Keisha had one pace in anything that she did – FAST and FASTER!

CHAPTER 10

Peter went to his favorite place in the world aside from the pickleball courts: his fitness room. He didn't have a particular workout regimen. He would randomly do push-ups, sit-ups, pull-ups, run on the treadmill, run on the elliptical... He just felt like the only comfort in his lonely existence was to keep moving. He had a huge, life-size mirror in which he constantly stared at himself, looking upon his body with both admiration and horror. Admiration for how great he looked for his age, but horror when he realized his age was a reminder of his own mortality. Peter thought of those he had killed. He relived the exhilarating joy he had felt when he had taken his pickleball-paddle-switchblade and struck his victims down. Peter had enjoyed the last few murders, but they hadn't felt the same as the Kansas City and St. Louis slayings. He felt glee recalling how those two victims begged him to stop and prayed for their lives.

"Why are you doing this? What have I done?"

"I'll give you whatever you want, credit cards, money, anything!"

Peter loved the begging. To know that their lives were in his hands made him feel as though he were God. He thought about how much better he was than other serial killers. He was very rich. He used his own handmade weapon made from, of all things, a pickleball paddle. He may not be some young guy in his thirties, but he was a seasoned, sophisticated killer. As far as Peter was concerned, other serial killers had nothing going for them. They were total losers. He was a self-made man who had created his own success. He had started out after college, tinkering on neighbors' faucets, and had built a business designing and building multi-million-dollar homes and businesses. It was rare to find anyone in the Wichita metropolitan area who hadn't heard of HEAVENLY HOMES INCORPORATED. Peter laughed while he ran his fifth mile on the elliptical, thinking how clever he was to have come up with the name HEAVENLY. Peter thought that he was more powerful than God and Satan. By day he played God, giving couples the homes of their dreams. By night he played Satan, taking human lives in a most horrific and nightmarish manner.

After his workout, he stepped outside onto his patio. His backyard was a gorgeous fenced-in area, equipped with the perfect lawn and a small pond filled with twelve-inch goldfish. The pond had a waterfall that flowed over rocks, and a bridge to walk across the pond. There was also a garden that flowed along the edges of the area, with a multitude of flowers such as tulips, carnations, and daffodils.

On the patio was a hot tub. Beside it lay a mini fridge with a boom box on top of it. He hit play and cranked the volume. WANTED DEAD OR ALIVE by Bon Jovi blared. He took a cold beer from the fridge and hopped into the hot tub to sip on a beer while admiring his self-made paradise. His mind ran towards his mixed doubles partner and the incredible sex they had together. Peter thought of calling Tasha to join him, but then he remembered the euphoria he felt when he took the life of the woman in the Hays hotel hot tub, and he realized sex in a hot tub would never be the same. Nothing could top the exuberant physical and mental passion of combining hot tub lust and murder. No Jacuzzi experience could ever match that feeling again.

Peter looked upon his mansion as he sipped his beer and thought to himself how amazing he was to have created all this: his company, his home, and his athletic legacy. He remembered where he came from, which reminded him why he hated the world.

Peter thought back to the horror of his childhood. He remembered sitting at the dinner table in a small, one-bedroom apartment. His brother, Tom, sat to the right of him. His sister, Angela across from him. Peter was six years old. His brother was eight, and his sister was ten. His mother was twenty-eight but looked about forty. She had raggedy hair and no make-up. They all wore clothes not even fit for a vagabond. His mother took a spatula and dumped some type of mush on his plate. Peter looked at the plate with dread. He did not eat it. In fact, he refused, shaking his head "no."

His sister looked at him as if to say, "Please, please, Peter. Eat the food." She so wanted him to eat it because she knew what would come next for her brother if he didn't. And sure enough, his mother didn't wait for Peter to take the time to make a decision to eat. She instantly decided to teach him a lesson for not enjoying the food she had cooked.

"I cook a meal for you, ya little bastard, and you don't appreciate it. Listen, you little bastard, I wouldn't have to worry about you if the married landlord didn't come over once a week and demand I put out to make up for not making the rent. And what do I get in return? Pregnant with YOU- An ungrateful little prick who won't eat my food. "

She picked up her cigarette, took a puff, and blew it in his face. She then smacked him on the right cheek. Angela cried, and in turn, she was hit in the face as well.

"Don't feel sympathy for the little bastard. Cry again, and I'll smack you both once more. You and Tom might be a slight step up in my eyes over your bastard brother, Peter. At least I was married to your father before he fucking overdosed on heroin. But don't think I won't send you down to the little bastard's level. Look at you, Peter. Look at yourself in a mirror tonight. You know what you'll see when you do? What everyone else sees- a Fucking Freak."

Peter did not cry. He just felt so lonely and sad. Angela wished Peter would obey their mother. She hated seeing him in emotional and physical pain. In contrast, his brother Tom laughed. Tom appeared to enjoy the agony that Peter endured. Their mother walked to the living room and pulled out a crack pipe. They waited for her to pass out before eating enough to survive and then dumped the rest in the trash. Angela took the garbage out so her mother wouldn't see that they hadn't eaten it all. Eventually, the landlord used his key to walk into the house without knocking. Peter, Tom, and Angela listened to him holler her name, Nancy, several times to wake her up. As she slowly opened her eyes, he demanded she take her clothes off. The landlord did not care whether the kids were in the room or not. Peter, Tom, and Angela left the apartment to play outside and try to keep their minds off what was currently going on in the apartment. All humans were shit in Peter's eyes, except for his sister.

Soon after Landlord Carl finished his sexual assault on Peter's mother, he opened the front door and hollered for Peter to come in while he zipped up his pants. He guided Peter into the bathroom to work on the toilet. Peter held a wrench sometimes, but mainly he watched his biological father, Carl, work on the toilet. Peter never knew whether Carl was teaching him handyman skills to help him out of guilt, or just to have the six-year-old fix things around the house so he wouldn't have to. It completely baffled Peter. But learning how to fix things did make him feel good. It was something so small, but it was something that he could embrace.

Peter was no longer sipping on beers while sitting in the hot tub but guzzling them. He did not feel gratitude towards his landlord father, although he did take pleasure knowing that it was the skills he had learned from his piece-of-shit father that had helped make him a millionaire. And what did Landlord Carl have? He had a two-bedroom, piece-of-shit apartment with a mean, ugly wife and four loser kids. And he drove a beat-up 1963 Chevy truck!

Peter recalled the time when he was eleven and Carl had picked him up and taken him to his shop a mile outside of town. Carl had Peter help him change the transmission in that same dump of a motorized vehicle. It had taken several hours, and Carl had a pizza delivered. Carl immediately binged on the pizza, eating six and a half slices. He had only allowed Peter to have the half of a piece that Carl had already eaten part of. Peter was starving, watching Carl scarf down the pizza. Peter remembered looking at Carl's plump body and thinking that starving might be better anyway. He wanted nothing to do with anything that might identify him with his biological father. Carl and Peter climbed back into the truck so Carl could give Peter a ride home. Carl had taken the box with the remaining pizza in it and thrown it in the back of the truck. Peter asked if he could have just one more slice, to which Carl replied with a hasty no, explaining that he was out of dog food and needed to feed the rest to his Doberman.

Carl started down the road. As they drove, he began having severe chest pains. Carl tried to pull over, but Peter had to take hold of the steering wheel from the passenger side and crank the old truck to the side of the road. Carl told Peter to switch places with him so Peter could take him to the emergency room immediately. Carl knew Peter could drive even at the young age of eleven, because he would often get so drunk on their garage outings that Peter would have to drive them home.

Peter drove down the road, but instead of continuing to make his way into town, he made a U-turn. Carl asked him what the hell he was doing. Peter did not look at Carl, as he stayed focused on the road. "Father, shut the fuck up!" Peter drove back to the shop, opened the garage door, and drove in. He then closed the garage door behind them. Carl, gasping for air, struggled to get out the words, "Ya needs to help me, boy. Get me to a hospital now, boy!" Peter hopped out of the truck, leaving the driver's door open. He grabbed the pizza box and took out a slice. Peter hopped back into the truck, took a bite of pizza, and smirked at Carl. "Guess the dog won't be eating tonight, asshole."

Carl continued to plead for help as Peter ate the pizza and watched him beg for his life. Peter thought his father's demise was more entertaining than watching a good movie in a theatre.

After finishing the pizza, Peter looked at Carl as he took his last breath. "Die, mother fucker, die!" And die, he did.

·········

Randall arrived at the Wilson's home and knocked lightly on the door. He did not ring the doorbell but knocked as lightly as possible to get Keisha's attention. He felt weird about the entire situation. Keisha let him in and guided him to the kitchen. To Randall's amazement, Mathew was sitting at the table. Randall asked Keisha what he was doing there.

Keisha explained that she had let Mathew and Elijah in on the investigation. In the middle of the kitchen table was her smartphone. It was on speaker phone, with Elijah on the other end. Keisha let Elijah know that Mr. Baines was now here to discuss the case. Randall was upset that Keisha had let both her brothers in on his serial-killer-pickleball-player theory, but Keisha would not listen to any of his concerns. She informed Randall that Elijah and Mathew would receive their share of the reward money when The Killer was caught.

Randall pointed out that their family would then receive three-fourths of the money, and he asked them to explain how that was fair. They gave some superficial reason about how it was an equal deal, which Randall didn't really buy. Personally, he didn't care about the money anyway; he just wanted to put up an argument as an obligatory, negotiation-type thing to do. He gave up the argument almost as soon as he started it. Keisha then explained her plan, which required the assistance of her two brothers.

Keisha wanted herself, Mathew, and Randall to play in the Wichita Open- a men's, women's, and co-ed doubles tournament held at a beautiful venue just outside of the city called Pondside Pickleball courts.

Keisha stated that the odds of Randall becoming a 5.0 player anytime soon were impossible, although she did feel that he was catching on faster with the dink game than she had expected. She stated that someone on their new crime-fighting team had to play with 5.0 players to be around them. Keisha had been in all 4.0 and 4.5 tournaments, but she believed confidently that she could move herself up.

Keisha knew she needed a legitimate partner to play 5.0 with. She thought Tasha might be able to play with her at 5.0, but Tasha had a work commitment on the day of the women's doubles. Keisha figured that she would probably end up playing with Robin. Robin would not be ready for the Wichita Open 5.0 tournament in three weeks. At best, she and Robin might be able to play 4.5, which would allow them to spend their time around more advanced players to help with the investigation; however, she knew she needed to play 5.0 to really be helpful.

Keisha hoped that Rusty might be a possible 5.0 partner in the co-ed division. Rusty's previous co-ed partner, Beth, had recently moved to Florida, as Florida was a hotbed for professional pickleball tournaments. Beth had invited Rusty to join her, but Rusty had not even considered accepting Beth's offer. He was still in Law school at Wichita State. Also, he sensed that Beth wanted something more from him than just being his pickleball partner, and Rusty did not have any interest in Beth in that way.

Keisha made it clear to Randall that it was still vitally important for her to continue to teach him the game so he could be around it and immerse himself in the whole "pickleball world." Keisha knew that it might be possible for Randall to get good in a speedy way. She knew that she had only been playing for a few months herself, but had caught on quickly since she had been playing tennis from the young age of four. The difference was that Keisha was young. Randall ate unhealthy foods, was a little out of shape, and in his seventies. With Randall's racket sport skills, Keisha thought there was a possibility for Randall to play in the Wichita Open tournament in three weeks at the 3.5 level. Mathew was a solid 3.5 player and he agreed to be Randall's partner.

Randall would still need a co-ed partner, though. Keisha suggested that Randall start playing with Sandy Rineheart. Sandy was a solid 3.5 player herself. She and her previous partner, Conner Thomas, had recently placed third in a large 3.5 tournament in St. Louis. Last week, though, Conner had let Sandy know that they couldn't be partners anymore. Sandy was an extraordinarily vivacious and flirtatious person. Recently, while practicing at Gabrielle Pickleball Courts, Sandy had hugged and gently kissed Conner on the cheek to celebrate a great shot. This happened just as Conner's wife unexpectedly walked onto the club courts. After this, Conner had felt it best to end his partnership with Sandy.

Keisha called Sandy to see if she would be interested in partnering with Randall. Sandy was reluctant to be Randall's partner at first. She told Keisha that she had been widowed after her husband's death from cancer three years ago, and taking up pickleball had given her something to look forward to. She was also starting to date, and the guys she would see were often naturally pickleball players. Sandy then explained that she was in her early fifties and would rather partner with someone younger. Keisha exaggerated Randall's pickleball skills and convinced Sandy that Randall was getting pretty good. She also suggested that winning with Randall might get other men closer to Sandy's age to want to be her partner. Sandy liked that idea! She reluctantly agreed to be Randall's co-ed partner.

Obviously, Randall had only played a few hours of net game. Keisha was playing her cards on pure faith.
"If Grandma Edna knew I was lying to get Sandy to play with Randall, she would have had me do ten thousand push-ups and say twenty thousand Hail Marys," Keisha contemplated with guilt.

With Randall's partners decided, Keisha explained to Randall that adding Elijah to the crime-fighting pickleball team was a necessity because he was the computer expert. She stated that Elijah was a statistics and numerical analysis guy who would come in handy when trying to narrow down suspects using dates, times, places, etc.

Elijah then said from the speaker on the phone, "I'm willing to be a part of this team, but I need assurance that you're not going to break into our home and assault us with any more Ken Follett novels. Are you?"

Randall laughed and assured Elijah that would not happen again. Keisha let Randall know that Elijah was not asking jokingly or sarcastically. After receiving Randall's sincere reassurances, Elijah agreed to be a part of the investigation and hung up. Keisha and Mathew explained that Elijah suffered from a serious anxiety disorder that had come about after their parents' fatal car crash. They went on to explain that he rarely ever left his room. He had become a computer expert by making computers his safe little world.

....

Keisha was up at four a.m. If she was going to make the attempt to move from 4.5 pickleball to 5.0, she knew that she needed to up her game. She went down to the basement.

The entire basement was a workout area, equipped with a treadmill and weights with dumbbells that ranged from five pounds clear up to fifty. The basement also held a rowing machine, pull-up bar, weight bench, and a bench press machine with all the necessary equipment.

She started out running three miles on the treadmill, with the machine set to an incline of eight, making it an uphill run. She had her headphones on, jamming to Drake. She especially loved the song, "Started from the Bottom." She felt it was an especially fitting song since she was trying to make the jump to 5.0, as well as training her younger brother and old man Baines into some sort of crime-fighting, tournament-champion, pickleball duo. One thing Keisha had never liked about sports was the way the media made athletes into heroes. To her, true heroes helped people in need. Sports played a different role. But combining sports with trying to catch a psychopath was beyond legendary!

    She did not really think that the monster was a pickleball player. She felt that Randall, in the process of trying to find himself after retirement, had used his wild imagination to try and find his purpose in life. There was; however, nothing in his outrageously insane theory that she could prove false. Until she could find evidence that his idea was absurdly wrong, she felt it her duty to play along and find out what she could. Keisha moved on to doing sit-ups while listening to "The Bees Knees" by Juice WRLD. The music she listened to might have a sweet beat, but the lyrics had multiple four-letter words. And those four-letter words didn't exactly spell out "kind," "nice," and "love." Eventually, she moved on to a full weightlifting regimen, followed by three hundred push-ups while she jammed out to "Hurt You" and "Often" by the hip-hop specialist named The Weeknd.

    Keisha was stretching out before heading upstairs to shower when she heard footsteps walking down the steps to the basement. She knew exactly who it was, and she knew precisely what she needed to do. Keisha switched from her downloaded hip-hop to YouTube, where she already had gospel music set to play. She was singing "How Great Thou Art," as Grandma Edna reached the bottom of the stairs.

Keisha pulled the headphones out of the phone, allowing her grandma to soak in the awe-inspiring Christian harmony. "That's why you're in such good shape, Keisha. You listen and pray while you work out. Jesus makes sure you burn double the calories listening to his love."

"You are so right, Grandma. Hallelujah!" Keisha thought to herself, "Truth is, if Grandma really knew what I was listening to, there would be no need to hit the shower. I'd be sentenced to a ten thousand push-up penance for my choice of tunes."

Grandma offered to make Keisha breakfast, but Keisha knew she wouldn't have time. She showered and headed to the club with Mathew and Mr. Baines to work with them on their game.

She knew she would just have to shower again when all was said and done, but she at least wanted to smell decent since Rusty would be her partner against Mathew and Randall to help them get them ready for the tournament. She told herself that she just wanted to stay feeling somewhat fresh, but deep down inside, she knew she had an infatuation with Rusty.

Keisha woke Mathew up. He stirred for a short time. She splashed a cup of water in his face. He complained, but she reminded him that if he wanted his share of the $2.5 million, he would get his butt out of bed and head to the club with her. Keisha rolled her eyes in disgust as she watched Mathew inhale a Pop-Tart. She thought about how that nasty stuff would go right into Mathew's system. In turn, Mathew watched Keisha crack an egg, dump it in a glass, and drown the raw egg with skim milk. She then shook it up and guzzled it. Mathew nearly threw up at the sight.

After their respective breakfasts, Keisha hopped in her car with Mathew and took off. After her parents' accident, she rarely wanted to drive. If Keisha was with her friend Robin, Grandma Edna, or Mathew, she insisted that they drive. But Keisha wasn't thinking much about her driving anxiety today.

She was on a mission to get Mathew and herself to the gym. Keisha didn't exactly have amaxophobia. She would drive when she needed to. She had driven Randall to Gabrielle Pickleball Club last night. But if she could, she took the bus or hitched a ride to save herself the worries. Keisha knew that between working out, perfecting her own pickleball game, finding time to train Randall and Mathew as pickleball partners, and working on the investigation, she no longer had time to deal with the logistics of finding ways to get from Point A to Point B.

Edna watched Keisha drive off with Mathew. Edna was happy that Keisha had chosen to drive but was also terrified, as memories of her son and daughter-in-law's fatal crash still weighed heavily on her mind. Edna was also suspicious of the reason that the two needed to leave the house so early in the morning. They had told her that they were in a summer club that was working to create a recycling system to help save the environment. While this might be something Keisha could be interested in, Grandma Edna was skeptical of Matthew's interest in such a cause.

When Keisha and Matthew arrived, they learned that Randall had already been at the club since it opened at 5:30 a.m. He had been working on his serve. He had already purchased a bag of pickleballs and a brand-new hybrid graphite paddle from club owner Mia. Rather than being impressed with Randall's ambition, Keisha was upset that he had started practice without her authority. She let Randall know that she wanted him to continue to work on his dink net game.

Rusty walked up and heard the end of the conversation. He interrupted Keisha's scolding of Randall and defended Randall, stating that coming in early to work on his serve could not hurt anything. Keisha shouted back at Rusty that while Rusty was her tutor and coach in the game, *she* was Randall's coach.

Rusty put his hands up as if to say, "Okay, then." Randall was surprised by Keisha's misgivings. He complained to her that he had been expected to complete a late-into-the-evening practice and then be right back at the court by 8 a.m., but here he was at the club, working hard at 5:30 a.m., and he was in trouble for taking initiative. Randall dared not question her authority too much; however, as he really didn't want another pop-in-the-head moment. Keisha relented and motioned for them to get started practicing.

Rusty and Keisha played the net with Randall and Mathew. They played for thirty minutes before Mathew complained that he wanted to play a game. Rusty said that was probably a good idea, to which Keisha disagreed.
"No. Randall is not ready."

Rusty, supporting Mathew, said he was getting bored himself. Keisha reluctantly relented, but to prove her point, she showed no mercy. Rusty tried to hit the ball lightly to them to get Randall and Mathew used to playing with one another and to help Randall learn the game.

But whenever Keisha was granted an opportunity to hit the ball for a kill shot, she drilled it as hard as she could into her brother's arms with pinpoint precision. Her aim was remarkable. And just to completely prove her point, she slammed a ball directly into Mathew's right cheek before he had any chance to throw his paddle up to defend himself. He then screamed at her, "Why do you keep hitting me? Drill Mr. Baines for a change!" Keisha smugly replied, "Randall never complained today and trusted my judgment." Randall laughed and said, "Yeah, I learned my lesson yesterday."

Randall pulled out his arms to show Mathew the marks and welts that covered them and changed the color of his skin to an ugly, black, and red mass. Rusty and Keisha destroyed Randall and Matthew 11-0, 11-1, and 11-0. Keisha then instructed Mathew to see Blue, the trainer in the club's weight room. Mathew said he didn't have any money to pay Blue. Keisha told him to put it on her charge account. She said that she and Randall would work another hour on dinks. Randall thought in his head, "If we hadn't played a game that Mathew and Rusty insisted on and just continued to work on dinks, I wouldn't have been sent to the principal's office to make up for the lack of dink work."

Rusty questioned whether another hour for Randall was such a good idea. He didn't want Randall to get burned out. He also mentioned that Keisha and Mathew both had eight lawns to mow during the week, and they would be exhausted if they continued to work out and play pickleball. Mathew did not dare butt in to help his own cause. He didn't want any more Wiffle balls drilled at his arms. Plus, he knew that he and Randall had to get real good, real fast, to help them contribute to catching a killer.

Mathew and Randall wanted to tell Rusty about their ulterior motives so that he might understand. But they knew that Rusty could not have any knowledge of the investigation. The more word got out that the Peanut Butter Freak could instead be a Pickleball Freak, the more likely the Pickleball Freak might be able to cover his tracks.

………

Elijah sat in his room. The rather dark room fit Elijah's rather dark personality. Elijah did laugh at times and had fun with online friends. He played board and card games such as Chess or Uno on occasion with Grandma Edna, Mathew or Keisha. But primarily, he was a loner. He had developed a subconscious belief that anyone he got close to would die. His parents had died in a car crash, and his grandfather, who had stepped into the fatherly role, passed away soon after. He really thought that Mr. Baines was a crazy man with crazy ideas. Elijah suspected that Mathew and Keisha were probably going along with his crazy pickleball killer idea because they were thrilled by the thought of chasing an imaginary pickleball killer, as it created more reasons for them to be around the game they so loved and adored.

Why would Elijah agree to help with the fantasy investigation? The answer was simple. He was so afraid to leave the comfort of their home, his own room for that matter, that he felt useless. Helping his brother and sister without having to leave the safety of his own walls gave him a sense of well-being and worthiness.

Although Elijah did suffer from agoraphobia, which is the extreme or irrational fear of leaving the house, he was capable of very basic necessities. He went to school; although he participated in no extracurricular activities, and while deathly afraid of cars, he managed to get through and pass driver's ed to obtain his restricted license. Knowing that his brother and sister needed him felt good. Since the accident, Keisha and Matthew had become closer than ever while he had withdrawn. He even felt a little comfort in knowing the nut-case neighbor needed him as well. He cared about the reward money, but more importantly, he longed to know that he was beneficial to someone for something, even if that something meant searching for a non-existent pickleball madman.

Elijah had four computers. Brandon and Stephanie both had life insurance policies for the children that amounted to forty-thousand dollars apiece. Edna would not let them touch any part of the money until they were twenty-two. They could probably go around her and take the money anyway, but they respected their grandma too much. Grandma Edna wanted them to work their way through high school and college, not have it all handed to them. But Grandma Edna had a few exceptions. The four computers in Elijah's room were one of those exceptions.

Edna by no means wanted Elijah to live his life in fear, confining himself to his own created prison. She also didn't want him to stray down a road of depression and misery. If his best friends were *Dell, Apple,* and *Intel* for a time, she could probably live with that. Edna just prayed that at some point, he would find his way out of his dark underworld.

Elijah did not start his venture with pickleball. He instead began his serial-killer-finding enterprise in the same manner that every FBI, KBI, city police force, private eye, and reward-money-wannabe-investigator in the country were looking – he searched for an association with peanut butter. He just couldn't fathom the idea that pickleball, of all things, would lead to a madman murderer. It just seemed more logical that it would be a disgruntled peanut butter factory worker.

He knew that Randall had searched for major name peanut butter companies associated with cities where the killings occurred, the same as everyone else who was involved in the investigation. Still, he doubted that anyone had tried to specifically tie in an individual who bought or sold peanut butter. Cogger Incorporated owned 2,321 stores. They were based out of Kansas City. The top grocery chain in the midwest, Costless, made up over half of those stores. He knew he would have to hack into either the Costless database, or, bigger yet, Cogger Incorporated to get the information he was seeking. Elijah googled the names of the shareholders of Cogger and discovered that the majority shareholder was Matt Delong. Matt was worth an estimated $1.7 billion. Finding information about Mr. Delong was not difficult. With the Cogger website, Costless website, Facebook pages, Instagram accounts, and even Tik Tok, he learned the name of Matt's best friends, family members, and every job he had ever had since he was twelve. He even learned the names of customers that he mowed yards for as a teen.

Elijah got on Facebook, now known as Meta, and pretended to be Mr. Delong's third cousin. Eventually, Harold Tieland, Matt's first cousin, provided him with Matt's personal e-mail account, Delong.Coggerceo.com. That was the easy part. Figuring out Mr. Delong's password was another story, but it could be done. He just knew it could.

CHAPTER 11

Over the next couple of weeks, Randall, Rusty, Keisha, and Mathew kept insane schedules.

Keisha arose every morning between 4 a.m. and 5 a.m. to work out. She then awoke Mathew so the two of them could get their share of the chores around the house finished early. After finishing housework, the two would run down to the club to play doubles. Keisha and Rusty would play against Mathew and Randall from 8:30 a.m. – 10:30 a.m. Robin would arrive at 10:30 a.m., and from that time until 12:30 p.m., she and Keisha would take on Rusty and Sandy. Moving Robin up to 4.5 required a lot of court time with the higher-end players. Sometimes when Sandy couldn't break away from work, Keisha and Robin would even take on Rusty and his usual men's doubles partner, Peter.

Keisha and Mathew had eight yards to mow each week. Mowing was a job they could do that did not require them to answer to anyone other than the homeowners, making it easier to slip away for workouts and pickleball. They mowed from 1 p.m. to 4 p.m. daily, no matter how hot and humid the weather might get. They made an excuse to leave every night after dinner by lying to Grandma Edna about a new part-time job helping a limestone artist move stones. They would instead rush back to Gabrielle Courts to play more pickleball.

In the afternoon, sometimes Keisha played with Rusty against Peter and his co-ed partner and part-time lover, Tasha. Other times she played with Rusty against Randall and either Mathew or Sandy. Matthew, Keisha, and Randall would then head to their homes. Matthew and Keisha would make small talk with their Grandma Edna and Elijah. After Grandma Edna went to bed, Elijah, Mathew, and Keisha would gather in Elijah's room for a short briefing on the investigation.

In what little spare time that he now had, Randall also worked out at the pickleball club with his new personal trainer, Blue. Randall had no idea what Blue's last name was or even whether Blue was his real name or a nickname. He never asked. Their conversations were short; Blue was all business. He had Randall lifting weights, running on the treadmill for thirty minutes, lifting more weights, running on the elliptical for thirty minutes…Blue worked Randall to the point that Randall often ran to the bathroom to puke. Blue was fifty-three but had the body of a twenty-three-year-old. He was bald with gold hoop earrings in his ears and a gigantic tattoo on his right bicep. The tattoo was a picture of Patrick Mahomes and the number 15 beside it, representing Mahomes' number. Blue had 80s heavy metal blaring through three speakers throughout the Gabrielle fitness area. Blue especially loved Mötley Crüe and Guns N' Roses. Most patrons went to Gabrielle's to play pickleball. Otherwise, there undoubtedly would have been complaints. Randall didn't mind the music, although he thought it too loud.

    Randall loved hard rock but was more into even older artists, such as Clearance Clear Water, Kansas, Jimi Hendrix, and the Stones. Sometimes Randall contemplated letting Blue know that since Blue was working for him, Randall should be the one choosing the background music. But then Randall would look up at the guy who could easily do Mr. Clean commercials and thought better of it.

    After his workout, Randall would get on his phone and talk to Mathew, Elijah, and Keisha through one of their iPhones, or the three of them would sneak over to Randall's house to go over the investigation. Elijah preferred to talk over a speaker phone, but he was starting to feel more comfortable joining them in person at Randall's home on occasion. Elijah leaving his computer to join the investigation next door may not have seemed like much, but to those who knew him, leaving his computer-based sanctuary at all was a step in the right direction.

Grandma Edna didn't think too much of Mathew and Keisha leaving the house every night, but it shocked her when Elijah began to join them. She didn't dwell on it, though, as she was just happy that Elijah was getting out more.

Had she known they were going next door to that lunatic Randall's house, she may have completely freaked out. She already lectured them every time they left the house that some Peanut Butter Devil had killed a wonderful Christian person in their neighborhood.

Twice a week, after the nightly debriefing sessions, Keisha would wait until Grandma Edna was asleep, and she would then sneak out to her Impala and drive over to Peter's mansion.

Peter lived about ten miles out in the country. He had a fuel tank at his country home and was kind enough to fill the car up every night Keisha visited, making it affordable to make the trip a couple of times a week. Peter had a shop about a quarter of a block away from his home, which he had turned into a pickleball court.

During these visits, Keisha played singles with Peter, three sets a night. She enjoyed playing pickleball with him, and they were very evenly matched. Peter generally won two of the three sets. Sometimes he might even win all three sets, but nearly every set was close. Rarely was a set won by a larger margin than an 11-8 score. And there were times that Keisha won two out of three, and even some rare occasions when she won all three sets. Peter would stop and coach her every opportunity that he could.

Peter was a narcissistic psycho killer, but there was something about Keisha that he found alluring. Sometimes he even hated the idea of wanting to help someone other than himself. He often tried to convince himself that what he was doing was selfish because he hoped to make Keisha his mixed doubles partner someday. But he knew that really wasn't the case, for he knew that his usual co-ed partner, Tasha, was still better, and he had sex with Tasha. Peter would remind himself that eventually, Rusty and Keisha would likely be co-ed partners, anyway. So, he knew deep down inside that he wasn't helping her for that reason, either.

He knew that he could help Keisha play better, though. It felt good to help her improve her game. He could not understand why he would want to do something for someone else without expecting anything in return, yet he found himself continuing to try and make her better.

Peter was correct in one of his assumptions; Keisha did have a deep-seated desire to play with Rusty. She loved playing doubles with him in practice. She was disappointed that he had not yet asked her to play with him in the upcoming Wichita Open 5.0 tournament. She knew that she had better start looking for a tournament 5.0 co-ed partner. She truly wanted to play with Rusty and, in more ways than one. This hurt because she had no desire to date anyone else.

Keisha had hoped he would notice her now that she was out of high school. Keisha tried to set aside her yearning for Rusty and reminded herself that she was running out of time to accept a scholarship with a tennis or track team. She knew she needed to accept one of the offers fast, while there were still a couple of offers left. Then she'd move out of the area, live in another city, and play tennis for tuition and room and board rather than for a true love for the sport. Keisha envisioned her only crush traveling the mid-west, playing and teaching pickleball.

Rusty was the club pro at Gabrielle Courts. With pickleball sponsorships, award money, and instructing clients at Gabrielle Club, along with giving some private lessons on the side, he was raking in about $65,000 a year. It wasn't a salary that would ever make him a rich man, but a healthy wage for simply coaching and playing pickleball. Keisha admired Rusty for finding a way to make a living entirely off of pickleball, although at the same time, she was often jealous of him. He had the kind of life that she longed for. She didn't have a real desire to attend college. That was more her Grandma Edna's dream for her than her own.

....

It was Friday. Randall had just rolled out of bed at 9:00 a.m. Generally, he would have already been up for a couple of hours. The workouts and the pickleball sessions were taking a toll on his body. He had lost ten pounds in less than two weeks because of pickleball and workouts with the Gabrielle Club fitness trainer, Blue. But he was feeling some serious pain. He took a couple of Advil and washed them down with a cup of coffee. Along with the afternoon/evening pickleball sessions and working out, he had just added 10:00 a.m. doubles with the lady scheduled to be his co-ed partner, Sandy. It was difficult for Randall. He woke up with his entire body aching. Randall wondered to himself whether he could really do this. He was receiving information overload from learning the game of pickleball and from the investigation.

Randall had not been happy with Elijah. Elijah continued to search more for a peanut butter-obsessed psycho freak rather than a pickleball player. Elijah kept stating that he was looking for a pickleball player, but whenever Randall would ask him about what he had found on his computer, Elijah would revert to information he had found that might support his own theory that it was a peanut butter guy. Elijah informed Randall that after heavily researching profiles of serial killers, it was his opinion that the psycho the entire nation was looking for was probably the obvious- a disgruntled employee of some peanut butter company. Randall argued with Elijah that he had already gone down that route and that Randall felt it was obvious that The Killer was not a peanut butter person. Randall continued to attempt to convince Elijah that if The Killer were related to peanut butter in some way, he would certainly have been behind bars by now, preparing to sit on an electric chair. With the entire world searching for a peanut butter guy, it was unlikely everyone would have overlooked such an individual.

Elijah bit back his opinion that the only reason Randall wanted the crazy bastard to be a pickleball player was because Randall wanted all pickleball players to seem crazy. Elijah did suggest that he thought Randall might be pursuing this theory to deter Keisha from the game, so she would quit banging the

Wiffle ball against the garage door on the weekends. Randall nearly laughed at that notion, thinking that it *would* make his weekends more peaceful, and he'd be able to read Follett's *World Without End* in peace. Instead, he realized he would likely never read the novel since Mathew and Keisha talked about the book so much that he was already finding out the entire plot. Mathew, of course, was obsessed with the building aspects, and Keisha loved the romance and fight for women's rights. Randall didn't know whether to feel sick to his stomach that he was probably never going to have a need to read the book or amused that he had gotten the two teenagers hooked on Follett.

   Elijah simply read all the footnotes and downloaded other synopses that told him everything about the novel in case Grandma Edna ever asked him about it. This made it very hard for Elijah and Randall to get along, as Randall didn't respect Elijah's "shortcuts."

   Randall had pickleball and Follett in common with both Mathew and Keisha, but he was not into computers. Elijah loved reading information but hated novels and sports. This led him and Randall with nothing to discuss but business, and neither could agree on that topic, either. Randall was truly feeling miserable in both body and mind. He was starting to regret the whole pickleball killer thing. Elijah was making Randall have second thoughts. He began to think that perhaps he had made the whole thing up in his head to try and get excited about something, to try to salvage his career reputation after being removed from his last case with the Wichita PD.

And now he was starting to think that due to his possibly delusional thoughts, he was going to end up exercising himself to death.

He was getting into great shape and starting to like the game, but it didn't escape his notice that every time he began to enjoy pickleball and feel good about it, Keisha would throw another "loop" into the mix. He had been playing for just two and half weeks, yet she was constantly having him reinvent himself as if he had been playing the sport for ten years. Keisha had told him that due to his previous racket sports experience, he was catching on in amazing fashion. She pointed out he had already established himself as a 3.5 player in practice; although playing 3.5 practice ball is a whole lot different than playing in a tournament, especially in the prestigious Wichita Open.

The Wichita Open was one of the more alluring tournaments in the area, drawing players from all over the mid-west. Randall had become really good, really fast, by learning to get the ball deep and rushing to the net to dink. This was a good basic strategy, but Keisha knew Randall would never rise to a 4.0 level or higher without elevating his game. Today he was supposed to work on a "third shot drop." The third shot drop is when the player tries to dink a ball over the net from clear back towards the end of the court. To make it even more complex, the player often needs to make this shot with a ball coming at them at speeds as fast as seventy miles per hour. This is comparable to a batter in baseball bunting, but instead of simply bunting the ball between the catcher and the first baseman, the batter would have to bunt drop the ball clear out in center field for a blooper hit over the second baseman.

The play was virtually impossible to learn after just a couple of weeks of playing the game, but the impossible had to be done if Randall was truly going to be around better players in the mid-west. Whenever Randall thought of quitting, he motivated himself with the overused cliché, "Failure is not an option."

The one bright spot that helped him get out of bed was the opportunity to see and play with Sandy. Sandy was in her early fifties, making Randall, at seventy-two, old enough to be her father. So, he felt there could never be anything between them as far as romance. But her electric personality just drew people to her. When he had met and played with her for the first time, he hadn't found anything about her physically that especially turned him on. Sure, she was pretty enough. But like most people well past their youth, she wasn't exactly model-material. She worked out daily and was in great shape, but she had more of a strong, athletic, tomboy figure yet still maintained her femininity.

Despite spending hours working out and playing pickleball every day, she was never to be seen without make-up. Her long hair was beautifully permed to perfection. Randall was a leg guy. He did wish that she wore shorts so he could see her long, beautiful legs. But to get a better workout and burn more calories, she always wore sweatpants. Regardless, Randall did enjoy looking at her round, firm ass. He stared at the clock and thought, "it's almost time to terrorize and destroy my body, but at least I'll get to see Sandy."

Rob MUNDEN

....

    Keisha and Mathew had just finished mowing a yard. They had ridden separately to the work site. She had driven her Impala, and he had driven his beat-up 1987 Vega. Keisha was itching to get onto the courts. She did not invite Mathew only because she knew he would be playing in the evening, and she wanted him to have some rest. Plus, she knew that if she invited him, he would feel obligated to say "yes" and join her. She knew that Mathew needed a shower, a short nap, and to play a few online video games with his buddies.
    Keisha had not reserved any courts. She had no idea who would even be there; she just wanted to play, no matter what levels of players were there. Keisha arrived at Gabrielle Courts around 2:30 p.m., but it was too late. All the courts in the main pickleball gym were taken or reserved. Four of her usual playing partners were on the center court. Randall and Sandy were playing Rusty and Peter's regular tournament mixed doubles partner, Tasha. It was three days before the Wichita Open. Tasha looked gorgeous, with her long, blond hair, large, double-D breasts, and long, thin legs. Although she had regular sex with Peter, he had never committed to her. She was divorced with two children. She had learned early on that Peter liked his life just the way it was: carefree, no wife, and no children to worry about. And since Peter was in his fifties, she knew that if he hadn't changed by now, he would probably never change. Due to Peter's lack of commitment, Tasha did

flirt with others. From the start of the match to the end, Tasha stroked Rusty on the cheek. She bumped into him every time they were within a foot of each other. When she picked up the ball and he was behind her, she made sure to bend over in such a way that she revealed as much as she could of her long legs and butt that floated outside of the short skirt she was wearing.

Keisha sat in the stands and tried to read Follett while waiting for a chance to play. She had a difficult time concentrating on what she was reading. She couldn't help but notice Tasha's flirtation with Rusty. Keisha kept telling herself that Tasha was Peter's girl, so there was nothing to worry about. Keisha also reminded herself that she and Rusty were only friends, so even if Tasha and Rusty had some sort of feelings for each other, it was not any of her business.

Sandy and Randall were beaten badly by the two 5.0 players, but they proved worthy sparring partners. In a short amount of time, they had learned how to stack when needed, which helped them avoid stroking the same ball, as Sandy was left-handed, and Randall was right-handed.

Their chemistry was coming together. Sandy, having played longer, was the better player, but not by much. She was very encouraging, often winking at Randall in a loving yet flirtatious manner when he made a great shot. And when he made a poor shot, she gently stroked his shoulder encouragingly. Sandy and Randall would eventually lose 11-4, 11-6 and 11-2 in the three sets they played, but Randall still felt like a winner, having spent time with Sandy.

None of the four had noticed Keisha in the stands since she was sitting in the bleachers a couple of courts away. Tasha kissed Rusty's cheek after the match and gave him a bear hug, purposely rubbing her large, soft-but-firm boobs against his chest. Keisha felt ill. She snuck out of the club and made her way to her car before they could see her.

Keisha knew how hard Randall had been working. He had been playing about five hours a day in addition to his workouts. She watched the chemistry between Randall and Sandy on the court and thought they were ready for the Wichita Open this weekend. She canceled the evening match she and Rusty were supposed to play against Randall and Sandy as well as the later one against Randall and Mathew. She decided that everyone probably needed a night off from the game.

Keisha, Elijah, and Mathew were still scheduled to meet at Randall's place at 10:00 p.m. for a debriefing session concerning any observations that might relate to the investigation, but Randall was not home. They went ahead and let themselves in. While waiting, Mathew and Elijah raided Randall's refrigerator. They stuffed themselves with cold pizza. Keisha sat at Randall's dining room table, tapping her hands and feet. She was very nervous. She continuously took out her iPhone to look at the time. Her friend Robin called a couple of times and rattled on about the day's big drama. Keisha tried to stay focused and listen to Robin, but she just couldn't. Not only was the girly-girly, gossipy conversation not really Keisha's thing, but she was worried about Randall. It was just not like him to miss a debriefing session.

PEANUT BUTTER PICKLEBALL AND MURDER

Despite her inattentiveness, Keisha sort of got the gist of the gossip session. Keisha caught that Debbie was seen kissing the captain of the football team, Kelly Seifert. This was big-time headline high school news since Kelly was dating Dara Keller, the captain of the cheerleading team. Robin was laughing because Dara was the snobby "mean girl" who acted better than everyone. Robin went on to say that Dara had heard about her boyfriend and Debbie kissing, so when she unexpectedly ran into Debbie outside of a convenience store, Dara had come up from behind Debbie and pulled the back of Debbie's hair while Debbie was talking to Katy. Katy then punched Dara to get her off Debbie and knocked Dara cold out. She said there was a crowd of other high school kids watching. When Dara finally regained consciousness, she did not know what had happened to her. None of the kids at the convenience store would tell her. The store manager had come out. All the students gathered around and said that she had tripped on her own feet and fallen. Robin seemed to think that the incident would elevate their pickleball group from "class nerds" to the "cool" people for a change. Keisha sort of doubted that, but she wasn't very invested either way. Keisha let Robin know that she was happy that she had just graduated and could leave all the high school drama behind. Keisha noted that although Katy had been defending her friend, concussions can become a serious issue, and it was not something they should gloat about. After this concern was brought to Robin's attention, she did feel some level of guilt for gloating about the incident. Keisha told Robin that her desire to brag was normal but that Dara was a person, too. Robin wanted to discuss it further, but Keisha was more worried about Randall's well-being. She ended the conversation and pondered, "Was it possible The Killer found out about Randall's theory that he was a pickleball player and decided to take him out?"

She contemplated the situation. What bothered her even more was knowing that she cared. She felt that Randall was becoming some kind of close companion. She didn't necessarily think it was a good thing to be buddies with the crazy, old, next-door neighbor. She looked again at the clock on the wall. She noticed Mathew and Elijah tearing into a full bag of barbecue chips. She found their eating habits disgusting and repulsive. Keisha did not stop them from eating all Randall's food because she felt it was not a good idea for the old dude to be eating that crap anyway. She looked down at her phone, hoping it would show a different time than the clock on the wall. It was only 10:17, but even seventeen minutes late was an eternity, knowing that there was some sort of peanut-butter-pickleball-whatever-the-hell freak out there that might be slicing Randall's throat at that very moment.

Eventually, Mathew and Elijah broke out the box of Little Debbie Cake Rolls. As their mouths were completely stuffed with the fattening, sugar-filled poison, Randall walked in through the kitchen door. Keisha jumped up and hugged him. She then whispered, "Thank God you're home!" She was immediately embarrassed when she realized that she had shown him so much emotion and care. She quickly let go of the hug and punched him in the chest, stating, "I mean, what the hell were you doing? We have work to do. Do you want to catch the creepy killer bastard or not?"

Randall paused, surprised at himself for being touched by the hug. He felt such a feeling of warmth and care. Since retirement, he wasn't even sure anyone knew he existed, including his one and only daughter. The neighbor girl who once annoyed him by banging the hard-as-rock Wiffle ball with the oversized ping-pong paddle against the garage every Saturday and Sunday morning had become his best friend. She then hit him again. "Well, I'm waiting. Where were you, Randall?"

Randall replied, "Uh, um, um…The one or two beers that Sandy and I had together kind of turned into five. I called a cab, so the car's still sitting there."

Mathew shouted out, "Way to go, Randall! Going for the younger babes, eh? Mr. Player!"

Elijah laughed, slammed Mathew a high five and patted Randall on the back, saying, "You animal, Mr. Baines! Didn't know ya had it in you!"

"Uh, um… it's not like that. We're simply pickleball partners. On a more disturbing note, how did you all get into my house?"

Elijah answered, "Oh, that was easy. I overheard a couple of conversations between you and Mathew over that stupid, boring sports stuff. I know your favorite football player is Travis Kelce of the Chiefs, and your favorite baseball player is Salvador Perez from the Royals. Kelce's number is 87 and

Salvy, as you Royals fans like to call him, is 13. Every old, washed-up, white guy athlete-wannabe makes their security code their favorite players' numbers. Your code is 8713."

"Hmm, I reckon you've left me speechless on that one, smartass!" Randall then gave them a dirty look as he noticed the Little Debbie chocolate crumbles mixed with crushed potato chips spread out all over the tile floor, with an empty pizza box sitting by the trash can.

"I see you boys must have been starving."

Mathew replied with embarrassment, "Um, sorry, Randall. We were kind of hungry."

"I see that."

Mathew then tried to change the subject. "On a more important note, how did your date with Saaaandy go?"

Randall blushed with embarrassment, "Enough of the Sandy crap. It was just a drink and dinner."

Elijah jumped into the conversation. He turned to Mathew and said, "I can tell if the old man was on a date or if he really thinks of Sandy as just a business friend with one question."

Mathew replied, "Go for it!"

"Randall, what did you have for dinner, and did you pay?"

"None of your damn business, Elijah."

Keisha stepped into the conversation. "Hmm, I think it *is* our business. If you're late for OUR business meeting, we have the right to know at least the very basics of what you were doing. It's a simple question. What did you eat, and who paid?"

Randall nervously replied, "Uh um, I paid, and we had grmmbm." He purposely muttered.

Mathew put his right ear close to Randall's mouth and said, "What was that, Randall? We couldn't hear."

Randall shouted out, "Steaks. Sirloin steaks, okay? We have been working hard and playing really well together. I believe that warrants a steak, damn it!"

Elijah instantly remarked, "Ahh, you paid for steaks! Our crazy, old, white neighbor is in loooove!" Elijah, Keisha, and Mathew all laughed.

Randall smiled slightly and said, "Ah, screw you guys. Let's get to work. Where are we at on the investigation?"

They all sat down at the kitchen table, but the three young siblings continued to giggle. Randall was trying not to laugh, but even he began to chuckle, as embarrassed as he was. He did recognize the humor in the situation.

After the laughter stopped and Matthew and Elijah had devoured everything remotely edible in Randall's kitchen, they focused themselves back on the investigation. Randall started the debriefing by looking straight into Elijah's eyes commanding, "Okay. Get out your daily evidence as to why you think it's still a Peanut Butter Killer and not a pickleball guy. Get it out of your system, Elijah, so we can move on."

"All right then, if you insist." Elijah then stated that when Randall searched for peanut butter companies in the cities where the killings occurred, Randall only looked up major peanut butter-associated products such as *Jiffy*, *Skippy*, and *Smuckers*. But Randall had not looked up minor, smaller peanut butter companies that could be found in every area with a victim. He then pointed out companies that most of the country had never heard of, such as the Peanut Butter & Jelly Company out of Kansas City, Mound City Shelled Nut, Incorporated out of St. Louis, and The Peanut Butter House in Galveston Island. He pointed out that even right here in Wichita, there was the Nifty Nut House.

    Elijah, for what seemed to Randall to be the hundredth time, mentioned the projected profile of The Killer. Elijah presented his data, which was the same as the FBI's. This data, of course, stated that The Killer was a white male between the ages of 21-39. The Killer was likely a disgruntled employee who worked for a peanut butter company and probably lived in the mid-west. Randall rebutted Elijah's theory with his own evidence, standing by his theory that The Killer was a white, middle-aged, rich male who was a borderline-expert pickleball player. Randall then demanded data from Elijah that focused on pickleball players who could be connected to the killings.

    Elijah did present some data that he felt was somewhat interesting, though he really thought it was just coincidental. Elijah stated that his research eventually led him to information that indicated that every city with a PB victim had a pickleball tournament within a two-hour drive within four days of the murders. Elijah bragged that he had done so much research that he had even found one church in St. Louis with a church-member-only tournament and an intramural tournament at Barton Community College, open only to college students. BCC was a little, two-year school located outside a small Kansas town called Great Bend.

Elijah then showed them a list of sixteen people who had entered pickleball tournaments in the areas of the killings at the times that the murders happened.

Randall, Mathew, and Keisha got excited. They pointed out that one of them could be the Killer with that many people being in those exact areas at the time of the killings. It seemed especially significant that sixteen of them had been in the Galveston area since Galveston was nowhere close to the other cities in question. On the other hand, Elijah argued that it was proof that The Killer was not a pickleball player because if a person wants to find evidence to support an agenda, they could easily find that data, making the data completely biased. Finding more than a dozen individuals who play pickleball and who were also within a two-hour drive of all the killings was not very difficult. To prove his point, Elijah searched for volleyball tournaments in the same areas at the same times as the killings and found forty-seven volleyball players who could have been near each of those cities due to their love of the game.

Randall then agreed that Elijah had a valid point, but he still wanted to know how many 5.0, or pure pro, circuit players would have been in the areas of every one of the killings at the time. Elijah immediately shouted, "NONE, ZERO, NADA!!!"

Randall then asked if any players were in the areas of the murders in all but one or two of the killings. Elijah stated that there were eight.

Randall then asked, "And how many are rich, or at least well-to-do?"

Elijah replied, "All have something going for them. Even though pro-level pickleball players aren't getting rich off the prize money, they do have enough connections and sponsors that none of them are exactly hurting for money."

Randall then asked, "And how many are middle age?"

"Three," Elijah remarked.

Elijah then revealed their names and gave a brief description of each. He gave a printed handout to Mathew, Randall, and Keisha. He read out loud the material he handed them that read as follows:

BERNARD JASPER

Forty-three-year-old white male from St. Louis. He is sponsored by Rammers Auto Repair out of St. Louis and by his own company, Over The Moon Security. Bernard lives in a ten-million-dollar mansion. He has an overall estimated net worth of twenty million dollars. He is married to Elisha who is six years younger than him. He has three adult children, one boy and two girls who have all graduated from high school and no longer live at home.

Bernard started his small business as the only member of his company. He is the number one suspect if you believe a pickleball guy is the murderer, only because he did work one month for a short-lived peanut butter company called Addus Butter Company back in 1995. He worked there as a security guard and was angry about making minimum wage. According to *Business Journal Magazine*, in the April 2014 edition, he took an old, beat-up, button-down, collared shirt from a local thrift shop and had a patch he had made put on it that said 'Over The Moon Security.' He then searched for small businesses that only needed one security guard.

    Eventually, Van Holly Loan Services gave him a contract to provide security for them. He eventually wanted to have some nights off and hired other employees. Over time, companies all over St. Louis wanted his services. Fifty security guards work for him now. His services are spread out, providing security all over the mid-west, including right here in Wichita. He did play in every 5.0 pro-level tournament the week or weekend a Peanut Butter victim was killed, except for Galveston. That includes Hays, and only our group, to my knowledge, has tied that murder to the Peanut Butter Killer.

Next, we have

SAMUEL TOWNSEND

Forty-seven-year-old white male who lives here in Wichita. He has no sponsor but also has no need for one. Samuel is not mega rich, although he has a net worth of three million dollars. Most of the money he inherited from his father. He was an only child. His father, John, was the head manager of a local *McDonald's*. He made decent money, but not a huge amount. Samuel's mother, Rene, worked as an assistant manager under John. They simply saved well and were very frugal with their spending.

John died suddenly of a heart attack at fifty-eight. Soon after, Rene, a heavy smoker, died of lung cancer. Between a life insurance policy and their savings, Samuel was set up well. Before inheriting his parents' money, Samuel spent most of his adult life working different odd jobs, enough to keep him going and pay child support for his son, Johnny. Johnny is sixteen and lives on Galveston Island with Samuel's ex-wife, Gina, who is forty-four. Samuel seems to be a fly-by-night guy who does what he wants. And the last couple of years, what he has wanted to do is play pickleball.

Samuel was in a 5.0 pro-level tournament in every town with a victim, including the Hays killing, except for St. Louis.

And next, we have a Peter Weatherford. Keisha quickly interrupted,
"Umm, I see that on this list you handed us. No need to analyze or investigate Peter." Mathew and Randall agreed. They explained to Elijah that he was a very close friend with whom they all played pickleball daily. Mathew said Peter was so harmless that he couldn't hurt a flea.

Elijah snapped back, "Okay, well, BTK was a compliance officer, head of a Boy Scout Troop, and president of his church. I'll bet no one considered him a psychotic, bloodthirsty nut case, either."

"Fair enough. We will hold onto your summary and keep an eye on him, but I don't believe we need to spend any real resources or time on Peter," Randall reluctantly replied.

Elijah nodded his head in agreement and said, "Fine with me. The less time we spend on pickleball players, the more time we have to focus on a peanut butter guy, who I still think is the obvious real killer."

Although Mathew, Randall, and Keisha stopped Elijah from verbally going over Peter's information, all three of them read the handout on Peter in their own time. The bio read as follows:

PETER WEATHERFORD

Fifty years old, single, never married. He is a self-made millionaire from building and selling houses as the founder and owner of Heavenly Homes. He is in incredible shape. He was a state champion in tennis for nearby Derby High School back in 1989. He was in and out of foster homes from the age of fourteen.

His mother eventually abandoned him, although she stayed with his brother and sister. She was investigated for child abuse against Peter on three different occasions when he was between the ages of five and fourteen. Once he reached the age of fourteen, she wanted nothing further to do with him. Elijah interjected his opinion into the report, pointing out that this might be a reason for Peter to have enough anger to kill.

In the report, Elijah also pointed out that Peter had a first name highly associated with a major peanut butter company. And his middle name, Branton, begins with a B, making the first initials in his name – PB.

Peter was in a tournament close to where each killing took place at the time, aside from the St. Louis murder. That would even include the Hays slaying.

Mathew and Keisha were heartbroken for Peter when they read of his turbulent childhood. It never crossed their minds that his upbringing, or anything else for that matter, could mean he had anything to do with the peanut butter murders.

After reading the handout, Randall, for the most part, felt as Mathew and Keisha did. But the violent childhood Peter experienced did indicate a legitimate cause to act out in anger. Randall still felt that any investigation of Peter could be put on hold. Peter was always polite and kind to Randall, Mathew, and Keisha, and it just seemed unlikely that such a seemingly nice guy could be the Peanut Butter Killer. Even with his stick-to-the-facts, leave-all-emotion-at-the-door, former detective attitude, Randall just could not bring himself to see good ole Peter as a serial killing machine.

After listening to Elijah and reading his information, Randall was; however, intrigued by Mr. Jasper's profile. Mr. Jasper had worked for a peanut butter company that he was not happy with, and he played pickleball, thus connecting him to both peanut butter and pickleball. Randall was reminded that Mr. Jasper made his fortune off being upset with the St. Louis peanut butter company, which would not exactly make him a disgruntled employee. Also, Elijah pointed out that Mr. Jasper had only worked at the peanut butter joint for a month. And that had been over twenty years ago. Elijah still adamantly insisted that Randall was reaching with what Elijah felt was a mere coincidence. He did acknowledge it was enough to warrant a more extended look, in contrast to the other pickleball player suspects. But once again, there was an argument between the two. Elijah was still persistent that Randall was finding a way for The Killer to fit into the pickleball world and Randall felt that Elijah was doing just the opposite, trying to find a reason why The Killer couldn't be a pickleball player. After the fifteen-minute cuss-and-discuss spat, they moved on to suspect number two.

They briefly discussed Samuel Townsend. The four did not officially eliminate him as a suspect as they basically had for Peter, but they did rely on Keisha's advice. Keisha had played with and against him in practice and open court sessions. She told them that he had a lot of issues with being on the crazy side: drinking too much and probably being a pothead. Despite these issues, though, she let them know that he just seemed to be easygoing and carefree; not exactly traits that create a monster.

She further stated that he laughed a lot and liked to play pranks. He was an all-around jokester and never seemed to grow up. She pointed out that his personality made his life hard. He was his own worst enemy. He had his faults, but being fun, carefree, and treating the world like one big party didn't exactly make for serial killer material. Keisha did concede that perhaps living for the moment and expecting immediate gratification should be criteria enough to keep him on the suspect list.

All three suspects were scheduled to play in the Wichita Open. Elijah tried to convince the three to drop the pickleball killer nonsense, pointing out that none of the suspects were at every tournament where each of the murders took place. But the other three decided they wanted to continue to pursue the pickleball murder connection.

CHAPTER 12

Bernard Jasper was not playing in Saturday's co-ed pro-level doubles tournament, but he was scheduled to play in the men's pro-am doubles tournament of the Wichita Open. His partner, Brance Jennings, was also a middle-aged man. The two had a losing record for the year the in non-age requirement, pro-level tournaments. They were both considering ending their partnership and getting younger teammates, as both were in their forties and struggling to keep up with some of the younger players. They were best friends, so making the move to split up was not something they were quite ready to do. They were receiving some prize money and keeping sponsorships due to winning nearly every single forty-and-over pro tournament that they had entered the past couple of years. But there were not very many age-related pro tournaments to enter. Many of the few such tournaments there were required both players to be a minimum of fifty years old, and they were not quite there.

Samuel Townsend was set to play in both the Saturday's men's doubles tournament and Sunday's co-ed pro doubles tournament. His co-ed partner, Elisa Briel, was a twenty-two-year-old, six-foot, blond bombshell of a woman from Great Britain. She had a cult-like following with her athletic ability and gorgeous looks. They had won one small tournament in Nebraska together, which was their only tournament championship, but they were both good-looking, fun, and energetic, which kept the sponsorship and fan interest up, making them a good team on a marketing level. Samuel's men's doubles partner was Andy Rice. Andy was a solid, thirty-three-year-old 5.0 player. He was no world-class pro-level player but could hold his own against most opponents.

Mathew, Keisha, and Randall discussed a plan to be near Samuel and Bernard during the open. Randall pointed out to Elijah that he and Mathew would be playing in the 3.5 men's tournament on Saturday and that he and Sandy would be playing in the 3.5 co-ed tournament Sunday.

All level tournaments would be played on the same Pond Side Pickleball Courts during the Wichita Open, so Randall and

Mathew would be in the area to observe some of the other matches. Keisha was trying to figure out how she could do her part and be around the two suspects on Saturday, but she was scheduled to play the 4.5 women's doubles with Robin on Saturday. They were all playing in the same complex which might help. Keisha had not registered for the mixed doubles. She had hoped to play 5.0 mixed doubles with Rusty on Sunday. The deadline to register had passed, but the tournament director had left a spot for Rusty in case he could find a partner. He was such a draw that the tournament committee wanted to keep every avenue open to allow a wild card spot for him. Keisha had made it clear to Rusty that she wanted to move up to 5.0, and she had thought he would have asked her to be his partner by now. To her disappointment; though, he hadn't.

………

Rusty owned his home. It was a nice, three-bedroom, two-bathroom home in the country, sitting on six acres. It was valued at around $225,000. Like many nice properties in the Wichita area, Peter's company had previously owned the house.

Peter made sure that the inspector discovered numerous problems with the home to justify selling it at a lower price. He didn't want the managers of his company to have any suspicion that he was selling this property to Rusty for $125, 000 just to keep the kid happy. Peter felt that he was a better pickleball player than Rusty, but Rusty was as good a partner as Peter was going to get.

Rusty had tried to convince himself that he was just lucky, but deep down inside, he knew that Peter was just doing him a favor for some unknown reason. Even so, Rusty had still been reluctant to purchase the home, knowing that professional athletes generally had short careers; not to mention pickleball wasn't exactly making him a wage that allowed him to stash tons of cash away for a rainy day. And he was in law school. Sure, his educational costs were being taken care of for now through scholarships and student loans, but at some point, he would have to pay those back. Also, most pickleball players would transfer their lives to Florida or California, where there were more sponsors and bigger and better tournaments. But he wasn't in a position to move to California or Florida anytime soon. It would be several years before he would finish at Wichita State, and he wasn't up for changing colleges.

Rusty also felt that if worst came to worst, he could sell the property for much more than he had paid for it. He poured himself a cup of coffee at around 7 a.m. and stood by his window, occasionally taking a sip and looking outside to watch a fourteen-point buck walk through his backyard. He admired the majestic prowess of the creature. He watched it traverse the bottom of the valley behind his house. Rusty was admiring the picturesque scene in peace until he heard the doorbell ring. He thought to himself, "Who would be at my door in the country at seven in the morning?"

When he looked through the peephole, he saw Keisha and immediately let her in. He asked her what was wrong. Keisha seemed baffled at the thought that there was anything awry.

Rusty reminded her that she had never been to his house and that it was out in the country. And it was seven in the morning. In truth, Rusty was shocked that Keisha even knew where he lived. She informed Rusty that Mathew had told her his address. Mathew had been out to Rusty's home to help him move in. Although Rusty had paid him a hundred bucks, Mathew didn't even care about the money. He had simply wanted to be near the one male figure he looked up to who was still alive. Keisha insisted that Rusty show her around.

Rusty stated that he needed to get dressed first. Keisha's attention was drawn to Rusty's six-pack abs and chest that were exposed where his robe gapped open. Rusty noticed that she was looking at his chest. Keisha was so mesmerized by the perfection of his build, she didn't even realize that she was staring until Rusty closed the robe over his chest. She turned away in embarrassment. Rusty told her to help herself to a cup of coffee, then rushed to his bedroom to get dressed. While he was getting dressed, Keisha looked at the pictures around his living room.

She was surprised that none of his pickleball championship trophies or medals was displayed. He did have lots of pictures, though. Some were of his parents and sister, but most were pickleball photos. He had some of himself and Peter and one with his co-ed partner, Anna, who had just moved away. Rusty also had a picture of himself and Mathew out on the courts practicing. But what Keisha found most intriguing was a huge photo. It was by far the largest picture in the room. It was of Keisha by herself, diving for a ball. Keisha remembered Rusty taking the picture. He had even shown it to her proudly after capturing it. He rarely carried his 35-millimeter camera with him, but when he wasn't playing and did have it on him, he took a lot of pictures.

Keisha then found another three-foot-by-two-foot framed picture of her simply holding her paddle and smiling. The two biggest pictures in the room were of her. Rusty came out of his bedroom, dressed in his pickleball attire, knowing it was close to time to begin the day practicing and tutoring.

Keisha immediately let him know that she loved his pickleball pictures. She teased him about the two photos of her. He mumbled in embarrassment about how he got the perfect shots, trying to make it sound as though it wasn't her beauty that gave her a couple of sacred places on his walls, but the images themselves. He pulled out his latest framed picture, a picture of Randall and Sandy playing together, smiling after they won a point against her and Mathew. Keisha loved the picture but laughed and let him know that it sucked that the perfect picture had happened after they won a point against her and Mathew. She then pointed out that it was Mathew who set Sandy up for the slam. Giggling, she remarked how cute Randall and Sandy looked together. Rusty rebutted by mentioning their age difference. Keisha looked Rusty in the eye and made it clear that age should not be a barrier to love.

Rusty ignored the obvious meaning Keisha had conveyed without words and changed the subject. After more small talk, Rusty came out with the burning question on his mind, "Keisha why are you here?"

Keisha quickly replied, "What? Can't I come visit my good friend?"

"Sure, you are welcome anytime. Even unannounced. But it's not exactly your style Keisha, especially when I'll see you later at the club."

"You say stopping by isn't my style. What is my style then?"

"I don't know, Keisha. It just seems like a bold move for you."

"Do you want me to leave?"

"No of course not. I'm just trying to figure out what you want from me."

"Who said I want anything?"

"I don't buy that you're here for a simple visit and a tour of the house. Am I right?"

Keisha then looked him in the eye, smiled, and said nothing.

Breaking the awkward but titillating silence, Rusty remarked. "You're just a kid."

"I'm eighteen and have graduated from high school. That makes me a full-fledged adult."

"Semantics," Rusty shot back.

Not getting the reaction that she had hoped for, Keisha reverted to her original purpose. She was outrageously nervous. Goosebumps, butterflies, and all other symptoms fitting a description of anxiety washed over her. Under normal circumstances, Keisha would not have had the tenacity to be assertive with the question that she was about to ask Rusty. But these were no normal circumstances. A murderer might be out there, and if that killer happened to be a 5.0 player who could be taking to the courts Saturday, she needed to be nearby to observe and investigate. She took a deep breath, chugged the cup of coffee that she had helped herself to, and finally, she blurted out, "Rusty, it's a few days away from the co-ed 5.0 tournament. I made it clear to you that I was ready to move up. Why haven't you asked me to play as your partner?"

After a long pause, Rusty replied, "You are running out of time to take one of the tennis scholarships you were offered. Most offers will soon be rescinded. You need to focus on tennis."

"That hasn't bothered you the past couple of weeks, Rusty. So why now?"

He mumbled back with a stutter, "b-b-because...uh, uh, um... I...we, we, we, we if we play well together and do well, umm, that will be it. You'll be off to college where you should be, where you belong."

Keisha then replied, "You need a partner, Rusty. I'm sure you can eventually find an older, more experienced player in the next couple of weeks. But there are only a couple of days until the co-ed tournament. You need me. This can be a simple, temporary fix. It's nothing permanent. "

After a long pause, Rusty sighed, "You are correct, Keisha. Just a temporary thing; just one pickleball tournament! We might as well sing Barry Manilow's song "Ships" afterward.

Bewildered, Keisha remarked, "You're getting a little weird on me, Rusty. And who the hell is Barry Manilow?"

Rusty then said with a chuckle, "Sure, Keisha. Partners it is."

He then reached out to shake her hand, but she ignored his gesture. Instead, she stepped forward, hugged him, and kissed the side of his cheek. Keisha had not meant to have that reaction. It just happened. She was embarrassed as soon as she realized what she had done. Keisha pulled back from Rusty quickly. "Good. Done. See you tonight, Rusty! Gotta go!" Keisha ran out of his house, jumped into the Impala, and sped out of his driveway flinging dirt everywhere.

Rusty smiled as he watched her drive off and thought to himself, "I reckon that tour of the house she supposedly wanted so badly isn't happening."

....

Later that evening, to help warm up and get Rusty and Keisha ready for the tournament, Mathew and Randall volunteered to be their so-called sparring partners.

Rusty and Keisha looked at each other with a smile when they entered the court. They had played together a hundred times or more, but this was different. Now they were practicing to play in a pro-tour event together. The thought that they would not only be training to play pickleball, but to fight on the pickleball tournament battlefield as one, instantly bonded the two in a special way that could not be put into words.

The match was an immediate disaster for Mathew and Randall. They were getting utterly spanked. Generally, Rusty eased up on inferior opponents, but not this time. He wanted

Keisha to feel their chemistry on the court together and to know he felt it, too.

Rarely did a volley ever reach more than three hits on a side apiece. Every volley, every serve by Keisha or Rusty either painted the lines or hit just inside them. Mathew and Randall could do nothing other than shake their heads in dismay. All five sets were easily scored 11-0.

CHAPTER 13

THE TOURNAMENT

It was a perfect day for an outdoor tournament. The morning temperature was sixty-three degrees, with a projected high of eighty-five by mid-afternoon. There was a slight breeze from the East. The lack of wind was highly unusual for any Kansas day, let alone tournament days, which seemed to attract it.

Randall had arrived with Mathew at 7 a.m., Elijah accompanying them. This was a big move for Elijah. Leaving the house for school and running next door to Randall's home was one thing. But now, he was hanging out with hundreds of pickleball players gathered at the Pond Side Pickleball courts.

Elijah still didn't buy into the whole pickleball killer thing, but he had committed to the work. He had brought his iPad so he could take notes on anything he might see that was out of the ordinary.

Although their first match would not start until 8:30 a.m., Randall felt so nervous that he worried he might piss his pants during the match. He had played in many racket-sport tournaments before with overall stunning success. But this was different. It was his first attempt at playing in a tournament in the fastest-growing sport in America. He was petrified of letting his trainers, Keisha and Rusty down, and the most terrifying thought of all was that he had to play while keeping his eyes wide open in search of a monster.

Mathew did not seem a bit nervous. He appeared to know everyone there; he had played against nearly all the 3.5 opponents. Most of the players were from the Wichita area, but there were some who had traveled from a couple of states away. Randall followed behind Mathew, looking like a desperate puppy following a child, searching for scraps that the kid might drop.

Randall was not only attempting to prepare himself mentally for the tournament but listening to everything around him. He cringed at the thought that The Killer might be in the vicinity. He tried to keep his mind off the whole catching-The-Killer-thing; only because he was convinced that if The Killer were a pickleball player, he would be playing on the advanced professional courts with other 5.0 players on the far west end of the courts, nearly half a block away. The main objective of the day was to learn the whole pickleball tournament process and make pickleball contacts. He figured that neither he nor any of the Reynolds clan would gather much useful information, particularly since they had no one playing in the men's 5.0 doubles.

They could somewhat observe from afar by watching them in between their matches. They would have done so anyway, to support Rusty and Peter. Matthew began talking to a couple of guys who needed to warm up. Randall and Mathew took the court with them. They dinked for twenty minutes, worked on serves, and played a quick rally practice game, meaning they could win a point when their team was not serving. Mathew and Randall then took a short break before their 8:30 match.

At last, stepping out on the court for that first match, they bumped paddles with two guys who called themselves The Planets. One guy went by the nickname Mars, and the other preferred to be called Pluto. They wore matching shirts with planets on them. Randall reminded the guy who called himself Pluto that Pluto was no longer considered a planet. The Pluto guy said that no one should take away from Clyde Tombaugh's work. Randall looked him in the eye and said, "Burdett, Kansas guy!"

Mr. Pluto was impressed, "Oh, looks like we have met someone who knows his Kansas History!"

As a result of Randall's planetary knowledge, he learned during a round of small talk that they called themselves Mars and Pluto to promote the astronomy classes they taught at

Friends University. Eventually, after the space small talk, they got on with the match.

Although a normal pickleball match is won by the best of three sets to eleven, this tournament pool play would require only one set for victory. But that one set would go to fifteen points, and the winning team must win by two.

Randall and Mathew won the coin toss and elected to serve. Randall felt his arm shake. He hit the ball straight into the net. Their two opponents quickly capitalized on the mistake. They immediately sensed fear in Randall, and they devoured their prey like a pack of wolves stalking a small, whitetail fawn. Every time they hit the ball, it was to Randall. The score was soon at an alarming 6-0. It was looking bleak. But then a miracle occurred. Randall turned around to a brilliant, radiating vision that suddenly appeared right before his eyes. Sandy and Keisha had arrived. The ladies stationed themselves behind the fence, directly behind Randall and Mathew's opponents.

Keisha ran her hand across her chest while raising her shoulders to tell him to breathe. Sandy blew him a friendly kiss that made him giggle. He thought if they watched, it might make him more nervous. But instead, knowing that two of his favorite people in the world were there to support him calmed him in a way he never thought imaginable. After seeing their faces, he returned an 80-mile-per-hour serve with a third shot drop dink.

This was almost unthinkable, as players typically want to keep their opponents further back, not close to the net. It was an amazing return. A third shot drop on a return that barely lands over the net is equivalent to a batter in baseball bunting for a base hit with no one on base. There was no rhyme or reason for Randall making the shot other than having caught the opponents off guard, and it worked. They were so far back that by the time it dawned on them to run up, it was too late. The ball dropped for the second time. Mr. Mars shouted with admiration for his opponent, "Great shot, sir! That was out of this world!"

Keisha and Sandy clapped. Sandy gave him a thumbs-up. Randall then served an 85-mile-per-hour serve to the back of the court that painted the line. It was never returned. Their planet opponents continued their strategy of hitting the ball only to Randall. That strategy had worked against a timid, nervous Randall. But this was a different Randall. This was a person who, a few minutes ago, was the hunted. But now he was the hunter. He tore his prey apart, point by point. The ball never returned to the other side of the court. Randall scored 10 points, and Mathew served out the final five, resulting in a final score of 15-6.

After Pluto and Mars congratulated Randall and Mathew on the victory, the two professors pulled out their cards and handed them to Mathew. Mathew tried to pleasantly let them down easy by telling them that Astronomy sounded interesting, but he wasn't really interested in majoring in it. Pluto told Mathew that he might change his mind by the time he got to the end of his senior year. Mathew politely nodded his head in agreement. He admired their original marketing skills, regardless of his lack of interest in the Milky Way.

Keisha ran up and gave Mathew and Randall both hugs. Sandy hugged Mathew but gave Randall a kiss on the cheek.

"I'll never wash this face again," he shyly replied.

"You will if you ever want to get kissed again," she flirted back.

After some small talk, Keisha said she had to go, as she and her partner Robin needed to get ready. Keisha was happy that she was playing with Robin, but she knew that she really needed to be around 5.0 players to help with the investigation. She wished that she was playing 5.0 with Tasha. Tasha had moved up to 5.0 three months ago in co-ed doubles with Peter. Her previous women's partners were no longer at her level, so she had not found anyone to play with her. Keisha had talked to her, but Tasha stated that she was already scheduled to work a 7 a.m. to 3 p.m. shift. She had no chance of finding another registered nurse to cover it. Registered nurses were already in high demand, let alone trying to talk one of them into working on a Saturday. Tasha agreed that it was time for Keisha to move up to 5.0. Without Tasha, Keisha would have to play 4.5 doubles with Robin. Robin was closer to a higher-end 3.5 player and had to "play up" to play with Keisha.

Keisha thought of having them play 5.0 together to help the investigation, but she was too scared it might hurt Robin's self-esteem if they did not do well.

Sandy said that her work needed her attention, which was why she wasn't playing. She apologized for not being able to watch them the rest of the day and acknowledged that she'd see them all tomorrow. She made a point to say that she was looking forward to playing in the 3.5 co-ed tournament with Randall. She winked at him, implying that it might not be just pickleball that she was looking forward to. Randall then realized that he would not have his best cheer team with him for the rest of the tournament, but he thought he'd be fine. He had just needed them to help him get through that first match. Soon, Rusty came by where Mathew and Randall had set up their lawn chairs. Mathew gave Rusty a play-by-play of the match. Randall and Mathew both laughed when discussing Randall getting smashed at the start of the match. Rusty joked that Randall was no longer a pickleball tournament virgin. An announcement over the intercom ended the pickleball talk among the three. "Reynolds/Baines versus Johnson/Barton; Court 4". Rusty followed them to watch the first couple of points, but then he had to get ready for he and Peter's first match.

Johnson and Barton were playing down. They were probably truly more 4.0 to 4.5 players, but neither were sanctioned by the United States Pickleball Association. This was because they played in a lot of recreation tournaments. Without any ranking, they could choose to play in whatever division they wanted. "Sand baggers" and "cheesy medal chasers" were the labels given to such people by most pickleball enthusiasts.

To start, Jacob Johnson and Mark Barton were up 11-5. Randall and Mathew closed the gap to 12-11, but Mark served out the match, defeating Randall and Mathew 15-11.

Randall and Mathew were both disappointed they lost, but they knew they had fought hard, played quality ball, and did what they could; they had just fallen short. The two went over what could be done differently. Mathew put his head down and stated that Barton and Johnson first served to Randall, assuming the new, older guy would be the one that got rocked, but they had quickly learned that Mathew was the weak link. Randall insisted that was not the case and that it wasn't Mathew's fault, but Mathew wouldn't hear it. Randall eventually reminded Mathew of the reason they were truly there, which was for Randall to learn, play, and be around the game. And the sole purpose of being around the game was to try to catch a killer. Winning wasn't as important as it was to look respectable enough to continue. Mathew nodded his head in agreement, but the disappointment on his face was obvious. Randall thought to himself how caring Mathew was. It was evident that he was upset about letting Randall down.

Randall thought, "I wish Mathew knew that I genuinely do not care." Sure, he had been extremely happy to win the first match, primarily because he didn't want to let Keisha down for training him. But losing to a 4.0/4.5 team signed up for 3.5 just to, in all probability, comfortably win a championship was not a big deal to him.

Finding the pickleball-peanut-butter-whatever freak was the reason for the season. They had about 45 minutes before their next match. Randall, Mathew, and Elijah walked over to the 5.0 match, where Rusty and Peter were set to play two guys from a small town called Pratt. The match had been delayed by five minutes, due to Peter running late. He continuously apologized while texting Rusty that he had a flat tire and had to change it. The two Pratt guys were very understanding. They pointed out that they had had their share of busted tires in the past. The tournament director arrived and stated that they might have to forfeit if Peter did not arrive soon, as the tournament had to move along.

The tournament director was more patient than she usually would be, as this was a 5.0 bracket with a $300 entry fee and a $3,000 purse for the winners.

Rusty was tapping his feet and chewing his fingernails when, at last, Peter ran onto the court. Peter was generally a clean-cut guy, as his image and ego meant the universe to him, but that wasn't the case today. He had a smudge of what appeared to be dirt on his face, and smudges on his hands, presumably from changing the tire. After a few quick, friendly introductions and just a few warmup hits, the match began.

As it turned out, the tournament would not be delayed due to Peter's tardiness. The two opponents from Pratt were no match for Rusty and Peter. In fact, Peter played most of the match left-handed to make it more challenging. Rusty whispered to Peter that playing left-handed might offend their opponents, but Peter remarked that they were so bad they wouldn't even know.

Rusty shrugged his shoulders as if to say, "Yeah, you are probably right."

Elijah took out his phone and snapped pictures. He took a few photos of Peter while he was playing, but very few. Once, the wind briefly picked up at the same time that Peter was reaching for a ball, causing Peter's shirt to briefly fly up the very second Elijah snapped a picture of him. Elijah stood and stared at that particular shot for a lengthy period of time. He then went back to taking pictures of Peter in-between points.

Randall turned to Elijah and said, "Why have you been taking pictures of Peter when they are finished with the point? Wouldn't it be a more interesting picture if you took it when Peter was playing?"

Elijah replied in a soft voice, "Not interested."

Randall followed up, saying, "That is strange, but even more bizarre is that you are not taking any pictures at all of Rusty. Why is that?"

Elijah once again replied in a soft voice, "Not interested."

Elijah took out his iPad and made a few notes. The match was finished within eight minutes. 15-3 was the final score, and if Peter hadn't played most of the match left-handed, it would have been a 15-0 skunk. The two Pratt guys were unsanctioned players who thought they were great because they beat up on everyone in their small town, rec-ball world. They thought themselves to be the best of the best; when in fact, they probably would have struggled to play in a 3.5 tournament. The Pratt guys realized that they had blown three hundred dollars to get into the 5.0 unsanctioned tournament, meaning they had not needed a resume to qualify for the 5.0 level. Any entry fee under the 5.0 level was just thirty-five dollars. Rusty thanked the two Pratt guys for playing. In contrast, Peter turned to them and said, "You all should probably go back to your granny Thursday night pickleball league, and don't forget your Depends."

The two Pratt guys laughed uncomfortably, but Peter was not laughing. Randall mentioned the comment to Mathew, pointing out that it was not cool for Peter to treat them that way. Mathew defended Peter, stating that perhaps the Pratt guys need to understand that pro-level ball was not the place for them. Randall, in turn pointed out that the scoreboard already told them they were in over their heads. Mathew nodded in agreement.

Randall and Mathew congratulated Peter and Rusty on the win. Randall let Peter know that the comment he made to his opponents was unprofessional. Peter agreed and said he was trying to kid around, but it probably did not come out right. Randall then giggled and said, "We all say things in the heat of competition that we might not have said otherwise."

Randall and Mathew started walking over for their third match in pool play when they ran into Keisha and Robin. Keisha said they had barely won a hard-fought battle, 15-13. Robin stated that she was happy they had won but was disappointed, as she felt that she did not carry her weight in the match. She pointed out that she had made too many unforced errors.

Keisha immediately struck down Robin's comments. She pointed out that nearly every point was hit at Robin, so naturally, she would eventually miss more, as she was hitting the ball more. Keisha said she thought Robin had held her own, overall, in the 4.5 level. She then added, "Never, ever, ever apologize for a win."

Keisha and Robin hugged. Mathew and Randall congratulated them and went straight to court six for their third match in pool play. Keisha and Robin had a short break before their second match.

Keisha wanted to sneak over and watch a 5.0 men's doubles match. It wasn't just any doubles match, but a match between two of their suspects: Samuel Townsend and his partner, Andy Rice, against Bernard Jasper with his partner, Brance Jennings.

She was hoping for something, anything, that could be a sign that either Bernard or Samuel were psycho-serial killers, but she saw nothing in the short span of time she had available to her. The match was at 7-all when she had to get ready for her own next match. She quickly found Robin flirting with as many young, handsome pickleball players as she could. Keisha giggled, realizing that Robin had already forgotten her worries over her play in the previous match at the sight of a few cute guys.

Robin and Keisha started out with a 7-0 count on their opponents from Tulsa, Oklahoma. The two Oklahoma girls were good, especially for two fifteen-year-old, identical twin sisters playing 4.5-level ball. Their father, Ron, also their coach, was watching the two. He made a gesture to them to hit the ball lower. He then pointed to Robin, which was his way of telling them to hit everything to her. The two Oklahoma girls, Angie and Rene, responded by scoring the next five points, closing the gap to 7-5.

Keisha called a time-out. She was going through all the clichéd statements that she could verbalize to Robin, such as,

"Relax, play your game. Be ready, they're coming to you. Slow down and let the game come to you," and "Don't try to do too much. Just take it one point at a time."

The whole time she recited these clichés, she was looking all around her. She was looking for anything suspicious she might notice. Although Keisha was trying her hardest to win, deep down inside, for the first time in her life, she was happy that there was a break in the action due to her team losing points. She found herself slipping into the role of a detective rather than a competitive athlete. Just a fortnight ago, she never would have thought that possible.

The only thing that she noticed was Randall and Mathew in the court beside her, taking a time-out. Randall was also looking around, not appearing to really be in the match, but more concerned about the surroundings. They spotted each other. Keisha and Randall each knew exactly what the other was saying to the other. They gave each other a nod as if to say, "See anything?" They both shook their heads "no" as if to say, "No, nothing."

Mathew watched the two, knowing that observation was the true reason for the time-outs. When Mathew and Randall were up 11-4, Randall called a time-out. Their opponents looked at each other, baffled and pleased, as they had already used their one-per-set time-out, and they were getting their butts kicked. The time-out helped them temporarily, as they did close the gap to 11-9. But soon, Mathew and Randall finished out the match 15-11.

Meanwhile, Keisha and Robin continued their dogfight with the identical twins from Oklahoma. The score was 13-13. Many spectators gathered around to watch the four young girls battle it out. All four ladies on the court were at the top of their games, playing relentless, fearless, high-quality pickleball. The Oklahoma twins even had to back off some on their strategy of hitting the ball to Robin at all costs. Robin was holding her own. She was starting to take batting practice on balls hit straight across the net to her, forcing Angie and Rene to go back to the fundamentals of dinking cross-court, no matter who would be on the receiving side of the shots. At 13-all, Robin was serving to Rene. Robin reared her arm back to make it look as though she was going to hit the serve long and hard. Rene backed up. But just as she swung at the ball, she stopped her momentum and dinked the ball over the net, just over the kitchen line, barely making it a legal serve. Rene made no attempt to hit the ball, for she knew that she had no chance at success.

14 -13 ROBIN AND KEISHA: A POINT AWAY FROM VICTORY!

Robin then hit a safe serve to try to close out the win. Angie returned it hard and low, right back at Robin's feet. Robin was barely able to scoop it up, just before the ball touched the ground to return it, but she scooped it too high, and Rene slammed the ball into Robin's left eye. Both Oklahoma girls immediately apologized and were genuinely concerned for

Robin's wellbeing. Their father, along with Randall and Mathew, rushed out to assist. After about five minutes, Robin said she was okay and ready to continue.

She could not open her eye, but she knew that the match couldn't be held up any longer. She would have to play with her left eye shut and tears streaming down her face forcing her to see with just her right eye.

Keisha still had a chance to serve and to try to close out the match. She knew that Rene would probably smash it right at Robin, knowing she couldn't see. Keisha needed to do something unusual. She whispered to Robin to run off the court after the serve. Keisha then served a high lob, twenty-five feet in the air, which would give her time to move to the middle of the court. Rene drilled the ball at Robin's side of the court, but Robin was not present. Keisha smashed the ball deep back at Rene. Keisha then ran up to the middle of the court. Robin was behind the back line, towards the middle, holding her eye. Keisha was hoping Rene would shoot too far to the left to keep it away from Keisha and have an unforced error, but instead, Rene surprised her with a hard, fast lob. Keisha didn't expect this. She reversed course as fast as she could but tripped and fell as the ball landed. Rene and Angie cheered as the ball hit the back of the line, but with the corner of her right eye, Robin caught the ball flying near her at the last minute. She quit rubbing her left eye and swatted at the ball. She wasn't even sure where it was exactly.

The ball caught the end of her paddle, curved far right, and then swung left onto the court. Before Angie and Rene understood that the point was not over, the ball had already struck the ground twice.

15-13 – MATCH TO TEAM ROBIN AND KEISHA

Mathew, Randall, and a crowd of around thirty people cheered. Even the father of the Oklahoma twins clapped and smiled. After the twins congratulated Robin and Keisha, their father told them that it was good that the match had ended this way because it taught them to never think a point is over until it is over. Keisha watched with some jealousy, wondering what it might be like if her father had not died in a car wreck. She also wished she did not have to hide this day from her grandma. She thought that Grandma Edna would have really enjoyed watching that match.

Randall and the father of the Oklahoma twins then tended to Robin's eye. After about fifteen minutes, she was able to open it. Not too many women in Wichita played 4.5. If they were pro-level, they played 5.0. If not, they all generally played 4.0 or lower, making just four sets of three team pools for the 4.5. Since Keisha and Robin won all their pool-play matches, they automatically made the top-seeded team in their bracket.

The tournament was set up so that the four pool-play champions would make the top Gold bracket, and there would be two wild cards that would make it. The other six teams would be put in a lower division, the 4.5 Silver bracket.

The 3.5 men's doubles tournament had four pools of four, with the top two doubles teams in each pool making it into the

Gold bracket and all the rest making it into the Silver bracket. Randall and Mathew really wanted to make the Gold bracket solely for the purpose of developing more of a reputation as good players. Good players tended to be around and play other good players, and being a good player was a pathway to becoming a great player. Being a great player was a way to play other great players, and being around great players was a way of being near the psychotic Peanut Butter Killer.

Randall and Mathew were confident that they would make the Gold bracket with just one loss, but it was mathematically possible to be dropped down in the bracket if three of the four teams all beat up on each other and went 3-1. Before they could delve deeply into the bracket to study their odds, Elijah walked up to them and pointed out the obvious. The top team of Jacob Johnson and Mark Barton had won all three of their matches and Randall and Mathew had only lost one, thus making it mathematically impossible for the other two teams not to have two losses. Mathew and Randall then hugged in excitement, knowing they had made the top bracket.

Elijah, Randall, Mathew, Robin, and Keisha walked to court ten where Peter and Rusty were playing. There they saw that they were up 5-3. Peter and Rusty were in a bracket that was identical to Robin and Keisha's, with four pools of three teams in each to a pool. If they won the match, they would win their pool, and they would be in. Court ten had bleachers to allow spectators to watch the match. Not every court had bleachers, but courts ten, eleven, and twelve did, as they were for top championship-level pickleball and were likely to draw more fans.

In the bleachers were Robin and Keisha's friends, Debbie and Katy, holding their signs and cheering on their favorite athlete, Rusty. Debbie held up a sign that said: "Never Rusty with Rusty," with a few rusty nails drawn on it. Katy held up a sign that said: "Hail King Rusty" with a drawing of Rusty wearing a robe and a crown on his head, holding a pickleball paddle.

Keisha and Robin both complimented Katy on her artwork, as they knew that she was the designer and creator of the posters. They were really impressed by how remarkably close the picture of Rusty on the poster resembled the real Rusty.

There was nothing remarkable about the match, though. Rusty and Peter did not completely blow their opponents away, though they won handily at 15 -9. As soon as the match ended, Rusty was surrounded by Debbie, Katy, and a few other teenage girls who made up the usual eight. He told Debbie and Katy how impressed he was with the posters. Keisha took some pictures of Rusty, while Randall went to Peter and congratulated him. Of the approximately forty-two people watching in the stands, it was only Randall who walked up to Peter to congratulate him right away. Soon after taking the pictures of Rusty, Keisha, Debbie, and Katy congratulated Peter. Peter was happy with the win but angry that hardly anyone had noticed him. Keisha, Debbie, Randall, Elijah, Mathew, Robin, and Katy all sat under a tree to relax. They had about an hour and a half before the start of the Gold bracket play-off tournaments.

After the match, Peter walked over to the bleachers. He remembered a scene from his childhood. On that day, he ran into the house holding a trophy. He rushed up to his mother. He had shouted at her,
"You refused to come to the Spelling Bee today because you said no eight-year-old could win. Well, I won! I wish you would have been there!"

He then set the trophy on the table in front of her. His mother picked up her glass full of whiskey. She chugged it down. Then she grabbed the trophy, poked it into his chest, and shouted, "You little prick. Why the hell would I care about you spelling out words? Don't you have something better to do with your damn time, Peter?"

She then hit the young eight-year-old across the face with the trophy. Peter immediately fell to the ground. She grabbed his hair, pulled him up off the floor with one hand, and clung to the trophy with the other. Blood dripped from Peter's head and onto the trophy. She shouted, "Watch your shitty trophy fly, you little prick!" Peter watched his mom toss the blood-covered trophy against the wall, smashing it into several pieces.

Just then, Peter's brother, Tom, walked into the room with a paper airplane and a smug smile on his face. Tom handed their mother the paper airplane. He said with excitement, "Momma, Momma! Look at the airplane I made!" She replied with joy, "Oh, Tom, that is the most beautiful plane I have ever seen in my life. Let's go outside and fly it, dear." She grabbed Tom's hand as she turned to Peter and, referring to the blood and the trophy pieces, shouted, "You had better clean up all this mess!"

Keisha noticed Peter alone on the bleachers. She left the shaded tree and quietly walked up to Peter, so the rest of their group did not notice. His elbows were on his knees with his head buried in his hands. She tapped Peter on his shoulder and asked with concern, "Peter, are you okay?"

Peter lifted his head up and said, "Oh yes, Keisha, just a slight headache."

Keisha kissed him on the cheek and said, "You are playing fantastically. I have some aspirin in my bag. I'll go get it."

Peter thanked her. As she walked back to the tree, he placed his hand on the area she had kissed. He nearly teared up. Sure, he had been touched by many women. He could get any woman his age that he ever wanted in bed. But this was different. He felt nothing sexual at all, but for only the second time in his life, he felt affection and love. He thought to himself, "Keisha is truly the only living creature in this world other than my sister that really matters. Everyone else can go to hell!"

Keisha came back with the aspirin and some water for Peter. She helped him up off the bleachers and guided him under the tree, where the rest of the group was talking pickleball shop. The number one topic that came up was Robin's amazing dink serve. Robin thought it felt great to be the center of the topic of pickleball. In the past, she had witnessed all the glory and compliments directed toward Keisha. Keisha loved the newfound attention Robin was getting as well. Keisha simply loved the game and wanted to win. She never sought any attention. It just came with playing the game well. Eventually,

Katy noticed Keisha tending to Peter. They walked over to Peter and Keisha to check on him. He assured them that he was okay. Peter didn't know whether their sudden urge of sensitivity towards him was genuine or obligatory, but it felt good all the same.

Eventually, they all returned to their pickleball chat. After a short pause in the game analysis, Randall suggested they all go to a nearby food truck selling some basics, such as hamburgers, hot dogs, French fries, and drinks. He expected Keisha to rip into him for even suggesting eating such unhealthy food. But before she could enforce her nutrition values on him, Grandma Edna appeared. Holding a picnic basket, Edna had snuck up behind all of them. She abruptly walked into the middle of their pickleball clique. Answering Randall, she exclaimed, "Now, nothing wrong with a big, greasy cheeseburger on occasion, but not in the middle of a tournament. I have some nice ham and cheese sandwiches with carrots, celery, and grapes for dessert."

Frightened, Keisha asked her grandmother, "Grandma, how did you know we were here?"

Edna answered, "I've known you all formed some kind of cucumber-ball-craze-cult-thing for a week or so. You can't fool me. Do you think I don't look out the window and see all of you kids sneak off to Randall's house every night? And every time my friend Betsy drives us to Bingo, I see either Mathew's Vega or your Impala parked by Randall's truck at the cucumber club."

She looked at Randall and said, "Put two and two together, and it's the only logical reason you kids would want to hang out with this fool. Well, at least in the case of Mathew and Keisha. Elijah doesn't even like sports, so I don't know what his deal is."

"So, you're okay with us playing pickleball now, Grandma?"

"No. Not really. Pickleball doesn't pay the bills; tennis scholarships do. But I suppose you can do both. Y'all must live your life at some point."

"Thanks, Grandma," Keisha remarked fondly, giving Edna a hug.

Elijah and Mathew did not get into the whole emotional, greet Grandma thing. They were too busy digging into the sandwiches. Grandma Edna had brought enough for everyone there.

She knew Keisha played pickleball with Debbie, Katy, and Robin, and had assumed they would be there. She suspected Elijah and Mathew were not really at Saturday morning Bible study, as they had said they would be. So, she deduced that Mathew was likely playing in the tournament as well, and Elijah was probably just hanging out there for some odd reason. It was just an instinct she had that Elijah was there since he so rarely ever left his room. But she had noticed him sneaking over to Randall's a lot, and she figured he was finally ready to get out in the real world and face his demons. She did not know Rusty and Peter, but whenever she ever packed get-away lunches, she always added enough for at least two more, just in case extras were needed. They all thanked Edna for the lunches. She simply replied, "You're welcome," then turned to Randall and said, "I knew I had to get you a lunch to pay you back for all those copies of that great Follett book."

Edna then looked at Elijah, "Yep, I've started reading what I am guessing is Elijah's copy I found on the hallway floor, as it looks untouched. I mean, really, did they have to make Caris a nun? I'm a good Catholic, but man, oh mighty, she's never going to hook up with Merthin at this rate."

Shocked, Keisha shouted, "What? Caris becomes a nun? That can't be. I've been so busy with pickleball and the investi…." Keisha paused as she realized she had almost given away that the whole pickleball improvement plan was a ploy to further the investigation.

"…and uh, mowing and what not."

"I can't relate since I donated ALL my copies to the Reynolds family," remarked Randall.

Elijah answered, "Um, donating and criminally assaulting us with them are two different things, Randall."

The entire group laughed. As they were eating their lunch, Edna and Randall conversed. Edna wanted to know why Randall had ignored them all these years, and now he was suddenly best friends with all her grandkids. He did not say much other than that retirement was giving him more time to spend with his neighbors. Edna didn't really buy into that statement. She knew that there had been plenty of evenings and weekends he could have at least said "hello," but she was not going to press the issue. She liked to think, at least somewhere in her mind, that praying for Randall every day had made him more caring and approachable. Randall did tell Edna that he was genuinely sorry about all her losses between the loss of her son, daughter-in-law, and husband. Edna thanked him, though she couldn't help but think that if he had really cared, he would have at least sent a card, or flowers, or something.

   Eventually, Mathew walked up to Edna to talk about Follett's book since he had found time to read it in its entirety. Keisha joined in the conversation somewhat, but since Mathew had read the entire book, and Grandma Edna was further along in the novel than she was, she couldn't contribute as much to the conversation. The book-of-the-month club talk helped Randall escape the tight situation he was in. He knew that he had no excuse for not outwardly paying his condolences for Edna's losses. Randall soon slid over next to Rusty and Peter to talk more pickleball. Debbie, Robin, and Katy had already started traveling around the area, looking for boys to talk to. Eventually, the brackets were officially posted.

   All playoff brackets were: win and you move on, lose and you are done. It is a best-two-out-of-three-to-eleven format. In the larger bracket, Mathew and Randall were scheduled to begin playoff play first. This gave the rest of their pickleball clan a chance to watch them. Mathew and Randall faced a very good team in John Seron and Paul Ledger. They had won their pool with no losses, as well.

   Mathew began serving. During that first point, the ball was dinked a total of seven times before Mathew and Randall lost the point. John then served a far deep shot to Mathew, allowing John and Paul to quickly approach the net. There was then a total of eleven dink volleys before Randall accidentally smashed the ball slightly too high, hitting Mathew right in the chest. John went on to serve a total of six points before losing his serve. Paul successfully served an additional three points before he lost his serve.

9-0 JOHN AND PAUL

Mathew served again. Paul caught Randall off guard by hitting a sharp, low shot down the baseline. Randall was unable to get any part of the paddle on the ball. Randall then served. In frustration, he tried to hit the ball too close to the back line to try and keep the Kansas City pair back, but the ball flew out of balance. John easily served out the set.

11-0 FIRST SET TO JOHN AND PAUL

Randall was not upset. He knew that, on average, there were probably about six volleys in every point. Randall felt they were both playing good quality ball, with very few unforced errors, but it just wasn't showing on the scoreboard. Mathew, on the other hand, was disappointed and embarrassed. He knew that Debbie spent most of her time watching pickleball, gawking over Rusty, as did all the girls. Plus, she was going to be a junior, two years younger than Keisha and one year younger than Katy and Robin, who would be seniors. But that was still a year older than him. Her long hair and cute red freckles made his heart beat a thousand times a second. In addition, it was the first time his grandmother had watched him play. She'd surely

make him put up his paddle and force him to completely focus on scholarship sports if he were to get crushed by the pair of thirty-somethings from Kansas City.
The second set started out an exact duplicate of the first set. Paul started out serving. He and John got four long, hard-fought points before losing the serve.

4-0 FAVOR TO JOHN AND PAUL

Randall then served. During the first point of his serve, there were eight dink volleys before Mathew, out of frustration, hit a short, inadvisable, high lob. John hit the ball into the net, missing an easy slam.

4-1 MATHEW AND RANDALL SCORE!

Grandma cheered, "Okay, men. We are on the board. Let's go!" Hearing Grandma cheering helped Mathew. It told him that despite her feelings about pickleball, she desperately wanted Mathew to succeed. The next point involved a lot more dinking, dinking, and more dinking. Randall eventually got frustrated and thought, "What the hell? Let's set him up for a slam again. What do we have to lose?" Randall then hit the ball straight up into the air, setting up an easy slam for Paul. Paul once again struck the ball right into the net.

4-2 JOHN AND PAUL

Randall called a time-out. He told Mathew, "I think Paul is frustrated. He overthinks every high ball. The sun is in his face. He's had easy slams, but he has been losing the ball in the sky because of the bright sun above him." Mathew nodded, "okay." When play resumed, Randall and Mathew continued to lob. They were getting the lobs deeper and further to the point that they were nearly hitting or striking the back baseline.

Paul missed hard backline shots on six of the next seven points.

8-5 RANDALL AND MATHEW

Keisha, Debbie, Katy, Robin, Grandma Edna, Rusty, and Peter all cheered. Mathew, noticing Debbie cheering for them, felt his confidence increase exponentially. He then started to coach Randall. Mathew whispered to Randall, "The set-them-up-for-a-slam-thing won't keep working, but if we totally abandon the net dink game now, it might throw them off. Hit hard or lob every shot."

"Works for me," Randall answered in agreement.

Throwing out playing the very basic playing techniques of pickleball and abandoning any type of dink game altogether would be a suicide mission at any level higher than 3.5. 3.5 players are generally pretty *good*. After all, playing levels go as far down as 2.0; however, 3.5 players are not *great* players. They're not 4.0 or higher for a reason. Mathew and Randall quickly learned that Paul and John were 4.0 or higher players when it came to playing the basics of the game, but they could not handle anything odd thrown at them. Randall and Mathew hit every ball so hard and so fast that they probably would have flown out of bounds if John and Paul hadn't struck at them. But the opposing team could not resist. John or Paul would strike at nearly every shot that would have been long. The two were so accustomed to hitting the ball back and dinking that they were not very good at anything else. Mathew and Randall went on to win seven of the next twelve points.

15-10 SET 2 GIFTED TO MATHEW AND RANDALL!

Mathew and Randall's support group cheered with excitement. Grandma Edna jumped up and down in a 360-degree circle. Randall smiled, watching her get so excited. He thought about how youthful she seemed and how well she had kept up her appearance and energy, especially considering all that she had gone through. Mathew found it amusing that his grandma was rooting with intense enthusiasm for two men playing a sport that she despised. Most of all, though, Mathew felt utterly giddy inside when he saw Debbie point at him and give him a thumbs-up. John and Paul were starting to settle down.

They were starting to adjust to the game and beginning to discipline themselves to let short and hard balls go. They realized that even though the balls were being hit low and hard, the speed would still force the balls to fall behind the back line before landing. But John and Paul had not completely adjusted yet. Both teams were battling back and forth. The Kansas City guys would get a couple of points in a row, but Mathew and Randall would come back with a few points themselves.

Mathew and Randall were starting to go back to playing a dink game, but whenever they felt that John and Paul were getting used to that style of game again, Randall or Mathew would slam the ball hard, thus throwing John and Paul off.

SCORE: 12-12

At this point, Edna was biting her fingernails and sweating profusely. Keisha was trying to observe everything around her, reminding herself that her primary purpose was to catch a killer. She found herself fascinated with the match, though, making it hard to focus on her main purpose. Robin leaned her head into Rusty's chest, trying to flirt with him while acting like she was nervous about the match. Rusty didn't particularly like Robin doing that but was too enthralled with the match to try to casually move her away. Debbie was staring at Mathew as if to say, "You got this."

Mathew served. John noticed Randall covering for Mathew, attempting balls that were not intended for him. This enticed John to return the serve down the baseline nearest Randall. Randall instinctively knew that John would try the baseline shot, though, and he never moved. He took the shot and slammed it right at Paul's feet.

13-12 IN FAVOR OF MATHEW AND RANDALL

Mathew then served a short ball to Paul's backhand to throw him off. Paul ran to the net and barely got to the ball, but when he scooped it up, the ball flew straight into the air, back to Mathew for an easy slam.

14-12 GAME POINT

There were nine volleys apiece from both sides of the net on the next point, making a total of eighteen volleys, nearly all being dinks. Eventually, Randall hit a ball that hit the top of the net. It felt like it was suspended at a complete standstill before deciding to land on the other side of the net. Paul dove for the ball. He was just barely able to get it back over the net, but the momentum from diving caused him to hit his shoulders on the net, disqualifying his team from winning the point.

15-12 MATCH TO RANDALL AND MATHEW!

All of their clan erupted in celebration. Edna ran out and gave Mathew a huge hug. She started to hug Randall but stopped and looked at him and said, "Sorry. I can handle my grandson's sweat, but sure in hell, not yours!" Edna and Randall both laughed and shook hands. The entire group ran onto the court to cheer for them, except for Debbie. Mathew looked over while walking off the court and saw her talking to some young guy in his twenties. Mathew was disappointed and jealous but still happy. He had made the upper bracket playoffs with other partners before, but they had never won a match. Now he and

Randall had won a match and were in the semi-finals. He figured that the red-haired, freckle-faced, Emma Stone lookalike was probably out of his league, anyway.

Soon, Keisha and Robin took court seven. Even though they won their pool, they did not have a large enough point differential to get one of two byes, forcing them to play earlier than they had hoped. The entire crew was there to support them, except for Elijah. Elijah did have a slight interest in watching his sister and Robin, but he thought that Mathew, Randall, and Keisha were losing focus on the task at hand. He felt that the three of them were not staying as observant as he would like them to be. They were getting much too interested in how well they played in the tournament and less focused on trying to catch a killer. His conviction that the Midwest madman was more of a Peanut Butter Freak than a pickleball enthusiast had not waivered; however, the mission was to play in this tournament to look for the pickleball/murder connection, regardless if they were all chasing a phantom, non-existent psycho or not.

Elijah walked around the entire Pond Side Pickleball complex. He went to the men's restroom. He looked around, but nobody else was in there. He saw nothing unusual. He then walked over to the women's restroom. He waited for a while until he was confident that no one was in there. He quickly walked into the restroom and looked around. He did not see anything unusual other than that one of the sinks appeared a little dirty. This would not be uncommon in a men's restroom, but it seemed slightly odd for a woman's restroom. He quickly took a picture of the sink. As he was taking a picture of it, Debbie walked in.

"What are you doing, Elijah?"

"Um, Uh, umm, it's an environmental project I'm working on. It deals with the flow of water in bathrooms and restrooms. Damn, we waste a lot of water in America!" he stated in horror.

"And how is taking a picture of a sink in a women's restroom helping slow the water flow in America?" she remarked.

"Uh, um, um...I already took pictures of the men's sink, and, um, the size of sinks can play a psychological factor in the decision as to how fast to have the water flowing when you wash your hands," he stated, off the top of his head.

"Hardly anyone can get you to come out of your room. Now you're not only out and about but you're doing creepy things in women's bathrooms. That's pretty scary and just plain wacked, Elijah."

Elijah put his head down and quickly exited the woman's bathroom in utter and total embarrassment.

Robin and Keisha were set to play. They were facing the two best 4.5 players from the Wichita area: Nadine Rouse and Jennifer Grain from Derby, Kansas, a suburb of Wichita. Nadine was forty-nine, and Jennifer was fifty-one. This was their last year playing in the nineteen-and-over category, as Nadine would soon turn fifty, making them eligible for the more winnable fifty-and-older tournaments. They were both looking forward to it because they were not quite good enough to play 5.0 or pro-level tournaments, but in larger fifty-and-older tournaments, they could make some serious cash and play senior division 5.0 pro tournaments.

The two middle-aged athletes immediately took the ball to Robin at any and every opportunity they had. Robin held her own okay, but they were just too much for her. Experience over youth was the story. Jennifer and Nadine won the first set 11-6.

Just as the second set was starting, Peter and Rusty began their match on court ten against pickleball killer suspect Samuel Townsend and his partner Andy Rice. Elijah made his way over to the court to observe Samuel.

The first set had a good flow. It was a back and forth battle until the score was eight all. Peter then served a deep shot that hit the very edge of the back of the line to Samuel's backhand. Samuel barely touched the ball, flinging it straight into the bottom of the net. Samuel threw his racket down, shouting a couple of four-letter words.

With it being a Gold bracket 5.0 match, a good crowd of around fifty fans was watching it. It surprised Elijah that Samuel had no concern for what the crowd might think of him swearing and losing his temper. Samuel thought using four-letter words in front of a large group of people was very careless at that level when a pro-level player would depend highly on sponsorships. Elijah thought it was particularly interesting, considering that Keisha described Samuel as a goofy prankster type of guy. Elijah was not seeing that side of him. Elijah took out his iPad, noting Samuel's anger. Rusty and Peter did not have to communicate with each other to know that the strategy to close out the match was to hit the ball at a very frustrated Samuel, and it worked.

After the next point, Peter served to Andy. Andy returned the ball to Rusty, who sent it straight to Samuel. Samuel was dinking the ball well, but after six dink shots in a row went directly to him, he lost his patience and went for a kill shot that went far out of bounds. On the next serve, Peter again hit a shot deep to Samuel's backhand. Samuel couldn't believe that Peter was able to get the serve deep to his backhand again. He barely made it to the ball, and it flew straight up to Peter. Peter hit it right into Andy's chest to win the set 11-8.

Elijah thought, "Hmm. Peter hit him right in the chest with no apologies, and it almost looked like he hit him on purpose to embarrass Samuel and Andy." Elijah took note.

Meanwhile, Robin continued to get bombarded with every shot. It was almost as if Keisha wasn't even playing. And yes, the middle-aged stars won the second set, eliminating Keisha and Robin from the tournament. But the score on the second set was 11-9. Robin was apologetic toward Keisha and told her that she was just out of Keisha's league. She stated that it would be in Keisha's best interest to find another women's doubles partner, but Keisha would have none of it. After Debbie, Katy, Mathew, Edna, and Randall all congratulated Keisha and Robin on a great tournament despite the loss, Keisha took Robin aside to talk to her.

She pointed out that in the past, a barrage of balls being struck at Robin would have led to her falling apart, even against 3.5 players. But now, at a nearly pro level, Robin was holding her own. Keisha pointed out that while she could find better players at a higher level than Robin to play with, virtually none would have Robin's potential for growth due to her age and ability. She then remarked that the only thing that would keep them from playing together might be Keisha heading off to college to play in the fall. They hugged and proceeded to court ten to watch the end of Peter and Rusty's match.

Keisha and Robin were impressed that Debbie and Katy, who had huge crushes on Rusty, did not head over to the match until it was over. It even surprised them a little bit that Mathew waited as well since he worshipped the ground Rusty walked on. As soon as the match was over, Grandma Edna went over to watch Rusty and Peter as if they were good buddies. But Elijah, who barely knew Peter and Rusty at all, hadn't watched his sister's match, but instead, was watching Peter and Rusty's match in its entirety.

Rusty and Peter continued to prey on Samuel's frustration and went on to easily win the second set 11-3, which allowed them to move on to the semi-finals. The crowd cheered as if they were rock stars. Peter smiled broadly. There were almost as many congratulating him as there were congratulating Rusty.

....

After half an hour of pickleball talk, Mathew and Randall headed to court three to play their semi-finals match against Rod Olsen and Trey Breese of Olathe, Kansas. Rod and Trey were two young guys in their late twenties. They had both learned early, from observing many, many games, that looks can be deceiving. Randall, at age seventy-two, was the more dominant player on his team.

They started the match by hitting the ball to Mathew. They took a 7-6 lead, although Mathew was holding strong. After six volleys from each side of the net, equaling twelve volleys total, Mathew noticed a shot just barely high enough to take a chance on, so he bent his wrist, twisting the ball overhand to the backhand of Trey. Trey could not return it.

7 ALL

From there, it was a battle royale, with no team leading by more than two points at any time. When the score was 10-9 with Trey serving the set, he served to Mathew. Mathew made an excellent cross-court shot to Rod. Rod hit a beautiful third shot drop to Randall's backhand that he was barely able to get back.

Then, after three dinks on each side, Mathew received a hard middle-of-the-chest shot. Mathew brought his paddle to his chest as fast as he could. He barely reached the ball, hitting it just at the top of the net. The ball fell on Trey and Rod's side of the court, but in the process, Mathew dropped his paddle, and the ball bounced high enough for Trey to get to it. Trey was only barely able to get it over the net. He would have liked to have aimed it straight at Mathew since he knew that Mathew did not have a paddle to hit it back with, but he didn't have enough time to aim it straight at his paddle-less component, so it floated over to Randall.

Randall dinked it cross-court to Rod. Rod hit the ball directly at Mathew. Mathew's paddle had landed on his left side, forcing him to pick it up with his left hand. Mathew hit the ball no more than a fraction of a second after picking the paddle up. He did not have the time to put any placement on the ball, so it sailed up over the net to set up an easy slam for Rod. Unfortunately for Rod, he was shocked that Mathew had been able to get to the ball at all, so he stood there stunned. Instead of slamming the ball in the air, he let it bounce.

After the bounce, the ball did not spring up as high as Rod thought it would, though he thought it was high enough to slam. He did not get his wrist over the ball well enough to hit it the way he wanted to, and the ball flew straight into the net. A crowd of about twenty erupted in cheer and applause.

A proud Grandma Edna shouted, "That's my grandson! That's my grandson!" Mathew appreciated the sentiment, but he was a little embarrassed.

SCORE REMAINS 10-9 ADVANTAGE TO TREY AND ROD.

Randall then served. Rod returned a shot straight to Mathew's backhand that was low and powerful. Mathew was just able to reach the ball, hitting it at the top of the net. It landed on his opponent's side. Rod dove for the ball but could not reach it.

10 ALL

Randall then served to Trey. Randall put in a safe, slow serve to the middle of Trey's side of the court, but Trey limped to get to the ball and hit it straight into the net. Trey was clearly hurting from diving for the ball that Mathew had previously hit.

11-10 ADVANTAGE TO RANDALL AND MATHEW

Randall found himself shaking with nervousness. He stopped, took a breath, bounced the ball twice, and served the ball to Rod, who hit the slow shot right back at Randall. Rod sensed Randall's nervousness. He hit the ball with the edge of his paddle, and it flew out of bounds. But Mathew still had his serve. Mathew, gaining confidence in himself, purposely served a long, hard shot to the back of the court to Trey. Trey got it back with a nice shot, but Mathew made a beautiful third-shot drop that floated just over the net back at Trey. He limped to get the ball, but he could not get to it with his injured knee.

12-10 SET AWARDED TO RANDALL AND MATHEW!

There was a good five minutes before the second set would start. Trey was trying to work his knee but found he couldn't get it to move well. He and Rod used the stacking technique to try and get through the rest of the match. Trey served, and then he would try and hop completely away from the court, basically forcing Rod to play one against two. This continued throughout the match. Rod was holding his own. Rod was very athletic. He was a former tennis player for Bethany College out of

Lindsborg, Kansas. He had just learned the game of pickleball a few months earlier, otherwise, he would have been playing at a higher level than 3.5. Despite his athleticism; however, he could not cover the entire court against two solid players. He helped keep them in the game, as it was 8-5 at one point, but Mathew and Randall soon closed out the match.

11- 6 - MATCH TO MATHEW AND RANDALL

Although the crowd cheered, it was a subdued cheer. Those watching were concerned about Trey's knee. He was taken to the ER for an x-ray. There was a lot of excitement around the fact that Mathew/Randall and Peter/ Rusty had made it into their respective championships. Randall tried to call Sandy, but she did not pick up. He told her over voicemail about the four of them being in the championship. He also let her know that Keisha and Robin hadn't medaled but had played at an extremely high level for such young ages. She texted back, apologizing for not answering the phone. She was busy with her work but was excruciatingly excited for them all.

They could not celebrate long, as the championship in the 3.5 category was scheduled to start in five minutes. Randall's entire body was sore. He so wished that the next match started later, but he reminded himself that there is always some form of turbulence when striving for success.

When they walked onto the court, they were face-to-face with the team they dreaded playing the most: Jacob Johnson and Mark Barton. This was the only team that they lost to all day.

Randall started out serving. Jacob immediately returned the serve low at about a sixty-mile-per-hour velocity. Randall was nervous since it was the championship, and the high-speed, low return was too much for him to handle. He hit it straight into the net. Mark then served to Mathew. Mathew returned it, but he hit it too high up in the air, allowing Jacob to smash the ball one foot from Randall's feet. He hit it so hard that it cleared the fence and hit one of the fifty-plus spectators in the shoulder. Jacob and Mark were relentless. They were the defending champs, and it showed. Randall and Mathew were wholly outclassed on seven straight points.

7-0 TEAM BARTON/JOHNSON

Randall and Mathew eventually got the ball back. They whipped off three points in a row. Two of the points were earned by patient, long point dinking, and the other by a rare, careless, missed slam by Jacob.

7-3 - RANDALL AND MATHEW DOWN BUT CLOSING THE GAP!

Unfortunately, that gap would not remain closing for long. Team Barton/Johnson served out the set unscathed.

11-3 SET ONE TO BARTON/JOHNSON

Soon after the set, Rusty and Peter made their way to court ten to play in the 5.0, nineteen-and-over championship. Peter and Rusty did not miss much, as set two for Mathew and Randall was more of the same. The match was basically over before it started.

11-4 - BARTON/JOHNSON REPEAT AS 3.5 NINETEEN PLUS, CHAMPIONS!!

There were some claps honoring the champs, but the crowd's enthusiasm was subdued. Not only did they like the young kid/old man partners, but the pickleball-educated crowd knew that if you were champions in a tournament as big as the Wichita Open one year, it was customary and ethical to move up one level, at the very least. The crowd thought that Johnson and Barton were in it more for a medal rather than to support the integrity of the game.

Mathew and Randall were not disappointed in the slightest. They were ecstatic to have reached the championship and to be able to stand on the second-place box on the podium to receive their silver medals. The only thing that was disappointing to Mathew was that he soon learned that his own brother, Elijah, had left the match early. Mathew felt as though Elijah had totally given up on him and Randall but made his way to court ten to avoid missing a second of Rusty and Peter's match. Mathew tried not to show his disappointment about his brother. Robin, Keisha, Debbie, Katy, and Grandma Edna stayed for his and Randall's medal ceremony before they moved over to support Rusty and Peter.

As the best 5.0 team that lived in the Wichita area, Peter and Rusty generally drew the largest group of fans throughout the tournament, especially with what those at the tournament had started to call the "Crew". The Crew referred to Rusty and Peter themselves, along with Debbie, Katy, Keisha, Robin, Randall, and Mathew, and although she wasn't around much today, most would recognize Sandy as a member of the Crew, as well.

Additionally, the Crew had even very recently added a pair of non-pickleball-player support system members in Grandma Edna and Elijah. But the two players on the other side of the net quickly gained their own set of fans as well.

Darin Pierce and Gus Rock were two mid-twenties kids. They looked like twin brothers, though they were not related. They both had shoulder-length blond hair. Darin was six-foot-three, and Gus was six-foot-four. Both were extremely fit. They wore black and gold shirts with a picture of a large mug of beer on them. Above the beer was their sponsor's name, Burdett Beer. The back of their shirts had their names at the top. In the middle of the back of the shirts were their numbers. Darin had the number 6. Below the number 6 was written, "Grab a six-pack at Burdett Beer." Gus had the number 7 on his shirt above the words, "You're In Seventh Heaven When You Drink Burdett Beer." Gus and Darin even had their own helper. She was a gorgeous, slender, African American woman named Lana. Occasionally, when Darin and Gus would make a great shot to win a point, Lana would turn to the crowd and throw out

Gold and Black hats that said in capital letters "BURDETT BEER". In small letters, the bill of the hat read, "Established in Branson 1987".

By the time the entire Crew had made their way over to the match, Rusty and Peter had just finished a long hard battle for the first game, losing in overtime.

15-13 SET ONE TO BURDETT BEER

Rusty started out serving in the second game. He tried to hit close to the back of the line, but it floated just a few inches out.

"DAMN IT!" shouted Peter.

Darin served to Rusty. Rusty hit the ball straight into the net. The hard-fought battle in the first set ended in defeat and wound through Rusty's head.

1-0 BURDETT BEER

Peter called a time-out. "What dorky freaking outfits. These two look like a couple of desperate puppies trying to get sympathy hugs from the crowd. I bet they're a couple of virgins who never got laid in their lives, so they gotta parade around in some type of Girl Scout shit with a fucking beer thrown on it just to try and get some play. What losers!" Peter followed up the ridiculous statement with a laugh.

After a long pause, Rusty laughed as well. "Those are some dorky ass outfits, huh, Peter?"

"Yes, they are! Now let's show these little Girl Scouts who we are."

After dehumanizing team Burdett Beer, the rock star image Rusty had of the Burdett Beer Boys was tainted. After the next serve and five volleys from each side, Darin hit a ball that grazed the top of the net but did not find its way over.

Peter looked at Rusty and whispered to him, "Girl Scouts."

Rusty nodded his head with a smirk in agreement. "Girl Scouts," Rusty repeated.

1-1 TIED UP

After a few dink volleys on each side, Gus was finally set up for a slam due to a rare bad stroke from Peter. Gus slammed the ball low between Rusty's legs. With remarkable reflex, Rusty took the paddle in his right hand, shot it behind his right leg, and dumped the ball just over the net. Gus was so shocked that Rusty had made that shot that he floated the ball into the air high enough for Peter to slam it. Peter ran up and chest bumped Rusty. Peter shouted, "YAAAAAAAA!!!!!!"

After the chest bump, Rusty said to Peter, "Girl Scouts".

"Girl Scouts," Peter repeated.

Rusty and Peter had shifted the momentum. They were playing with confidence, whereas Darin and Gus were playing with the taste of bitter beer in their game. Rusty and Peter went on to win the next eight points.

9-1 RUSTY AND PETER

Darin called time-out. He and Gus discussed strategy. Peter and Rusty used the time to continuously repeat two words back and forth to each other, "Girl Scouts". The time-out helped Team Burdett Beer settle down, and they scored the next six points.

9-7 RUSTY AND PETER STILL LEAD

Peter knew Rusty's game was getting tight. He couldn't call time-out, as the rules only allowed for each team to call one per game. After finally getting the serve back, Peter lobbed an extremely high serve to the back of the line to Gus. It was slow and high but it threw Gus off, and he slammed the ball into the net.

10-7 GAME POINT

Peter then served a deep, hard shot to Darin. Darin sensed that his opponent was nervous. He hit the ball low and hard back at Rusty, who swung at the ball, but was so aroused with nerves that it hit the tip of his paddle. It caused the ball to fly far right, but still remain on the court, making its way to Gus. As Gus was swinging at the ball, it flew back to the left. He completely missed the ball as it bounced twice on the court. The crowd had grown to over one hundred people, and they all cheered. Peter turned to Rusty and remarked, "Better to be lucky sometimes than good."

"GIRL SCOUTS!"
"GIRL SCOUTS."

11-7 SECOND SET TO RUSTY AND PETER

The third set would be a dogfight. The lead switched back and forth, with neither side ever holding more than a two-point lead. Whenever Peter sensed that Rusty's nerves were getting to him, Peter simply said the two now-infamous words "Girl Scouts." He tried to say it just loud enough so that Darin and Gus would hear, but not loud enough that the crowd could, to keep up the image to the public that Peter and Rusty still treated pickleball as a gentlemen's game. Despite the newfound confidence Rusty was feeling, eventually Burdett Beer would gain two chances to close out the match.

10-9 BURDETT BEER – CHAMPIONSHIP POINT!

Darin served to Peter. Peter drilled a ball right over to Gus's backhand. Gus fired it back to Rusty. Rusty sent a drop shot to Darin. Darin hit the ball into the net, but it just barely made it over the net to Rusty. Rusty got to the ball and dinked it over the net and back at Darin. Darin saw how close Rusty was to the net, which gave Darin the idea to lob the ball hard and deep over Rusty's head. Rusty had no chance to get back far enough to get it, but Peter instinctively guessed Darin's plan, and Peter rushed back to get to the ball. He got to the lob just in time, but he only had the chance to reach the ball while facing it straight on, forcing him to hit it over his own head and backwards. The ball came to Gus's backhand. Gus hit the ball right onto the top of the net. It rolled across the net in a suspenseful and miraculous fashion. The crowd gasped! By some sort of miracle, it then landed on the side of Burdett Beer, and the crowd erupted in applause and whistles.

Rusty and Peter were able to fight off one match point. Gus then served to Rusty's backhand. Rusty not only hit the ball back, but he hit it deep to Darin with great force. It was a very gutsy shot with the game on the line. Nerves got to Darin, and he uncharacteristically hit the ball right into the net, giving the serve back to Rusty and Peter.

TWO MATCH POINTS SAVED

Peter served a mediocre shot down the middle. Ten dink volleys from each side ensued, making a total of twenty volleys before Rusty hit an amazing cross-court shot to Gus that barely cleared the net and hit the line to Gus's backhand side. Gus could not quite reach the ball.

10-10 TIE

Julie Kennedy and her news crew were there filming. The Wichita Eagle was snapping pictures. About every fifth person was filming from their phones, a couple streaming to Facebook Live. The crowd was cheering so loudly that one might think it was a Friday Night Football game between two undefeated rivals. Keisha had her hands clasped, and there were butterflies in her stomach churning in pure madness. Mathew looked over and noticed Elijah on his iPad, as he had been the entire match.

Mathew leaned over to Elijah. "I Know you're not into sports, but this is so intense I don't even know how you can possibly be so disinterested that you can't put that stupid iPad down."

Elijah simply shrugged his shoulders. He then turned to Mathew and asked, "What kind of car does Peter drive?"

"Why ask a question like that at a time like this, Elijah?"

"Can you please just answer the question?"

"He drives a black Mercedes. I think it's pretty new."

"Thanks"

"Elijah, this is the most intense pickleball match I have ever seen in my life. It's a pro-level 5.0 tournament and suddenly you're into cars. You a damn weirdo, bro, but I love ya anyway."

Elijah then got up from the bleachers and started walking away.

"Hey, I'm sorry, brother. I was just kidding. Surely you aren't going to leave now?"

Noticing her grandson's exit, Grandma Edna also remarked. "Yeah. Are you actually leaving a match like this?"

"Um, uh, yes. My stomach is hurting. I got to go to the restroom."

Debbie chimed in, "Well at least make sure it's the men's restroom this time, creep-o!"

Elijah was embarrassed by Debbie's comments but said nothing in response. He ran off to the parking lot, away from the pickleball courts.

After Elijah left, Grandma Edna asked Debbie why she would say something like that to him. Debbie apologized. She told Grandma Edna that it was just an inside joke between them, but she admitted that it had probably embarrassed him. Grandma Edna was not sure what to think about Debbie's comment or explanation, but she decided it was none of her business. Edna had never seen Debbie as a bully, so she figured that the comment was just some ill-placed joke that wasn't appropriate but had no malicious intent to it.

After Peter's next serve, Gus hit the ball to Rusty, who responded with a cross-court dink shot to Darin. Darin hit a cross-court shot back to Rusty. They continued to dink cross-court to each other as if they were playing a game of singles. Rusty hit his eighth cross-court shot to Darin. On Darin's eighth cross-court shot back to Rusty, Peter noticed the ball went farther over, closer to the middle. So, he took a chance and ran to Rusty's side.

Peter shoved Rusty over with his shoulder and slammed the ball into Gus's chest. Peter never apologized to Rusty for knocking him over, nor to Gus for hitting him in the chest. The crowd cheered and Rusty could have cared less about Peter's rudeness. It had worked and that's all that mattered to him.

RUSTY AND PETER UP 11-10
CHAMPIONSHIP POINT

Peter wanted to put the game away, and in turn found himself trying to do too much. He swung a serve hard and low that hit the net. "DAMN IT," shouted Peter.

"Don't worry about it." Rusty reassured Peter.

Peter rolled his eyes and thought, "Who the hell are you to tell me anything about the game, you little prick."

Rusty had not served yet, so they still had one more chance.

Rusty hit a safe cross-court serve to Darin, which Darin had anticipated with the game on the line. Darin aimed the slow, safe, middle shot toward the edge of Rusty's backhand at around seventy miles-per-hour. Rusty dove, falling to the ground but reaching far enough with his backhand to get the ball over the net with a mid-court set-up for a slam shot to Gus. Gus slammed the ball in an attempt to hit Rusty, knowing he was lying on the court, but he just missed him. Peter anticipated Gus's aim for Rusty, so he had already run at a full sprint to make his way behind Rusty before Gus even hit the ball. Peter did not have time to move his right arm over to hit a backhand shot at it, forcing him to switch hands. He was just able to reach the ball with his paddle using his left hand and drilled it right back at Gus. Gus assumed the point was over, but h literally didn't know what hit him. The ball struck his right knee, and the crowd went insane. The one hundred-plus fans stormed the court.

12-10 - TEAM RUSTY/PETER TAKES THE 19-OVER 5.0 CHAMPIONSHIP!

After the crowd somewhat subsided, it didn't surprise Peter that Keisha came to him first to congratulate him. But it caught him off guard when Katy, Robin, and Debbie hugged and patted him on the back before taking their usual flirtatious positions near Rusty. Mathew shook Rusty's hand first, but quickly moved to shake Peter's hand soon after.

Even Grandma Edna gave Peter a big hug and told him that she was inspired to see a middle-aged man hanging out with the kids. The Crew felt an enormous amount of pride, as a pair of their own was going home with a championship and three thousand dollars. They all got into a circle and shouted, "Crew, Crew, Crew, Crew…" The Crew gathered around for a picture that another pickleball player offered to take for them.

One Crew member; however, was not present for the picture. They all looked around for Elijah so he could join in the shot, but they couldn't find him. Debbie felt bad that she had kept calling him creep-o. She thought that might have embarrassed and scared him off. Debbie thought Elijah was strange and a loner, but she didn't really think he was a creeper. Her gut feeling was that there had to be a logical explanation for him taking pictures of a sink in a woman's restroom. Guilt sent her thoughts spinning. "Perhaps his strange explanation of the environmental, water usage thing was real," she thought. Not to mention, he had already revealed to Keisha and Mathew in the past that he was gay, making the possibility of seeing partially clothed females in restrooms appealing unlikely.

Rob MUNDEN

After a short search for Elijah, the Crew went ahead and had the pickleball player take a picture of them. Everyone attended the medal stand ceremony for Peter and Rusty and engaged in more pickleball small talk on how the day's tournament had gone. The crowd gradually moved to the parking lot. Standing between Edna's old, blue Buick and Peter's Mercedes was Elijah, who was bent down, looking at one of the tires on Peter's Mercedes. He had his camera in one hand, as though he had just taken a picture of the wheel. Edna saw Elijah as she approached the car. "Those are some nice rims."

Elijah, startled, hopped up from the ground, "Uh, um, Yes, they are, Grandma."

"I'm real proud of you, Elijah. You made it through the whole day here with all these people. That's a gigantic step for you."

"Yep"

"I'm also pleased you're right here at my car, ready for me to take you home instead of going with Keisha or Mathew. That shows me that some people still like spending time with their grandma."

"Yes, that's true, Grandma. You are the best. I'll text Mathew and Keisha and let them know I'm heading home with you. Let's get out of here."

A few minutes after Elijah and Edna left, Peter got in his Mercedes and started down the road. Right behind him were Robin and Mathew. Peter had left his bright red, hybrid graphite paddle on the court. After discovering it, Robin and ran after Peter to return it. Mathew watched Robin run after the Mercedes waving the paddle, and ran after her. He could not keep up with her. He was amazed at her ability to sprint that fast after playing an entire pickleball tournament. Mathew thought that maybe he should put the chips, dip, and candy bars aside and eat healthier like Robin and Keisha. Then he laughed to himself and thought, "Nah. I'll stick with the chips and dip."

Peter drove off so fast that he did not see either teen. Robin told Mathew she knew where Peter lived because she and Keisha had played on Peter's personal court on several occasions, so she would run it out to him later. Mathew commented that she probably better not wait too long, as Peter might panic when he realized it was missing, knowing he had mixed doubles tomorrow. Robin let Mathew know that she would get it to him soon, as she also needed to go to bed early. She revealed that she was to drive to her dad's house in Topeka to spend the day with him and would need to hit the road early. Mathew asked Robin if it was wise to try to drive that "old, shitty" Volkswagen van all the way to Topeka. He reminded Robin of the trouble the van had going to Hays and back. Robin thanked Mathew for his concern. She was excited to tell him that the reason that she was making the trip was that her dad had bought her a 2003 Honda CR-V and she just needed to make it to Topeka to see him, pick up the CR-V, and head home in her much newer and incredibly safer car. She was going to leave the van there for her father to sell for scrap. Mathew let her know that he was relieved that she was obtaining a more reliable means of transportation.

Mathew then turned to face Robin and boldly stated, "Robin I'm happy that you're getting to see your dad and getting a better car, but I think at some point you should consider playing co-ed."

"Oh yeah, Mathew? And with who?"

After a short pause, he shyly answered, "Me."

"That sounds like a great plan… If you're sure you could keep up with me?"

"You nearly ran down a Mercedes after a long day of physical activity. I'd say I'm probably out of luck on that one, Robin."

She laughed.

Rusty told Keisha he would walk her to her car. For safety reasons, ha had always walked Keisha to her car, but this was different. Being in a crowded park at 5 p.m. was a whole lot different than walking out of the Gabrielle Club at eight or nine in the evening. Even more striking, during the last several steps to her car, Rusty took Keisha's left hand in his right, holding on until they had reached the car. Rusty thanked Keisha for cheering him on and said he couldn't wait to play as partners with her tomorrow. She looked into his eyes. He looked in hers. He opened the car door for her and told her that he would see her tomorrow.

Keisha didn't know if Rusty had held her hand out of friendship, encouragement, or something more, but either way, she blushed with excitement. Happiness filled her heart; something she hadn't felt so intensely in a very long time.

CHAPTER 14

Tasha met Peter at his home later that evening. She congratulated him on his championship and let him know that she would present a titillating award for him. She rubbed his genitals and led him to his bedroom. She took off her bright red dress, revealing nothing underneath.

Peter had walked in the door just minutes before Tasha arrived. He was still sweaty. At first, he didn't understand why she wanted to be with a guy who smelled like a sewer plant, but he quickly replaced that thought with another, "Of course, she would want to be with me, under the circumstance."

He quickly entered her. She was amazed at how fast and hard Peter was. Although he was in great shape, most men at his age couldn't go straight from winning an entire tournament to making love to a younger woman within moments of her presenting herself to him. He did not last long. Peter's objective was to enjoy the pleasure of an orgasm and move on.

Tasha complained to him that she wasn't finished. She asked him if he would at least go down on her, to which his response was simply, "Why?"

Peter then grabbed some fresh gym clothes. As he was putting them on, he commanded Tasha to get dressed. He reminded her of their co-ed doubles match tomorrow and that she really needed to work on her backhand. Tasha didn't question his

215

authority and got dressed. Peter grabbed his pickleball bag and searched for his paddle.

After noticing it was gone, he remembered that he had left it on the courts at Pond Side. He didn't think much of it. He still had three paddles of the same make and model in his bag. He generally threw his paddles away or tossed them out in the crowd after a couple months, anyway.

As soon as they had their gym clothes on, Tasha and Peter were on his personal pickleball court. Tasha was hitting backhand strokes delivered to her at a fervent pace by Peter.

After twenty minutes of a fusillade of pickleballs being fired at her left side, he had her work on her dink game. He then suggested she work on her serves, followed by lobs, and finishing with a game of skinny singles. Skinny singles is a game that only uses half of the court. It was a game played primarily by out-of-shape pickleball players who like singles. In this case, Peter and Tasha were using it strictly to work on precision-made shots. After an hour and a half, he told her to go home and get plenty of rest. She asked if she could join him in the shower. His response was cold, telling her that anymore time she spent in his home would be a distraction, and winners can't be distracted. She let herself out. He hit the shower.

....

It was 9 p.m., "The to-catch-a-killer" portion of the Crew met in their usual briefing room. Mathew decided to raid Randall's kitchen. After opening the refrigerator, he gasped in horror. He boisterously complained that there were no chips, cookies, cold pizza, or any other delicious poisons that Elijah and Mathew loved to stuff themselves with. Mathew nearly threw up at what he saw - Brussels sprouts, salads, grilled chicken, apples, oranges, and celery.

"Oh my God, Randall, you're starting to live like a fairy princess or some kinda shit!"

"Don't panic. I just needed them out of my sight. All the suicide toxins for you and Elijah are in the fridge downstairs. There's frozen pizzas, chips, chocolate cake, and cookies. I totally hooked you up with all that garbage. "

"Oh, thank God! Come on, Elijah!"

Mathew ran downstairs in a blaze so fast that he didn't even realize his brother wasn't following. Elijah remained seated at the kitchen table with his iPad open and a notepad beside it. Elijah was studying every note he had made with great attention to detail. Keisha and Randall seemed not to notice him. They could not stop talking about the pickleball tournament. Randall was showing Keisha their silver medals that were lying on the kitchen counter. The two talked about how well Robin had played and how she was starting to show her true potential. They spent at least five minutes discussing the incredible shot that Peter had made with his left-hand dive shot to win the 5.0 Men's doubles.

Mathew eventually made his way up the stairs with two bags of chips in his left hand, an entire chocolate cake in the right, and a Ziploc bag of sugar cookies on top of the covered chocolate cake. Partly smashing the cookies was a six-pack of cola.

"We most certainly know where you got the coordination to play so well today, Mathew," Randall remarked before he and Keisha started laughing.

"Elijah, you could have helped!" Mathew replied as he dropped all the goodies on the kitchen counter.

"Some of us aren't here for socialization, grub, and small talk!"
Keisha then remarked,

"We just had a big day today. Can't you be happy for us and celebrate, Elijah?"

"And how is that going to catch a killer?"

"You don't even believe the Peanut Butter Killer guy is associated with pickleball anyway, Elijah, so why do you care?"

"Maybe I don't, but it is the task at hand!"

Randall stepped in, "Elijah is right. Everybody at the table. Let's get to work. "

Mathew carried a bag of chips to the table with him but just before sitting down, he hesitated, threw the chips on the table, and grabbed a piece of cake and a can of pop. He started to sit down again but went back to the counter and grabbed the cookies.

Elijah then started the meeting. He went around the room asking the Crew what they had observed. Embarrassingly, all three had nothing.

Trying to lighten the moment, Mathew shouted, "Yeah, but we played a kickass game of pickleball, didn't we?"

Keisha and Randall gave Mathew a high-five and laughed.

Elijah picked up his iPad and notebook. He then shouted, "When all of you are willing to catch a freaking psycho serial killer, give me a call. I got work to do." He left Randall's house.

Keisha thought Elijah was just jealous and pointed out his obvious lack of athletic ability. Mathew didn't think that was the case. He felt that Elijah's behavior was due to the fact that he was a "weird duck" and thought that he was strictly at the tournament to observe. Mathew went on to say, "It's not that he's not happy for us, he just doesn't understand why it was a great moment."

Randall then remarked, "I don't understand why he was there to observe when Elijah's part of the investigation is to find statistics and patterns with his computer skills. The pickleball observation stuff was to be left to us, as the pickleball players."

"But the problem is that Elijah probably felt we were too into ourselves and our games to take any kind of pickleball player killer notes today. And perhaps he was right," Keisha added.

The three of them put their heads down in shame. In just a few short minutes they had moved from euphoria to abashment.

The phone rang. Picking it up soon added to Randall's distress. "Oh, dear! Oh, oh no! Can I get you anything and bring it over to you? Are you sure? No, no, don't worry about the tournament. It's okay. There will be plenty of competitive opportunities for us to play together. Okay, okay. Take care of yourself, Sandy, and if you need anything, don't hesitate to ask. Bye."

Randall hung up the phone and turned to Mathew and Keisha.

"Guess I'll have more time to focus on the investigation at the tournament tomorrow."

"Is Sandy, okay? What's the matter?" Keisha asked with concern.

Randall let them know that Sandy had become very sick. She was suffering from a migraine and had been vomiting for the past couple of hours.

Mathew and Keisha walked up and gave Randall a hug. They knew how close he and Sandy were becoming, and they had hoped that playing in the tournament would draw them even closer.

Randall acted as though he was fine, but Keisha and Mathew knew better. The siblings asked several questions about Sandy's condition, but Randall assured them that she was sure that she had probably just caught a tough, twenty-four-hour bug and should be fine.

Keisha heard some thunder and looked out the window. Keisha told Randall that it had just started raining and that she had seen earlier on her weather app that it was possibly going to rain all night. She was trying to make the point that Randall probably wasn't going to get the chance to play with Sandy anyway, to try to make him feel better.

Randall asked why there was not an indoor backup plan. Keisha informed him that there originally was. Gabrielle Courts was supposed to be the tournament backup plan, but owner Mia Gabrielle was offered three thousand five hundred dollars last week to rent out the courts to a group holding a family reunion in town. They had a place for their reunion but came up with the idea just before to also meet at Gabrielle's to play pickleball. The reunion organizer decided that sitting around a hotel swimming pool, drinking all day and night, and reminiscing about the old times might not be the best of ideas. Gabrielle had already been paid four hundred dollars by Pond Side Pickleball Courts for access to the club if they needed them. She told Pond Side Courts that to get out of the contract, she was willing to give them back the four hundred dollars plus an additional five hundred. The Pond Side Courts committee looked at the upcoming weather forecast and saw clear and sunny skies predicted throughout the weekend, so they agreed.

   Keisha then turned to Randall and said, "I reckon they forgot they all live in Kansas!"

CHAPTER 15

Peter was tormented by the happiness he was feeling. For the first time in his life, he thought about being part of a team that won a tournament. In the past, he had viewed their wins as something he had earned, with Rusty as the handsome sidekick who mopped up all the credit with his charm and good looks. Peter was a handsome man himself, but he knew that he was aging.

After practicing with Tasha, he jumped in the shower and saw the light purple birthmark that covered the left side of his body. Memories of his mother calling him a freak or a monster because of the unusual birthmark helped him to forget his warm feelings of winning with Rusty.

He wanted to feel anger and hate. To Peter, anger and hate were easier to deal with than happiness. He convinced himself that happiness would not last, but hatred could be embraced and last forever. His mind drifted to Keisha and their wonderful singles play dates on his pickleball court. He usually saw a person like Mathew as someone who had maxed out his potential. But now, Peter found himself contemplating strategies to help make Mathew better, too. Even Edna, someone he had known for a short time, had touched him. Peter could feel the love and care she had for all of them.

He remembered taking a bite of one of her tasty sandwiches earlier in the day. It was perhaps the best sandwich he had ever eaten. Additionally, Peter found himself immensely impressed with a guy in his seventies playing at a 4.0 - 4.5 level in just a few short weeks. Peter wanted to replace the feelings of worthiness with malevolence. The torment of joy continued to creep into his mind.

The doorbell rang. "Who in the hell would be ringing my doorbell at nearly midnight?"

Peter jumped out of the shower and wrapped a towel around his waist. He grabbed his classic Colt M 1911 pistol from underneath the recliner that sat near the living room door. The paranoid Peter took the safety off the already loaded gun. Peter looked through the peephole. After seeing who was on the other side of the door, he re-engaged the safety, tossed the gun back behind the recliner, and opened the door.

"Robin, what on earth are you doing here at this time of night? And what happened to you? Hurry. Get in here out of this rain." Robin was soaked in mud and water.

"I'm not playing co-ed tomorrow, and you left your paddle on the court. Mathew and I tried to wave you down as you were leaving, but you didn't see us. I gotta leave early in the morning to visit my dad in Topeka. I wanted to get it to you before the tournament. I left earlier for your house but got stuck in the mud on the way out here. I couldn't find my cell phone to call for help. I tried for an hour driving back and forth trying to get my beat-up van out. Finally gave up and walked here. I'm starving, muddy, miserable, and just want to get home." Tears flowed from Robin's eyes.

Peter rushed to get her a couple of towels to dry off with. She saw the birthmark on his chest but didn't think much of it. She was more concerned about her van and getting home. Peter took her to another bathroom in the house, not the one he had just used. It was connected to a bedroom. He stated that while she was in the shower, he would find some of Tasha's clothes that would probably fit her. There were clothes he could have chosen that would have covered more of her body. Those were not the clothes chosen for her.

Robin walked out of the bathroom into the connecting bedroom and saw, lying on the bed, a white tank top that had the word "WANT" across the top front. He left her no bra. The tank top was thin; her nipples were visible through the fabric, bursting out of the shirt. And the sides of her boobs were also exposed. Beside the "WANT" shirt was a pair of very short, red shorts that barely covered her thighs. She put them on. Robin then walked out to the living room area where Peter was sitting. He stared at her bright green eyes and beautiful blonde hair. He found himself mesmerized by her golden, voluptuous breasts. He stared at her nipples popping out of the white shirt and then peered down to look upon her thin, athletic legs. "You look stunning."

Embarrassed and trying to cover more of her breasts with the tank top, Robin said, "Uh, um… Do you have anything more um, uh…conservative?"

"Don't be frightened, girl. You are wearing exactly what you are supposed to for what we're about to do."

"Um…Uh, um…Peter, I'm not that kind of girl. Please! Don't do this!"

"We will do this. You want me, and you know it!"

"Peter, you're scaring me!"

"You should be scared. I want you to feel scared. Scared it will be." Peter then took her arm. He walked her out of the living room. She begged him to stop. He tried to kiss her, but she pulled back and slapped him in the face.

"Please, please, Peter, let me go. I won't tell anyone!"

"Come on, baby. Nothing wrong with an older man. I got the goods."

"I'm a virgin."

"Oooh, even better. I haven't had a virgin in decades."

With his right hand, he grabbed her right breast. She sank her teeth into his wrist. She tried to run as he screamed in pain, but before she could reach the front door, he grabbed her hair with his left hand and dragged her out of the room.

"You want to leave, do ya? Well, then, you got your wish. We'll leave." Peter threw on some clothes while keeping her beside him so she couldn't escape. He then grabbed her arm.

Robin was demanding to know where she was being taken. Peter said nothing but continued to pull her with him. She scratched his left arm and attempted to bite him again, but before she did, he punched her in the eye that was already hurting from the Wiffle ball that hit her during her pickleball match. Peter took her to a large garage where he had stored several vehicles, ranging from an old Model T Ford to a 1967 Chevy. He threw her in the front seat of a jet-black 2012 Colorado. She screamed. He stuffed a rag in her mouth.

He pulled some handcuffs from his backseat and bound her hands together. He made her give him directions to her Volkswagen van and drove to where it was stuck in the mud. As rain poured down on him, he scampered around in the mud until he found what he was looking for; her cell phone. He grabbed it and stuffed it in the right pocket of his gym shorts. He took a chain from the back of his truck and secured her van to the truck. The door was open with the key in the ignition. He put the car in neutral and pulled it out of the mud. He then took off her handcuffs and removed the rag from her mouth. He took out the 357 Magnum he had hidden under his seat.

"Please, Peter, don't do this, please! I don't want to die; I'm begging you," she said, as tears rolled down her cheeks. "Rape me. Anything, but please let me live. I won't tell anyone."

"Shut that shit up, Robin. I don't take a female that doesn't want me. Fear is the reason that you've been a 3.5. Sure, you played alright at 4.5 earlier today, but you didn't win shit, did you? Why? Because you can't handle pressure. You're more worried about boys and your stupid, beat-up Volkswagen van than winning. Keisha deserves better. No, you're going to get in that van and then drive to Cheney Lake. I know you know where that is since I've heard you talk about some of the parties you have been to out there with your so-called friends. I'll be right behind you, so no funny business."

"Uh, um, uh…yes, sir!" After getting into her van, Robin didn't know whether to feel relieved that she was alive or petrified, knowing that Cheney Lake would be a great place to dump a body. While driving in the heavy, pouring rain, she struggled to stay stable on the road. She was so nervous that she trembled furiously. Every time Robin crossed the center line, Peter pulled out the 357 Magnum and shot into the air just above her van. It was difficult to stay focused, but she managed.

After thirty minutes of driving, she arrived at Cheney Lake. Peter pulled her over. He then told her the exact spot he wanted her to go to, directing her near a boat ramp. She drove there without incident. Robin was about a block from the boat ramp. Peter handcuffed her left hand to the steering wheel. She again begged for her life. He screamed at her to shut up, then gave her a key to the handcuffs. He told her that he had a radar gun in his hand and flashed it in front of her face. He let her know that if his radar gun did not pick up that she was driving 60 miles-per-hour before flying off the boat ramp, he would walk into the water and shoot her. He got out his pistol. He had the radar gun in one hand and his pistol in the other. He aimed the pistol at Robin and said, "Start driving, Robin. You've got twenty seconds to hit sixty off the ramp starting in 3,2,1 –GO!"

"Uhh, umm, uh…ya, um…" The van already had her at a slight disadvantage. She hit the gas but realized that she had instinctively hit the parking brake instead. She kicked it while screaming…

15 SECONDS!

Robin was off. Quickly she hit 25…

10 SECONDS

Up to 31 miles-per-hour…

8 SECONDS

Now at 39 miles-per-hour …

5 SECONDS TIL DEATH

44 miles-per-hour with just thirty feet to go…

3 SECONDS

55 miles-per-hour…

1 SECOND

59 miles-per-hour as she entered the water.

As the van sank, Peter shrugged his shoulders. "Too bad. I kinda liked her. She was just one second away from me jumping in with my extra cuff key in my hand to save her. Oh well. Sucks to be her!" Peter watched the car slowly sink into oblivion. Soon the last bubbles arose, and the van could be seen no more. He turned his back to the lake and slowly walked back to his truck.

....

Robin took a deep breath before the van hit the water. She was a certified lifeguard, giving her an advantage over others who might find themselves in a similar situation. She had no experience with unlocking handcuffs, however. She only had her right hand to work with as she frantically tried to fit the key and twist it correctly to open the cuff securing her hand to the steering wheel. She was turning blue. Robin twisted the key in the hole back and forth, what seemed like a hundred times.

She finally stopped. She was beginning to accept her fate. Water began seeping into her mouth. She felt peace and acceptance within. But then, as more water started bleeding into her lungs, she remembered all the tragedies that Keisha had dealt with, having lost her parents, grandfather, and now her best friend. She worried about her own mom and dad. She was an only child. Her time between them might have been divided, but they loved her more than life itself.

Now three minutes had passed since she had been underwater and one minute since the water had started running in her mouth. She coughed. She didn't want to fight on, but she knew that she must. If not for herself, then for her parents and Keisha. She tried one more time to twist the key in the cuff hole.

This time it clicked and loosened. She had little strength left but managed to pull the cuff off her left hand. Luckily the driver's side window was down. She pushed through it. Robin could faintly see moonlight dancing upon the water stage. During her journey to the light of the moon, she kicked her shoes off to make the trip faster.

    She had about a twenty-foot swim to the top. She, at last, managed to get her lips inches above the water and felt a sliver of air seethe between them. She pushed on, incessantly struggling to get her head fully above water. She had almost no energy left, but her heroic determination helped her find a way to the top. She gasped for air, profusely coughing up dirty, muddy water that gushed from her lungs and out of her mouth. Repeatedly, Robin coughed up the disgusting lake water. She could barely move her arms and floated on the surface for a while to catch her breath.

    At last, she approached the bank. She turned herself right-side-up so she was not face-down in the water, but she had drifted away from the dock to a steep bank. Robin had no energy left to pull herself out of the water and to the bank, but she was able to propel herself onto a flat rock that was barely submerged underwater. It was just high enough that the top of her body, and more importantly, her head, was not covered by water. Robin was relieved that the rain had abruptly stopped, preventing more water from entering her mouth. She coughed up considerably more H20. She raised her head up to cough again. Her head slammed back down onto the rock. Her head struck the rock so hard that she felt herself losing consciousness. Her final thoughts were, "Sorry, Mom, Dad, Keisha – I tried. I really tried."

Peter tore out of the lake area as fast as he could. If he got out of there in time, no one would see his truck which he rarely used anyway. People would probably think that Robin committed suicide. The investigation would take five days, tops.

Authorities would see that the handcuff was attached to the steering wheel, indicating that she likely did this to herself. She was in the driver's seat, going nearly sixty miles-per-hour into the lake.

He did not feel any thrill with this killing. "All I wanted to do was fuck her," he thought. Her turning him down had deflated his ego. He had considered raping her at first, but he felt that the rape of a young woman was not a tasteful killing. "I'm a serial murderer with morals. What kind of nonsense shit is that?" he thought as he continued to contemplate his reasoning for not defiling her.

He was also disappointed knowing that this murder was one of his most creative, yet the Peanut Butter Killer wouldn't even be associated with her death.

The authorities in Hays had not linked the murder of the cheating wife to the Peanut Butter Killer, either. He began to feel sorry for himself. He was finally getting the credit he felt he deserved in the pickleball world, but in the killing world, he had now been severely defeated twice in a row.

Peter made a most ominous villain who would, nonetheless, not be awarded recognition for his last two slayings. He was driving along the top of the hill when he looked down at the boat ramp where the killing occurred. He glanced to the west section of the bank by the ramp. He saw something large and in the shape of a body. He slammed his brakes to take a longer look. Peter scrambled frantically under the driver's seat and pulled out his binoculars. When he locked them on the shape he had seen, he recognized the body of Robin Lebbin. "Shit, shit, shit! How the hell did she manage to get out of that damn, ugly-ass van?"

Looking through his binoculars, he did not see any signs of life. He thought about taking off, but even if she were dead, it wouldn't look as much like a suicide with her having fought so hard to live. Peter drove back down to the boat ramp area, but instead of driving to the ramp itself, he shifted left, closer to the rock that Robin lay upon. Peter drove the truck as close to the water as he could. He parked at the edge of the bank. Five feet further out in the water was the bank that Robin's body lay upon.

He scampered into the water to her. Peter checked for signs of life and found none. Having verified that she was dead, he ran back to his truck to take off. Just as he opened the driver's side door, he noticed another truck about a half a mile away driving towards the area. Peter thought it best to get the dead body of Keisha's young friend completely out of sight. It might take weeks, if not longer, to find the van, but the body would be discovered at sunrise. It would not take long for the authorities to find out that she came over to his house to give him his paddle. He had been operating under the assumption that anyone involved with the investigation, in the absence of the van and a body, would assume she had run away. Running away did fit her fly-by-the-seat-of-her pants kind of personality, he thought. So, fleeing town seemed like a rather logical conclusion.

He jumped back into the water, grabbed Robin, and pulled her to the bank. He let down the tailgate. He lifted her up and threw her into the truck bed. Peter slammed the tailgate closed and sped out of the area.

He looked back through the rearview mirror and spotted the other truck approaching the road by the ramp. He was relieved that it continued to drive past the ramp area but was also concerned that the vehicle might follow him. Peter saw a fork in the road. He continued to monitor the truck, which was now just a quarter of a mile behind him.

Peter approached the spot where the dirt road split into two different roads. Peter chose the more obscure route to the left. His pulse trembled at record speed. Watching the rearview mirror more than the road itself caused Peter to fly into the ditch.

Robin flew up and back down in the bed of the truck. Her left arm was cut by the edge of the side of the truck. Blood gushed from the lifeless body. Peter overcorrected and nearly flew into the other ditch on the opposite side of the road but managed to get the truck under control before doing so. Seconds later, he saw whoever was behind him slow down and turn right. Peter took a deep breath of relief. He was confident that they had not gotten close enough to him to see his truck or suspect any foul play.

After arriving back at his ranch, he was drained. He had played in a long tournament, had sex with Tasha, and conducted pickleball drills with Tasha. And then he had gone to extreme measures to murder his friend Keisha's best friend in what seemed like a tropical rainstorm, which had started back up again. He contemplated what to do. He considered burning her body, burying the ashes, and cleaning up the crime scene, but it was now 1:00 in the morning not to mention it would obviously be difficult to start a fire under such wet conditions. Peter wasn't sure he had the energy, though he was running out of time.

Then suddenly, to his surprise, Peter heard a ding on his phone. It was a text from the president of the Wichita Open Tournament. The message said that the mixed doubles co-ed portion of the tournament was officially delayed from 8 AM. to 1 PM because of the storm. The text further noted that the tournament would be canceled if the rain continued until morning. Peter was elated.

He considered simply leaving Robin's body in the truck until morning. But then he figured the rain could wash out a lot of the blood. Peter opened the tailgate, tossed the body over his shoulder, and carried it to his barn. The large, yellow barn was the home of his one and only tan, thoroughbred horse. He dumped Robin on a pile of hay. He tore off his shirt that was now soaked in Robin's blood, and tossed it next to her. Peter then stumbled back to his home. He knew he must rest for a few hours, and then he could dispose of the body. Peter stumbled to the couch in the living room near the front door. He fell upon the sofa and instantly fell sound asleep.

....

The horse looked upon the lifeless body and the red hay dyed from Robin's blood. The cut on her arm was not terribly bad, as the blood eventually stopped flowing from it. The gorgeous tan, white-chested thoroughbred trotted up to the edge of the pile of hay. She was curious. The horse took her head and nudged Robin in the chest. She sniffed and nudged the girl again. The determined creature took her right hoof and tapped Robin a couple of times. In the process of trying to wake Robin up, the horse unintentionally crushed her ribs by stepping on her chest. Although the animal damaged Robin's body in the process, the 1250-pound horse also managed to flush a gush of water from Robin's lungs and out of her mouth.

After the gush of water, there was a long silence. And then a miracle happened. A faint cough was heard by the thoroughbred. She licked Robin's face. More water was coughed up. Robin groaned in pain. Her chest felt awful, like a cement boulder had been dropped two hundred feet onto her ribs. The painful coughing continued for two more hours. Robin suddenly opened her eyes. Her first sight after awakening was two big eyes framed by flowing hair, an elongated nose, and huge, white teeth inches from her face. She would have screamed if she was capable. After a minute of paralyzing terror, she finally became focused enough to realize that it was not a monster in front of her eyes, but a lonely, goofy horse simply longing for some attention.

....

7:35 AM

Rusty was thrilled to see that the rain had stopped. Trees across the Wichita metropolitan area were down. Some power lines needed to be restored. But overall, the heavy rains did not do any severe damage. He was happy that the tournament was still on. Rusty had tried to call Peter a few times to set up a morning pickleball warm-up session to keep everyone loose before the now-delayed tournament.

Rusty called Tasha, who hadn't been able to get ahold of Peter either. Tasha told Rusty that she'd had to call Peter and leave a message to let him know that they would be unable to play co-ed doubles today, since the tournament's later start would run into her shift at work. But she did say that she could still play with Peter this morning to help get Keisha and Rusty ready for the afternoon tournament. Rusty suggested they all show up at Peter's home to check on him and play on his court. Tasha agreed. She worried Peter was upset with her for not playing in the tournament with him, but at the same time, she wanted to see him and do what she could to make things right. Such an impulsive move, like making an unannounced appearance at Peter's house, was not typically Rusty's style, but he wanted to see Keisha. He knew that he would see her in the afternoon tournament, but it suddenly wasn't enough. He couldn't believe that just two years ago, he had seen Keisha as just a kid who loved pickleball and asked him way too many annoying questions during their personal instruction sessions. Now she was a young, beautiful, confident woman he couldn't keep his mind off of.

CHAPTER 16

Robin struggled to get to the barn door. She opened it slightly, trying to be quiet, but she grunted in pain, holding her broken ribs. She was nearly all the way out the door when she saw Peter coming out the back door of his home. He drove the truck back into the car storage garage. She peered out the barn door and watched as he began walking from the garage straight towards the barn. Robin went back into the barn and attempted to bury herself under some hay.

Peter was talking to himself as he walked to the barn, "Time to dispose of a body. What a sensational way to start a Sunday morning." He entered the barn, his heartbeat thumping uncontrollably. "Surely, she's not still alive!" Peter furiously looked throughout the barn.

The horse stood remarkably silent. Generally, it pranced about the barn nervously while neighing if things were out of order, but this time she remained eerily silent and calm.

"Damn it! Damn it! Damn it! Where is she, Jiffy? Where the hell is she?"

Peter saw Robin's footprints. He followed the tracks in the dirt to the barn door. He walked outside, searching for more footprints, but did not see any outside the barn. He then walked back into the barn and found more footprints that led him to the hay that Robin was buried in.

After brushing the hay aside, he revealed a struggling Robin curled in a ball and attempting to breathe. He smirked at the sight of the girl holding her ribs. Peter laughed in a most sinister manner, "Nothing like finding a beautiful Robin all snuggled in her nest. You have more strength than I ever guessed. I've come to admire your tenacity and spirit. But as much as I've become fond of your will to live, I just can't let you do that, Robin."

Barely able to get the words out, Robin replied, "Please, please, Peter. Don't!"

"I have your phone. Not sure why you didn't put a lock on it. Your mother texted and asked where you were this morning. I texted back, pretending to be you, of course, to let her know that you couldn't sleep and left earlier than planned to visit your father in Topeka. I then texted your father to let him know that you were running late. Later, I'll text him back with some lame excuse as to why you can't make it at all. By the time they find out that you're missing and they trace the texts back to here, I will have all my millions stashed away in a Swiss bank account while I'm drinking cocktails somewhere in the Caribbean on a nice warm beach."

"Now, I could do things the easy way, like take a pistol and shoot ya, but it's time you pay me a nice agonizing death for giving me so much trouble."

Peter grabbed a rope hanging from a spike in the barn and ran upstairs to the loft with it. He carefully tied the rope to a rail. He took the end of it and created a noose. He then dropped the noose off the loft. It dangled about five feet from the floor of the barn. All the while, Robin lay in the hay below, watching in horror. Peter ran downstairs and faced Robin. "Now, I could have just dragged you to the top of the loft and thrown you off with the noose around your neck, but then the noose would snap your neck on impact, killing you instantly. I prefer, instead, to watch you die a looong, painful death. And come to think of it, I'm not going to burn your body after all. An artist must get credit for his work. Perhaps I'll leave you in some park, hundreds of miles away in Kansas City or somewhere tonight, sitting you up on a bench with your new peanut butter make-up job. You are a pretty one, but you could use a little more color in your face. I don't think that with the condition you're in you will go too far. I will be right back."

Before walking out of the barn, Peter turned toward his horse and said to the thoroughbred, "Now now, Jiffy, keep our guest entertained. I'll be back shortly." He laughed again with sickening pleasure.

Peter ran into his house. Robin crawled to the door, but he was already back before she could attempt any type of escape. He had a jar of peanut butter in one hand, and with the other, grabbed her by the hair and dragged her to where the rope was hanging. He pulled a paintbrush from his pocket. Peter carefully began painting her face with peanut butter. Robin attempted to fight him, but that soon stopped after a punch to her broken ribs. She grunted in agonizing pain. With smooth precision and care, he brushed her entire face with that brown, buttery goo. He was sure to do so carefully; the peanut butter covering her skin smoothly and evenly.

As Robin's peanut butter-covered face stared at him with horror, he smiled, relishing in his insane craftsmanship. "You look even more ravishing than before." He proceeded to kiss her gently on the lips. He took his tongue and licked around his own lips, tasting the fragments of peanut butter that had fallen on him from his forced assault. "Ahh, generally I prefer a good Kansas, medium-rare, ribeye steak, but there are some days nothing beats the simple flavor of peanut butter."

Peter draped Robin over a large steel table that he used to clean fish. He grabbed Robin by her hips, further inducing pain in her ribs, and tossed her onto the table. He jumped onto the table next to her and grabbed the noose with his left hand. He struggled to pick Robin up with his right arm. He put her on his shoulders, balancing himself on the table. Peter wrapped the noose around Robin's neck. Suddenly, he heard a car slam. He continued to hold her up while listening. He soon heard someone knocking on his door, probably after giving up on ringing the doorbell. He then heard Rusty's voice. "Peter, are you anywhere around here?"

Robin gasped out the word, "Help," but she was in so much pain that the cry came out as nothing more than a whisper. "What on earth is Rusty doing out here?" Peter softly asked himself. He then turned back to Robin, "Well, lucky for me and unlucky for you, it will be kinda hard for you to cry for help at all when you're choking on this noose. Sorry, Robin. I'd normally let you say a few last words like they do in the old western movies, but we haven't the time. Goodbye, now."

Peter then dropped her from his arms. He jumped off the table and kicked it away. Peter rushed out of the barn, where he saw Tasha, Rusty, and Keisha outside near the front door. "Hey guys, just feeding my horse. What brings all of you out here?"

Rusty explained that he and Tasha had tried to call before coming out. Then he asked if he and Keisha could play a couple of games with him and Tasha to warm up. Peter couldn't really say he was busy when he would have been scheduled to play in the tournament that morning anyway, so after a long pause, he reluctantly agreed. Tasha asked Peter if he had received the message that she couldn't play with him in the tournament since it had been moved to the afternoon when she was scheduled to work. He said that he had gotten the message. Tasha was worried he would be angry, but he said that he really didn't care. Normally he would have been furious, but in this case, he preferred not to play so that he could dispose of Robin's body.

Tasha, Rusty, and Keisha grabbed their pickleball bags out of Rusty's green 2017 Horizon. Peter already had plenty of pickleball equipment in the shed where the pickleball court was. As they walked to the shed, Keisha started to veer towards the barn. "How is good ole Jiffy doing, anyway? I should go say 'hi' to her."

"No, uh, um…that's why I was tending to her. She is not well. She needs some rest. "

"Ahh, that's why you weren't answering your phone; you were more concerned with helping your horse. You're such a kindhearted soul, Peter. Perhaps we came at the wrong time."

Peter knew the wise thing to do would be to use that as an excuse to get rid of them. And he would have done just that if he'd really thought all of them would leave. But he knew Tasha would make a fuss and insist on staying to help nurse Jiffy. It would be quicker and easier to play a warmup game or two and send them on their way.

"No, no. I think she's fine. I noticed an apple with vomit on it. I think Jiffy swallowed the apple whole. It's out of her system now. She will be fine, but she needs peace and quiet, and rest."

Tasha went up and kissed Peter on the cheek. "You are sweet, Peter. I think I'll keep ya."

The three of them then entered the shed to play. Back in the barn, Robin was pulling hard on the rope as it was furiously choking the life out of her. She managed to pull hard enough with both hands to briefly relieve the pressure from her neck. Her forearms were in agony as she continued holding onto the slack in the rope. Shockingly, it had not broken her neck yet, which kept her hope alive. She held on for what seemed like hours. It had only been about forty seconds.

With her crushed ribs and badly damaged body from drowning, she finally gave up. She said a little prayer in her mind, mostly asking God to take care of her father and mother. Robin wished they had never divorced and hated splitting her time between them. And now, she thought, she would no longer see either of them at all. She slowly let go of the rope.

Jiffy watched her slip away as Robin's face turned blue. She choked until she had no air at all and lay in mid-air, looking completely lifeless. The horse slowly walked up to her. Jiffy lowered her head to position Robin above and over Jiffy's neck. Robin slid down Jiffy's neck onto her back.

The horse sensed that if she made one slight move, Robin would fall off to her death. With the noose still surrounding her neck but no longer applying pressure, Robin could faintly breathe. The most disciplined horse would not step even an inch.

....

Peter and Tasha were not playing well. Tasha was too worried about what Peter was thinking and was still scared that he was upset with her about not being able to play later in the tournament. Peter could handle pressure better than any of the four of them when playing under normal circumstances, but with a dead body in his barn awaiting disposal, it was difficult to concentrate. In his own mind, he blamed Tasha for handily losing to Keisha and Rusty.

They played two games and then decided to call it quits in order to save energy for the tournament. As they walked back to the car, Tasha asked Peter if she could at least check on Jiffy. Peter was adamant that no one other than himself look in on her while she was sick. Peter walked them all back to Rusty's car.

Peter thanked them for the games and said it had helped get his mind off his horse. Rusty suggested Peter come with them and go out for a light lunch. Peter told them he was too concerned about his horse and admitted that he was sweaty from the morning pickleball session. Not to mention, he had already obtained a wretched smell from spending so much time in the barn with Jiffy. Tasha noted that they had all played pickleball as well, and probably didn't smell the best, but that he should join them anyway. Peter declined firmly and stated he would rather stay behind.

Keisha walked up to Peter, kissed him on the cheek, and let him know how sweet she thought he was. Keisha then begged Peter to go with them. He knew that he probably should not wait any longer to dispose of Robin's body, but Keisha was the one person in the world whom he found it nearly impossible to say "no". Then he had a plan.

"Okay, I'll go to lunch with you, but I don't want all of you to have to run me back to the ranch. I'll meet you wherever you are going. "

"Good compromise, fair enough," Keisha responded.

Peter ran in the house and changed his shirt. His plan was to then cover Robin's body at least with hay, on the off chance someone, for some very odd reason, would walk into his barn.

But when he walked out, he saw Rusty behind the wheel with Keisha on the passenger's side.

In the back seat, Tasha rolled her window down. "Are you ready, hun?"

"You all didn't have to wait on me."

"We wouldn't have but we never actually said where we were eating. Unless you object, we're heading to Sam's Sandwich Shop on North Douglas."

"Sounds good to me. See you there." He looked back at the barn, turned his head toward his Mercedes, then back at the barn. He reluctantly got in his car and followed them there.

Keisha knew that the rest of the Reynolds family was probably at church, making it impossible to invite them for a pre-tournament luncheon at Sam's Sandwich Shop. But she did think it would be nice to invite Randall. She was worried about him anyway. She knew that he had been looking forward to playing with his crush, Sandy before she became ill. After answering her phone call, Randall said he would love to join them, but just as he was accepting Keisha's invitation, he heard the doorbell ring, followed by a banging at his door. He rushed to see what the matter was. After looking through the peephole and noticing it was Elijah, he quickly opened the door. Elijah, out of breath, told Randall that they needed to talk.

"Is that Elijah in the background?" Keisha inquired.

"Yes, Keisha," Randall answered.

"Put him on!"

Randall handed the phone to Elijah. Keisha asked her brother why he wasn't in church. He told her that he had been up all night and was not feeling well. He then stated he was starting to feel better and needed to get out of the house, which is why he was currently at Randall's.

Keisha laughed and said, "Guess we both ditched church. I was honest and told grandma I needed to warm up for the tournament since it was moved to the afternoon. She actually let me. I guess she's really okay with pickleball now." Keisha then invited Elijah to join them for lunch, but he pointed out how outraged Grandma would be if he was not there when she came home. After all, he had been too sick to go to church.

Keisha agreed and felt dumb for not realizing the obvious. Elijah then stated that Randall would not be able to attend the luncheon either, to which Keisha was confused. She said that didn't make sense, as he just said he could. Elijah told her that Randall didn't have the time. He then casually wished his sister good luck on the tournament. Keisha was dumbfounded, but she just shrugged her shoulders, figuring there were other things to worry about. Elijah asked if Peter would be joining them.

Keisha answered, "Yes, of course. Why?"

There was a long pause, "Um, and where are you eating at?"

"What would it matter, Elijah, if you're not going?"

"Just curious, never mind." Elijah then hung up the phone.

Randall turned to Elijah, "What that was all that about?"

Elijah let his neighbor know that they had a lot of work to do. Elijah grabbed his briefcase that was sitting at his feet and walked straight to Randall's kitchen. In the kitchen, Randall's radio was playing some soft rock in the background. After sitting down at the table, Randall observed as Elijah opened his briefcase. But before Elijah could present his findings to Randall, the phone rang again. Elijah instructed Randall not to answer it. Randall showed Elijah the caller ID. The phone displayed the name "SANDY."

He pleaded to Elijah, "She's been sick. I've got to take this."

"Okay, but make it quick, Randall. No hot, blonde babe that you're in love with is any reason to impede this investigation." Randall answered the phone. Sandy informed him that she had been taking Advil all night, along with some antacids. She said that she was starting to feel better and wanted to give the tournament a go.

Randall admitted to her that he had already called and canceled their participation in the tournament. Sandy said she would see what she could do. Randall felt his heart race. He was euphoric, knowing that he would get to spend time with Sandy if they could get back in the tournament.

After they hung up, Elijah went straight to work. He first asked Randall if anyone had been alone around Peter lately. Randall told Elijah not that he knew of. Randall demanded to know why he cared. Elijah pulled out a sheet with his findings.

The teenage boy reviewed the information that Randall already knew about Peter, which was that Peter had been at tournaments in the vicinity of all but one of the murders, which was the one that happened in St. Louis. Elijah stated that this was Peter's alibi. He intentionally made this clear, as he wanted Randall to know that he didn't think Peter was The Killer. Randall yelled at Elijah, acknowledging that he knew where

Elijah was going with this, since Randall knew that a "but" was coming.

Elijah nodded in agreement. Randall pointed out that at first, Elijah had been insistent that the pickleball killer thing was ridiculous, and now he was trying to convict one of their closest friends. Elijah asked Randall to allow him to continue, who reluctantly nodded his head in agreement. Elijah then began making his case. He had worked all night to find out the information on the "grocery store."

He said that he was able to, at last, break into the President of Coggins Incorporated, Matte Delong's account. Elijah stated that he eventually discovered that Mr. Delong's two chocolate labs' names were Jack and Jill. He bragged that after deductive reasoning and a little bit of luck, he got Delong's password. He had deduced the password would be Jill&Jack1. Randall looked annoyed, "Go on, Elijah."

Elijah informed Randall that after hacking the account, there was only one odd grocery sales discrepancy in all of Coggins Incorporated stores. Peanut butter sales at the Costless grocery across from Gabrielle's Pickleball Club were up 06% over the last year. Elijah was surprised that no single person on the committee had associated the peanut butter sales with the Peanut Butter Killer through the sales reports.

Randall was intrigued but not surprised. Randall told Elijah that finding a killer was probably not on any grocery company board meeting agenda, as such a thought would be too horrifying to contemplate.

Randall then remarked that 06% was significant but not an outrageous number. He further informed Elijah that increased sales of peanut butter couldn't necessarily be related to a couple of jars of peanut butter used to paint a few victims' faces. Elijah agreed but still thought it noteworthy. He made the case that it could relate, because if The Killer was obsessed with himself and his association with peanut butter, The Killer might very well use peanut butter as a symbol of his killings.

This might cause the Peanut Butter Freak to collect and eat more peanut butter than usual due to the taste, smell, and sight of the creamy substance. This was because The Killer might look upon it as some sort of trophy associated with the killings.

Elijah then showed Randall his notes on Peter's odd demeanor during the Wichita Open. Randall acknowledged he was taken aback by such things as Peter making fun of the two Pratt guys that he and Rusty crushed. Elijah further pointed out how intelligent and successful Peter was, despite coming from a broken home, in which Elijah could find no evidence of a father in Peter's life growing up. Elijah thought that money, power, and intelligence had helped Peter get revenge on a society that probably didn't treat him so well in his younger days. Elijah thought that if Peter was The Killer, coming up with the Peanut Butter Killer thing was clever.

Randall was intrigued. His anger at Elijah for even presenting a theory about their friend being a murderer diminished as he was drawn into Elijah's theory. Randall had so hoped that Elijah was wrong, but at the same time, Elijah had enough evidence that the possibility of Peter being the Peanut Butter Pickleball

Freak just might have some weight behind it. Elijah then pulled out some pictures that he had taken of Randall. The photos showed that Peter did have dirt on his face during the first match as evidence that he had changed a tire. But then Elijah showed Randall the pictures that he had taken of Peter's Mercedes, including the tires.

Randall was dumbfounded and remarked, "Not an ounce of dirt on the car and no donuts on any of the tires."

Elijah added, "There are regular tires that can be used instead of donuts, and it is possible for a guy to change a tire without it looking like it has been changed, but it's something to keep in mind."

"Agreed," Randall replied, just as his phone rang.

"Hey, it's Sandy. I have good news and bad news."

"What's the bad news, Sandy?"

"We cannot get back into the 3.5 tournament. They already filled our spots."

"And the good news?"

"There is one opening at one level left in the tournament due to a recent cancellation."

"And what level is that, Sandy?"

"5.0".

"No! Not a chance!"

"We can do this, Randall. I'll even pay the three-hundred-dollar pro-rate entry fee."

"You've been in two tournaments in your life."

"But I did well in one of them, Randall. I won a bronze medal in St. Louis."

"But when we went out for drinks that one night, you said that was a 3.5 tournament, Sandy. And I was just in my first yesterday."

And then Sandy said the one thing that Randall could not say no to. "I want to spend time with you, Randall."

After a long pause, Randall replied, "Okay, Sandy. Let's do this."

After some more small talk and encouraging words to each other, Randall said goodbye and hung up. Elijah normally would have teased Randall, calling him "lover boy" and whatnot, but he went right back to the business at hand. Elijah said he was happy that Randall would be in the tournament so he could be around the game and make observations. Music from the radio continued to play softly in the background. Suddenly, in the middle of a Stevie Wonder tune, the radio went silent. Then, "This is JR Freed reporting for KAR Radio news. We interrupt this program to bring you Breaking News on the Peanut Butter Killer. Sources report that some DNA was found at the scene of two of the victims. The DNA was not a match for anyone already in the system; however, it does provide evidence that the Peanut Butter Killer is a white woman of European descent. We will report any additional news regarding this case as it becomes available. We now take you back to your regularly scheduled program."

Randall and Elijah stared at each other with bewilderment.

"Hmm, reckon I was wrong about your friend Peter."

"I guess you are, Elijah. I guess you are. "

Rob MUNDEN

CHAPTER 17

At the restaurant, Keisha and Rusty sat next to each other. On the other side of the table sat Peter and Tasha. They all ordered light meals. Keisha and Rusty both had salads. Tasha and Peter had salads as well but also ordered half-sized sandwiches. Peter tapped his foot incessantly. He looked nervous. He swung his eyes back and forth and constantly turned his head left and right, scanning the restaurant. The others assumed he was worried about his horse, Jiffy.

Peter was concerned about disposing of Robin's body, but he found himself more agitated about not playing in the afternoon tournament. Peter suddenly wished that Tasha didn't have to work in the afternoon. He was itching to play. He thought of trying to find some 4.0 partner and making her play up just to get out on the courts. Peter was surprised at himself. He was no longer very concerned about getting rid of Robin. He had been thinking about it and figured that any immediate concern of Robin was irrational. Nobody was going to head out to the country and randomly decide to snoop around a barn just for the hell of it. "There were better odds that lightning would strike a person twice in one day," he mused.

Peter walked away from the table and made calls from his phone a couple of times. He told his lunch companions that he was communicating with Jiffy's veterinarian.

Tasha rubbed Peter's back, attempting to soothe him between calls. Peter was annoyed by Tasha's touch. He only wanted her attention in bed or on the court. Otherwise, he had no use for her. But in this case, he did not want to come across as abrasive. He needed to look the part of the concerned animal trainer.

After finishing their meals, they all sat around for a while to talk and relax. Keisha and Rusty's relationship had transformed overnight from a serious, business-like attitude towards each other to being much more than pickleball companions. They kept telling each other jokes. And each constantly giggled, regardless of whether they found the other's jokes funny or not. Rusty looked under the table and was awestruck by the essence of Keisha's legs. They were dark, solid, and illustrious. He quivered at the sight. Keisha caught him looking. He turned his head in embarrassment. When he turned back to look at her, he saw her smiling at him as if to say, "It's okay. Look all you want." The conversation moved to a discussion about their amusement regarding Robin's improvement on the court. Keisha commented that Robin had gone from some boy-crazy, giggling flower child to a shark out for blood on the court. While laughing at the comment, Rusty took a chance and lightly touched Keisha's leg.

She smiled at him, and he bravely progressed from a slight touch to rubbing his palm across her right knee. Keisha grabbed Rusty's hand. He thought that she had become offended. He felt his heart pounding as he thought of how stupid he had been. But suddenly, he discovered his hand moving further up her leg. She was guiding him as she took his hand and helped him stroke her. The hand nearly found its way to her crotch. Rusty's eyes watered in ecstasy. They wanted each other so badly.

Peter and Tasha didn't know exactly what was going on, but both had a pretty good idea. Peter had thought that the two were slowly becoming closer over the past couple of weeks, but he had hoped that it wasn't true. He thought Rusty was unworthy of a creature so talented, intelligent, and beautiful.

Out of nowhere, he declared that he had to go. Tasha asked for a ride. Rusty insisted that he could take her home since he had brought her, but Tasha sensed that Rusty and Keisha wanted to be alone and insisted that Peter take her. The last thing Peter wanted was to run Tasha clear over to her home on the other side of Wichita when he had a killing to clean up. But he also did not want to draw any suspicions, so he reluctantly agreed.

Keisha and Rusty stood by his car. They engaged in meaningless conversation until Peter and Tasha drove off. Rusty then took Keisha's hands. Fingers intertwined, they stood and stared at each other until Rusty took his hands away from Keisha as she leaned against his car. He put his right hand around her waist, and his left hand gently touched her cheek. He leaned over and kissed her.

At first, it was a gentle kiss, but then he took his tongue to meet hers as he squeezed her closer to him. Their lips were bound together as one for nearly ten minutes. Keisha finally pointed out that it was 12:15, and they better get to the Pond Side Courts. For the first time in their lives, they both wished they weren't about to play in a pickleball tournament.

....

Mathew and Grandma Edna returned home from church. Since they had eaten a big breakfast, neither planned on eating lunch. Edna instructed Mathew to check on Elijah since he was sick. Mathew let his grandmother know that he would, but then he was going to head over to the tournament to watch Keisha & Rusty. After checking his text messages, he also realized that Randall and Sandy were back on to play mixed doubles. Edna stated that she would meet Mathew there. She told her grandson that she would have ridden with him, but she needed to go to the grocery store afterward. She knew how Mathew disliked hanging out in the store unless he could get his hands on junk food, which Edna rarely allowed.

She found it surprising that she was suddenly becoming such a big pickleball fan. Two days ago, she had despised the sport, and now she was obsessed with following the members of the "Crew."

Elijah informed Mathew that he had just returned from Randall's and wasn't really sick but needed to work on the investigation. He let Mathew know that he and Randall both thought they had a top suspect until they found out that the

Peanut Butter Killer was a woman. Randall had then taken off to play in the tournament with Sandy.

Mathew asked who they had thought might be The Killer. Elijah reluctantly said Peter. Mathew proclaimed the theory ridiculous and insulting. He was shocked that they had even slightly entertained the thought that their friend was a psycho serial killer. Elijah then sighed, "I know the news just reported that DNA found at two different locations of victims supposedly proves that The Killer is a woman, but I still have my suspicions. I just don't buy it. All signs point to Peter."

Mathew told Elijah he was spending too much time in his room and needed to get a life. Elijah then pleaded with his brother to look at the evidence. Mathew, with some hesitation, agreed. After hearing what Elijah had to say, Mathew apologized, agreeing that there was nothing conclusive, but there was enough compelling evidence to not rule Peter out.

Elijah said that DNA from a woman being found in the Galveston and Kansas City murders was compelling, but it wasn't a fact that The Killer was a woman. The PB Freak might have an accomplice. Mathew informed Elijah that while Tasha sometimes flirted with other men, even including his young self at times, she probably wouldn't do so if Peter committed to her. So, it wasn't a reach that she might help Peter if he was The Killer, to impress him.

Elijah asked Mathew if Peter had been around anyone over the past twenty-four hours who might be in danger. Mathew said he knew that Tasha, Peter, Keisha, and Rusty had all spent the morning together playing pickleball and going out to lunch.

Elijah noted that The Killer would likely only murder a stranger after his pickleball tournaments.

But Elijah still wanted to be sure that everyone from their clan, or the "Crew" was okay. Mathew assured him there was no one he knew of who had been near Peter and not been accounted for.

Elijah continued to look at his accumulated evidence while questioning Mathew, who noticed that Elijah kept focusing on a picture of Peter with half his shirt off. Mathew asked Elijah if he had some sort of crush on Peter, and perhaps that's why he was obsessed with him. Elijah stated that although he might find Peter attractive for "an old guy," that was not why he kept looking at the picture. Elijah showed Mathew Peter's stomach. "I wanted to show Randall this one, but he had to run off to play with Sandy in the tournament." He zoomed in on the picture as closely as he could. After seeing the birthmark, Mathew agreed that it was fascinating, noting how it covered half of the left side of his body and stopped in a near-perfect line that split through the middle of his chest through his belly button.

Mathew stated, "Enthralling indeed, Elijah, but what on earth would his freakish birthmark have to do with anything?" After a short pause, he answered, "I don't know. Maybe if by some chance he is The Killer, his anger stems from a complex over his looks or something. Though admittedly, it doesn't seem like a reason to be that angry. I am baffled. I just don't know. But if the birthmark gives him some form of complex, combined with his rough childhood, it could lead to a very, very angry Peter."

Mathew then remarked, "Or you are using your overactive imagination to try and force Peter into fitting a pattern he doesn't – a female psycho?"

"Mathew, I hope you're correct. I hope that I'm the crazy one with these thoughts. But for now, I want to make certain all of us are safe. There's no one else who might have been around him?

"No. No one, Elijah… uh, well, I guess not *no one*. "

"What do you mean, 'uh, well, I guess not no one,' Mathew?"

"Well, supposedly, Robin was going out to his ranch briefly last night to drop off a pickleball paddle he left at Pond Side."

Alarmed, Elijah then exclaimed that it was critical to check on Robin. Mathew had her number. He tried to call her a couple of times, but he only received a text back. She said she couldn't talk, as she had just met a guy and was walking with him in the park. Elijah then made it clear that a text was insufficient and that one of them needed to hear her voice. Mathew did not have the phone numbers for either Robin's mother or her father, but he knew Keisha would have them.

………

Keisha and Rusty arrived at Pond Side Pickleball courts. They pulled out their lawn chairs and set them down at the back of the crowd that had already gathered, listening to the tournament director.

The director reiterated the modified rules. No best out of two out of three to eleven, and no games to fifteen, with the late start. Each match would be one simple game to eleven during pool play.

The crowd then laughed when the director congratulated everyone in the 5.0 division, noting that the worst any of them could do was third in their pool since there were now just two pools of three. Only one winner out of each pool would advance to a one play-off match, a championship game to eleven.

Keisha felt like such a naughty rebel. This was the first tournament she had ever been to, where she was running late. They were getting ready to run out on the court for their first match when they ran into Randall. They teased him about moving into the 5.0 big leagues after only having played a few weeks.

Randall then said that he hadn't seen Sandy, and they were about to go out on the court. Keisha and Rusty said they hadn't seen her either. Randall slowly walked out onto court seven, alone.

There he saw a husband-and-wife team in their mid-twenties on opposite sides of the net, dinking together. He greeted them. They introduced themselves as Ron and Jennifer Krocher, from Chicago. Randall informed Ron and Jennifer that he wasn't sure where his partner was, but he was sure she would arrive soon. They let him know that they could wait, as the brackets were down to six total 5.0 teams. Most of the 5.0 pros had gone on to catch flights back home or to other cities that their sponsors ordered them to play in. In most cases, the pro players had private lessons and pickleball camps to put on for the week, that paid more than taking fourth or fifth in a pro-level tournament.

Therefore, hanging around, hoping the weather would cooperate so you and your partner could place, made no sense.

   Sandy eventually made her way to the court. She apologized for being late. She winked at Jennifer, whispering to her that she had a woman's issue to take care of. Ron and Jennifer found her so fun and delightful to converse with briefly.

   She brought up the craziness of attending Wrigley field, which swept the couple right off their feet. Attending Cubs games was their favorite topic. They were impressed that Sandy had been to five games at Wrigley in her life. Sandy's personality overcame any possible ill thoughts that the couple would have had towards her due to her tardiness.

   Sandy served first to Jennifer. Jennifer cross-court shot the pickleball right back to Sandy. Sandy smoked a bullet to Jennifer's backhand. It sailed high in the air, and Sandy put the ball away with a slam that hit so hard it bounced clear over the back fence and into the back seating area. Sandy then served to Ron. Ron followed Jennifer's pattern and hit it cross-court to Sandy. It was blatantly obvious that their strategy was to hit it to the girl every time. It was a method they soon lived to regret. Sandy not only took the next serve and smashed it directly into Ron's chest before he could raise his paddle, but she was the primary reason that the next six points went to her team. Randall's paddle touched the ball just four times during that entire stretch.

                       8-0 Randall and Sandy

Sandy finally lost her serve. Ron started out serving to Sandy. Sandy bulleted the return to the right-hand corner of the court, straight to Jennifer's backhand. Jennifer could barely get to the ball. It flew straight up in the air to Randall. Randall slammed the ball right into the net.

8-1

"Damn it, Randall!" Sandy shouted.

Randall was caught off guard by Sandy's anger. "Sorry, Sandy."

Sandy realized that she was taking things to seriously and kissed Randall on the cheek. "You goober. I'm just teasing, my love."

Randall went from feeling intense embarrassment to giddy feelings of joy. After the ball was served to him, he returned the serve right down the middle of the court. Ron and Jennifer ran into each other with their paddles colliding. The ball went straight into the net. Jennifer then took her turn serving. Being down eight to one in a match to eleven put Jennifer on the nervous side. She served the ball long and out of bounds. Then Sandy served. Randall noticed that she hit the ball with her right hand. The ball's velocity increased when she served using her opposite hand. The quick, hard serve to Jennifer's backhand caught Jennifer off guard. She barely edged the ball. It flew behind her.

9-1 - TWO POINTS FROM VICTORY

Sandy served to Ron. He drilled the ball with an eighty-five mile-per-hour shot to Randall's chest. Randall flicked his wrist with amazing instinct and tenacity. He edged the ball back to Ron's side of the court, striking the outside line inside the kitchen. Ron dove for the ball, planting his face straight into the court floor and missing the shot. Ron slowly got up and made it clear he was okay. After Sandy served the ball to Jennifer, Jennifer drilled the ball to Randall. Randall was able to get the ball back but left it a little high. Jennifer slammed the ball. It flew to the right of Sandy, and she had no chance at a backhand shot, but instinctively tossed the paddle to her right side. She caught the paddle by the handle with her right hand.

With her opposite right hand, Sandy drilled the ball right back at Jennifer. Jennifer managed to get the ball over the net with an okay dink to Randall, but it was far enough over the net that he was able to dink the ball just over to Ron. Ron hit it back to Randall. Ron and Jennifer had changed strategies from 'hit to the woman' to 'hit to the old guy.' Randall handled the pressure well. He dinked the ball eight times during the point with exceptional patience.

Eventually, Ron became frustrated and tried to zing the ball with all his might right at Randall. Randall threw his paddle to the side and dropped to the ground dodging the ball. It missed him by inches. The ball flew three feet out of bounds.

11-1 MATCH TO THE 5.0 ROOKIES – SANDY & RANDALL!

......

Keisha and Rusty surprisingly found themselves all business. They were facing two opponents in their mid-thirties from Denver. The two had won about half of their matches on the 5.0 pro tour. Their game was solid with few unforced errors on the court, but they did nothing special. Keisha and Rusty had both privately thought that their newfound interest in each other off the courts might affect their game. As it turned out, they were both so competitive that their morning tryst crossed their minds occasionally, but winning was the task at hand. No kiss in a breakfast parking lot would hinder their quest for a championship.

7-3 KEISHA & RUSTY WITH THE LEAD.

Keisha took a deep breath before serving. Her face radiated with joy to see Sandy and Randall there to support them. Since she knew the other two were playing 5.0 that morning, she assumed they had quickly lost their first match. She felt bad for them but proud that they were willing to put themselves out there to play at such a high level for the experience. She was also excited to see her Grandma Edna, Debbie, and Katy in the stands again today to watch. But Keisha was disappointed and a little annoyed that Mathew was not there for her. Not to mention that they needed to be at the courts to observe anything and everything to progress the investigation. After winning another point on her serve making the score 8-3, the match tightened up some. But the Denver duo was really no match for the two.

11-7 KEISHA AND RUSTY WITH THE WIN!

The crowd of around thirty-five cheered. After talking some to Edna, Katy, and Debbie, Keisha was ecstatic to find out that Sandy and Randall actually won their match. They were happy to know that they were in different pools. If they were in the same pool, it would force one side of the "Crew" to force the other side of the "Crew" out of the tournament.

Keisha did ask her grandma where Mathew was. Grandma Edna let Keisha know that she was concerned herself. Edna told Keisha that Elijah was sick, and worried that Mathew might have caught a bug from him. Keisha, of course, knew that Elijah was supposedly sick but didn't tell Edna that she knew. Grandma Edna said she tried to call and text a couple of times but received no reply from Mathew.

......

Neither Mathew nor Elijah knew Robin's parents' numbers to verify the texts from Robin's phone stating that she was safe in Topeka. With Robin refusing to answer the phone and only texting, Mathew was getting a little frustrated.

Mathew knew that Keisha would have Peter's number, but she was not picking up. He knew that she was probably in the middle of a pickleball match, so her phone was not on her. He left several texts as well as a couple of calls. He also noticed his grandma trying to contact him, but Mathew did not respond because he just wasn't sure what to say to her as an excuse for his absence.

   Mathew had been to Peter's ranch once to play a pick-up game of pickleball. He told Elijah that he was going out there. Elijah insisted on going with Mathew, but Mathew convinced his brother that it would be better for him to stay on his computer.

   Mathew wanted Elijah to continue to research and go through all documentation and journaling he had conducted that might point in the direction of Peter.

   Also, Mathew explained to Elijah that Peter would not suspect anything particularly weird if he came out unannounced, as Mathew could always use the excuse of wanting to play a game of singles with Peter. Elijah accompanying him would not make sense. Elijah reluctantly agreed, only because he really didn't believe that Peter was The Killer. He was just acting on a theory with remedial evidence. And Elijah further knew that evidence was now very thin since DNA pointed to a woman.

....

   Randall and Sandy were preparing for their next match. Randall mentioned jokingly, "Are you going to play right-handed or left this match?" Sandy giggled, "Yes, I reckon I was a little lucky with those right-hand shots."

"For such a sweet, bubbly, fun personality, you sure do have a fighting spirit and tenacity to win."
"I just want to win so badly for you, Randall."
Sandy grabbed Randall's cheeks and kissed him on the lips. It was not a long kiss, but it was made with both passion and affection. Randall then proclaimed, "Let's kick some 5.0 butt!"

Randall and Sandy were taking on the co-ed 5.0 defending champions Kyle Taylor and Renee Thompson. The pair was from Tulsa, Oklahoma. They were a couple in their early thirties that had been dating for five years. The pro pickleball tour took too much of their time to stop, marry, and create a family.

Kyle started out serving to Sandy. She swatted the ball deep and with speed to Renee's feet. She was barely able to scoop the ball up enough to get it high to Randall, who slammed the ball right to Kyle's backhand. Kyle had great reflexes to get to the ball.

Randall started out serving to Kyle. Kyle went straight to Sandy. Sandy dinked it to Renee. Sandy showed patience when needed but with power and conviction. She was not afraid to go for a kill shot as well. Randall, for the first ten minutes of the game, was a non-factor. Sandy had no problem with the one-on-two battle. Kyle and Renee realized their strategy wasn't working. They called a time-out. Randall and Sandy had worked up a healthy lead.

7-3 RANDALL AND SANDY UP

Yesterday, the crew was cheering their comrades in full force, but today, many members were not present. Only Debbie, Katy, and Grandma Edna were cheering them on. Rusty and Keisha were supporting Randall and Sandy between their own matches. Elijah and Mathew were noticeably absent. All thought Peter was taking care of his sick horse, and Robin was assumed to be in Topeka with her father. Keisha did think Mathew and Elijah were rude for not being there to support them. She felt that Elijah was just Elijah, who was supposedly ill, but it wasn't in Mathew's character to not be there to support her and his mentor, Rusty. Mathew was nowhere to be seen. Keisha thought of calling him, but she decided he probably had a good enough reason to be AWOL.

Keisha did reason that Mathew worshipped Rusty. So, it wasn't like he wouldn't want to be here.

Renee served to Randall. Randall hit it cross-court back to Renee. Renee went right back to Randall. There was a total of twelve volleys a piece. The crowd of nearly ninety people gasped in awe. On Randall's thirteenth volley, he hit an unexpectedly hard strike to Kyle. Kyle never raised his paddle. He was taken completely off guard.

8-3 RANDALL AND SANDY

......

Keisha finally looked at her phone. She saw several missed calls and texts from both of her brothers. She walked away from the match for privacy and called Elijah, who asked her if she knew where Robin was. Keisha said she was in Topeka. Elijah then asked her if she had had any communication with Robin since she left for Topeka. Robin assured him that she had. She said that Robin had texted her about the excitement of meeting some boy in Topeka. Elijah then asked if Keisha's information was based on texts, not phone calls. Keisha stated this was, indeed, the case and that she had not spoken to Robin. Elijah asked his sister for the phone numbers of both of Robin's parents so he could call them and confirm Robin's whereabouts. Keisha became worried and said that she would make the call.

Elijah told her that she needed to concentrate on pickleball as there was probably nothing to worry about. He assured her he could handle checking up on Robin. After getting the numbers from Keisha, Elijah asked her a peculiar question. "Do you think there's any chance that Peter might actually be a girl?"

Keisha laughed until she caught on that Elijah was serious. She then said that there was no way Peter was anatomically a woman because one time, after playing singles at his home, Keisha had accidentally walked in on him naked She said that after they played, they had gone into his house and sat down to drink a glass of water and relax. Peter told her that he needed to take a shower, and Keisha had told him that she needed to get home anyway. Just before leaving, she decided to go to the bathroom. She had assumed that he would go to the master bathroom to take his shower, but instead, he had gone to the main one. She explained to Elijah that she had accidentally walked in on him and was so embarrassed and apologized profusely. Peter had said, "No worries." Keisha had closed the door and left. She then stated to Elijah once more that Peter was all man and not a woman. She asked if there was anything else Elijah wanted to know.

He asked one more question. "Keisha, I noticed the birthmark across his chest when he had it exposed briefly yesterday. When you saw him naked, did you notice anything unusual about it?"

Confused, Keisha replied, "I don't know where all this is going, but yes. I mean, I didn't look that thoroughly, for obvious reasons, but I did see he has an unusual birthmark that runs halfway down his body and cuts off in an exact line." Keisha asked Elijah why that was so important.

With hesitation, he replied, "I'm trying to figure out his motives in case, uh, in case. um..."

"In case what, Elijah?"

"In case he's the Peanut Butter Killer." Elijah explained his suspicions about Peter. But he reassured Keisha that he was most likely wrong because breaking news revealed that DNA evidence pointed to The Killer being a woman. Elijah did let Keisha know; however, that Peter clearly being all man did not completely clear him from being The Killer, as Tasha or another woman could still be an accomplice.

....

Keisha wasn't sure what to think of her brother's remarks. On one hand, it seemed like it could be the result of the overactive imagination of a guy who spent too much time on his computer.

But on the other hand, if he was insistent on continuing to search for information on a pickleball guy, it was probably something that should be taken seriously. Keisha knew that if stubborn Elijah was willing to swallow his pride about the pickleball killer thing, there was probably a good reason. Elijah didn't say much about why he thought Robin might be in danger, but it weighed on Keisha's extremely concerned mind.

Keisha returned to watching the match but had a difficult time enjoying it after the call. Five minutes before, she had been on top of the world. She had a new romance developing with her crush and had just won her first 5.0 match with him. She was watching two of her best friends take apart two highly experienced 5.0 players. She should feel happy and on top of the world, but instead, she was nauseated and bewildered by her conversation with Elijah. Was Elijah crazy and paranoid, or was it possible one of her other best friends was a serial killer who might have harmed Robin?

Randall served a long, high lob at match point. Kyle took his time to slam the slow lob back, but the slow, high lob threw Kyle off, and he hit the ball hard towards Sandy.

She swerved out of the way as the ball flew past the back line.

11-9 MATCH TO RANDALL AND SANDY!

All the Crew members present cheered loudly, except for Keisha. She clapped, but the clapping was subdued. Randall and Sandy hugged. Many of the other spectators cheered them on, as well. They loved the story of the old guy who had only played a few weeks, teaming up with a woman who had played in just a couple of 3.5 tournaments and suddenly finding themselves in the championship of a 5.0 tournament. The crowd members were already fans of Randall's after watching him and Mathew in the 3.5 championship yesterday.

In the meantime, Keisha slithered away under a tree to call Elijah for more information. She and Rusty's semi-final match was scheduled to start in ten minutes, but pickleball was the last thing on her mind. Elijah informed her that there was still no confirmation regarding Robin's whereabouts. After obtaining the numbers for Robin's parents, Elijah quickly discovered that Robin, or whoever had her phone, had manipulated Robin's mother and father. Through texts, Robin's mother was led to believe that Robin was with her father in Topeka. Robin's father was told that Robin had to skip the Sunday with him in Topeka due to illness. Robin's father and mother were in pure panic mode. They questioned Elijah extensively as to why he would have possibly suspected that Robin was missing. He hesitatingly told them there was some suspicion that she might have had contact with the notorious Peanut Butter Killer. Immediately, Robin's mother called 911.

While talking to Keisha, Elijah was also looking at some of the photos that he had downloaded to his computer from the previous day. He was zooming in on the picture of the dirt in the sink in the woman's bathroom. He said there was something about it that kept him looking. He said he would send the picture to Keisha to see what she thought. Keisha said that she had to get ready for the next match but would look at it as soon as it was over. She thought of forfeiting, but that could lead to suspicions, as well.

CHAPTER 18

Mathew drove up to Peter's home. He rang the doorbell and knocked loudly. He even yelled out Peter's name several times. Robin was still in the barn, lying on Jiffy and praying the majestic creature wouldn't move because she knew that if she did, she would fall off the horse and hang from the noose to her death.

She heard Matthew hollering for Peter. She tried to yell but could not talk loudly enough for anyone beyond a three-foot radius to hear. She struggled, trying to get the noose off, but she could barely move. She had little strength left after the beatings she had taken, and she didn't want to make any movements anyway, as it could drive Jiffy to move away from her.

Mathew peeked through the windows and banged on them, trying to get Peter's attention. At one point, he slammed his hands against the south kitchen window so hard that it shattered. He cut up his hands and bled profusely. He looked intently at the window for a moment. He then thought he might as well peek inside. He pulled himself up on the windowsill. In the process, the broken glass cut through his shirt and into his belly. He was now bleeding from many places, all over his body. He thought, "I'm a dead man. Either Peter will come out and kill me because he is the Peanut Butter Killer, or he will kill me because I broke into his house and bled all over it."

He opened the kitchen cabinets. He wasn't sure what he was looking for, but he looked all the same. He looked under the sink, in the trash can. Then he opened the pantry. He thought his heart would stop beating. In horror, he looked inside the entire pantry.

THE PANTRY WAS FILLED WITH NOTHING BUT PEANUT BUTTER PRODUCTS!

An odd collection, every type of peanut butter imaginable, *Peter Pan, Smucker's, Jiff, Planters*, and even classic, discontinued peanut butter jars like *Koogle* from the seventies, and a jar of vintage *Beach-Nut* from 1926. Mathew had no clue why Dr. DNA was attempting to reveal the Peanut Butter Killer as a woman, for The Killer was clearly a man named Peter!

Mathew feared for his life and even more so for Robin's. He knew that it might draw attention from Peter, but with unfathomable logic, Mathew decided that if Peter were in the house, he would have already appeared and cooked Mathew up for dinner.

So, Mathew hesitated very little before screaming out.

"ROBIN! ROBIN! CAN YOU HEAR ME? ROBIN!"

Mathew continued to scream her name while frantically running through every room of The Killer's home. Mathew looked through closets, under the beds, and even the bathtubs. He was beginning to panic. He called Elijah and told him of the freaky peanut butter pantry. Elijah yelled at him to get the hell out of there. Mathew told his brother that Tasha must be mixed up in the whole thing since Peter is a man.

Elijah let Mathew know that he had done some more digging and discovered Tasha had been working as a nurse in Wichita and not playing doubles with Peter in Kansas City at the time of the murder there. He reminded Mathew that Kansas City was one of the two cities where white female DNA was found on the victims, which would clear Tasha. The two continued to talk on the phone.

Mathew started to get in his car but told Elijah that he had decided that he might look around in the shed where the pickleball court was. Elijah made it clear to Mathew that staying in the area was dangerous, but Mathew refused to listen. Elijah continued to argue with his brother, to no avail. Elijah then said he had to get off the phone as the authorities were trying to call in to question him because of Robin's mother calling 911.

Mathew continued to bleed from the window glass cuts. Blood had not only spread throughout Peter's house but all over his ranch area.

Mathew looked through the pickleball shed, leaving more blood throughout it. Aside from the pickleball net on the court, the shed was empty, only revealing a small bar with a couple of bar stools and some lawn chairs. The bar was equipped with two mini-refrigerators. One was filled with Crown and Jack Daniels, the other with beer and water. He then noticed that underneath the bar was a pickleball bag. He carefully unzipped it. He found duct tape, knives, scissors, a couple of towels, and a pickleball paddle. Mathew pulled out the paddle. He was amazed at how heavy it was. He noticed a lever in the middle of the handle. Mathew pulled up the lever, and the triangular switch blades immediately shot out. One of the blades cut deep into his left forearm, nearly hitting bone. He fell and screamed in pain. The blade was still stuck in his arm, rendering him unable to move. He felt weak, as though his life was fading away. But he knew that he must hang on. He lay on his back while the ceiling moved in circles. He fought hard to not pass out, as passing out would mean never waking up. Mathew took the handle of the pickleball paddle and attempted to pull the blade out of his arm without success. He then looked at the lever on the handle. With his right hand, he pushed down on the lever. The blade was slowly cutting further into his arm as it was pulling back into the paddle. He only had the lever halfway down. Mathew took a deep breath and pushed with all his might to get the lever to pull the blade all the way to the bottom of the paddle.

"AHHHHHHH"

Mathew screamed in agonizing misery. Blood gushed out of his arm. He grabbed the pickleball bag and took out both towels. He held one to his left arm to slow down the bleeding. The towel turned from white to blood-drenched red in a matter of seconds. He grabbed the duct tape and laid it beside his left arm. He then reached over to the fridge with the alcohol. He took the bottle of Crown, opened it, and poured the alcohol on his left forearm to clean the wound.

"AHHHHHH EEEE UHH"

He again screamed in agony as the alcohol burned into the deep wound. Mathew then rolled the duct tape around his forearm until the wound had been covered three times. He then wrapped the duct tape around his bloody, cut-up hands, and took the second towel and covered his stomach where it was also cut from the window. He wrapped the duct tape around his waist and the towel. Mathew thought how ironic it was that the duct tape that was likely used to help Peter kill people was now a formidable aid in helping save his own life. He grunted as he arose off the floor, using the bar to pull himself up. He reached down and grabbed the pickleball-paddle-switch-blade-weapon for protection. He stumbled out of the building. Mathew walked by the barn. He stumbled and fell to the ground and again screamed in pain.

"OHHHHH"

Robin heard the scream. She tried as hard as she could to yell the word "help." She was running out of time. The horse was a most disciplined horse, but she could only stand in one place for so long. Robin again whimpered out the word "help". It was useless. The horse, sensing her frustration, neighed loudly and hard. She neighed three times until at last, Mathew heard the horse and became curious. He stumbled to the barn and nervously opened the barn door.

There he saw a young woman with peanut butter covering her face, a noose wrapped around her neck, lying on top of a horse. Mathew saw that the girl was alive. He was unsure of who it was, but he had a pretty good idea.

"ROBIN?"

"M-M-M-M-Mathew. D-d-don't move, M-M-M-Mathew. You'll scare the horse, and then I'll drop from the rope to my end."

Mathew slowly crept towards the horse. "Good girl, good girl. It's okay. I won't hurt you." He crept closer.

The horse started to walk away. "Woo, horsey. Stay, buddy. Please, just stay still. I won't hurt you."

"H-h-her name Jiffy."

"Jiffy, it's okay. Stay still. I know I look pretty scary right now but trust me. I won't hurt you."

At last, Mathew made it to Jiffy. He slowly petted her face and mane. Mathew laid the switchblade pickleball paddle on Jiffy's back and tried to pull the tight noose off but realized he couldn't. The horse was creeping forward. Jiffy then became spooked and started to run forward. Robin fell off. But as she was falling and the horse was taking off, Mathew instinctively grabbed the paddle off Jiffy's back and pulled up on the lever of the pickleball paddle still in his right hand. The triangle switch blades flew out. He swung the blades inches above the noose, coming awfully close to striking Robin's neck, but detaching the rope from the noose.

   Robin fell painfully face down, further crushing her already broken ribs. Mathew ran to her. It took several minutes, but he managed to get her up on her feet. "C'mon, Robin, we have got to get out of here."

....

   Keisha and Rusty were out on court five for their semi-final match. They were up against suspect Samuel Townsend and his partner Elisa Briel. Although Samuel was on the Crew's suspect list, they were almost exclusively focused on Peter at this point in their search for a killer. Rusty noticed Keisha's nervousness. He was disappointed that she was being so serious and not flirtatious. Rusty wondered if he had done something wrong. Keisha assured him that he had not, and claimed she was just worried about the match. The problem was that pickleball was the last thing on her mind, and it would not take long for the score to show it. Right out of the gate Elisa and Samuel preyed upon her nervousness…

5-0 – SAMUEL AND ELISA TIME-OUT CALLED.

Rusty used their one allotted time-out. Keisha expected some type of tutoring lecture on her play. She put her head down while walking up to Rusty during the time-out, ready for what she figured was a well-deserved scolding. Rusty looked up at the stands. "See your grandma up there? If she's going to get into the whole pickleball world, she really needs to dress the part."

Edna had not changed from her church clothes and was wearing her Sunday best.

Keisha laughed. "I suppose she's a little too fancy-schmancy for a pickleball affair."

"What do you say we take her pickleball shopping this evening? Clothes are on me."

"Great idea, Rusty! It sounds like a plan."

The humorous distraction worked. Keisha drilled a return from Samuel down the baseline, straight at Elisa. Elisa hit the ball back at Keisha. Keisha dinked to Elisa and then back to Samuel, then back to Elisa again. When Elisa and Samuel fell into the pattern of Keisha hitting it back and forth, she changed it up and hit it to Samuel twice, but the second shot in a row to him was delivered with power and ferocity. Samuel was caught off guard and unable to get the ball back.

At last, Rusty and Keisha were given the opportunity to serve in the match. Rusty served to Samuel. He and Elisa continued their strategy of attempting to pick on Keisha, but that strategy had played itself out. A whole new Keisha was on the court. She continued her odd approach of dinking back and forth, taking turns between Samuel and Elisa, only this time, when she changed it up, she did so with a lob over Samuel. It caught him so off guard that he was not prepared to run back and was too late to get the perfectly lobbed ball.

5-1 ON THE BOARD!

Rusty then served to Elisa. Instead of the customary tactic of keeping the serving team deep, Elisa dinked the return to Keisha, who stayed alert and was not tricked by the awkward move. Keisha recognized that her back-and-forth, every-other-shot routine was messing with Samuel and Elisa's minds. This time, she changed it up with a hard shot right down the middle. Neither player saw it coming.

5-2 BACK IN THE GAME!

After Rusty's next serve, the couple realized that Keisha was getting hot and had worked out her kinks. They then decided to work on Rusty. Rusty handled the barrage of dinks extremely well. He stuck with the game and never stopped dinking, even when he saw an opening. He just kept at it, and when the ball went to Keisha's side, she would do the same. Samuel and Elisa felt like they had hit a wall. Point after point after point continued to go Rusty and Keisha's way.

The score turned in Rusty and Keisha's favor.

6-5 RUSTY AND KEISHA WITH THE LEAD!!!

Keisha was pleased that she was playing better. Rusty's well-planned, humorous therapy time-out instilled the couple with a newfound vigor. However, the time-out did not keep Keisha's mind from her concern about Robin's safety. Her thoughts again strayed from the game and to the whereabouts of her best friend. After Rusty's serve, Samuel drilled the ball low and straight to Keisha. She did not react in time and hit the ball straight into the net.

Keisha was shaking as she served. She hit the ball far right, but a gust of Kansas wind blew it sharp left. Elisa threw her body back and missed the return, injuring her hip in the process. She was slow to get up.

7-5 RUSTY AND KEISHA

Keisha then served to Samuel. He cross-court shot the ball right back at Keisha. Keisha attempted a third shot drop just over the net to Elisa, but the ball sailed a tad too high. Elisa rushed to the net and slammed the ball to the edge of the sideline by Rusty for a winner. But after striking the ball, she grabbed her right hip in pain and fell into the net, forfeiting the point.

8-5 RUSTY AND KEISHA

Samuel, Rusty, and Keisha rushed up to the net, concerned for Elisa. She struggled to get up. She said she wanted to go on, but Samuel would not let her.

RUSTY AND KEISHA ADVANCED TO THE FINAL

Samuel congratulated Keisha and Rusty and apologized for not engaging in small talk but was adamant about getting Elisa help immediately. Rusty and Samuel carried her to Samuel's car so he could take her to the hospital. Rusty thought it odd that Keisha did not walk to the car with them. Out of the corner of his eye, he caught sight of her talking on the phone. Rusty knew that not failing to pay attention and assist with an injured person wasn't in her nature. Baffled and perplexed, Rusty sensed that Keisha wasn't being herself, and thought he had a good idea why. Rusty got Samuel's phone number because he wanted to call to check on Elisa's condition. He then wished them well and walked up to Keisha. She was hanging up just as Rusty approached her. Keisha dropped her phone, picked it up off the ground, and quickly put it in her pocket.

"Uh, umm, umm, uh... how is Elisa? Is she going to be okay?"

"Yes, Keisha. She will be fine. I'm a little more concerned about you at the moment."

"And why is that?"

Rusty then went on to point out that she had been uncharacteristically jumpy and on edge. He acknowledged that they might have lost the match if not for Elisa's injury.

Keisha became enraged. "I think we have a whole lot more to worry about here than some damn pickleball match, Rusty!"

"I know, I know, Keisha. I know why you're feeling so trepidatious."

"You do? Why is that?"

"It's because I've turned our wonderful, business-like pickleball relationship and overwhelmed you by throwing in a restaurant-parking-lot-kissing-session. I'm sorry, Keisha. I'd rather have you as nothing more than a pickleball buddy than not have you in my life at all. I can assure you that our championship match in twenty minutes will be nothing but business. I'm sorry, Keisha. See you on the courts in just a few." Rusty then began walking away.

"But, um, uh...Rusty, wait!" Rusty stopped and turned around to look at Keisha,

"Yes, Keisha?"

The phone rang again. "Uh, um...I'm sorry, Rusty. I've got to take this. I'll see you on the court."

Keisha wanted to dive into Rusty's arms and let him know how wrong he was, but for now, she had much bigger fish to fry. Rusty walked away with his head down. She gave him a solemn look but answered the phone and turned her head away to listen to what Elijah had to say.

"Keisha, stay on the line and get Randall as soon as you can. Go someplace private and put him on speaker phone, ASAP!"

"I'll get right on it, Elijah!"

CHAPTER 19

Mathew took the pickleball switchblade paddle and stuffed it in his sweats, leaving one half hanging out. He hoped the paddle would stay there and not fall out or hinder him, but it was his only weapon, so he had to hold onto it. Mathew and Robin, both in severe pain, helped each other escape the barn. The horse followed them. The two struggled to get to Mathew's car. He discovered that somewhere down the line through his strives and strains at Peter's ranch, he had lost his keys. They both gasped in despair. Mathew and Robin dropped to the ground in pure exhaustion, feeling alone and defeated.

The horse licked Robin's cheek. This sparked an idea. "Mathew, there is a way out of here." Robin then looked up at the horse.

Mathew groaned, "You gotta be kidding me."

"If I can get on that horse, Mathew, I can ride bareback. Many years of 4-H have taught me well."

"There probably isn't a need for such drastic measures. Elijah said the police have been contacted and notified of the suspicions regarding Peter. They're aware you're missing and probably came out here last night to give him his pickleball paddle. It's only a matter of time before they reach this property and save us."

"The man is r-r-relentless. We c-c-can't chance it. Gotta get outta here now."

"But your ribs are crushed, Robin. We'll never make it."

"As God is my w-w-witness, we will."

"All right, Robin, let's do this."

Robin and Mathew struggled but made it to the hood of the car. Robin patted her hands to motion for Jiffy to come closer to the hood. "C'mon, girl. C'mon, Jiffy, over here."

Eventually, Jiffy lined up next to the car's hood as if she understood what Robin was asking of her. Mathew gave Robin a push. She crawled up onto the horse. With his torn-up body, Mathew utilized all his might to climb up onto the horse behind Robin. He held onto her waist. She slumped forward on her stomach, too damaged to sit up straight. Mathew lay over Robin's back.

"What's the plan from here, Robin?"

"L-l-l-logic would tell us to get to town for help. But Pond Side Courts are just a few miles away on this country road. P-p-p-peter's gotta go where the action is. He's there somewhere, putting the several hundred p-p-people there in danger. L-l-let's go find the son of a bitch!"

"Robin, you've got to be shitting me."

"I'm not. I-I-I-I want the bastard's b-balls on a silver platter! Jiffy, giddy-up!" With the two teenagers clinging on for dear life, Jiffy listened to her newfound master. And Master Robin had commanded Jiffy to leave the nest.

．．．．．．．

"Okay, Elijah, what do you need to know? Randall is with me. We are away from the courts, but we go on to play in the championship in five minutes."

"By we, you mean Randall, Sandy, and Rusty?"

"Yes," Keisha answered.

"Wow, from what I've learned about pickleball, that's a pretty impressive feat, considering Randall hasn't ever played 5.0 or pickleball at all until three weeks ago, for that matter… But enough of the useless sports gibber. Looking over the evidence, at one of the two tournaments where DNA was found at the crime scene, Tasha was working at her nursing job. Scientifically speaking, there's no way that she was involved."

Randall then quipped, "That's good, because if she wasn't involved and there was female DNA found, Peter couldn't be involved in the peanut butter murders either! "

"Not necessarily. Listen, I've been looking at the journals I've kept since we started this case, including yesterday's tournaments and the practices I've sat in on. Did you know I am unable to find any records of a Sandy Rineheart? As all of you know, Peter was not in a pickleball tournament in St. Louis at the time of the murder of Charles Ogafer. But you know who was?"

"Sandy?" Randall questioned.

Elijah then continued, "I cannot think of a time that Peter and Sandy have ever been in the same room together. Can either of you think of a time, either in practice, personal life, anywhere that they might have been in the same place at the same time?"

Keisha and Randall replayed every moment they could think of over the past couple of weeks and even months in Keisha's case. They both discussed their interactions with Sandy and Peter. They finally agreed that for a short time, Sandy was at the tournament watching Randall and Mathew.

Randall then thought about it and said that she was never at Peter's matches, but she had briefly been at his and Mathew's first match. Randall said there was a small window between the match that Sandy watched and the time that Peter and Rusty started theirs. He pointed out that it was very brief.

Randall then mentioned that Peter was uncharacteristically late for the start of his match. Elijah remembered the dirty faucet in the women's restroom and switched the phone call to Facetime to show Keisha and Randall a picture on the computer. Elijah asked Keisha if perhaps that was not dirt on the faucet but rather make-up. Keisha noted that it looked like make-up.

Elijah flipped from the computer picture of the sink to one of Peter's first match. Elijah zoomed in on the brown coloring on his face. He asked, "Keisha, is that dirt from changing a tire or make-up that matches the make-up on the sink?"

Keisha completely stunned, replied, "It's the same make-up from the sink." She asked Elijah if he was insinuating that Sandy was actually Peter, to which Elijah said yes.

Keisha reminded her brother that all the media reports said the DNA indicated The Killer was a woman. She then informed Elijah that Peter/Sandy could not be The Killer since Peter was clearly a male. She reminded Elijah of the time she accidentally walked in on him naked in his bathroom at his ranch, confirming his manhood.

Elijah let Randall and Keisha know that there was a possible explanation for that. He then pulled up the computer photo of the birthmark on Peter's chest. "Remember the perfect line birthmark we discussed earlier, Keisha?"

"Yes, Elijah, what is the point?"

"The birthmark that covers virtually half of his chest is a sign of an extremely rare condition called chimerism. In fact, only approximately one hundred cases in the entire history of the world have been discovered. If a human has chimerism, they are made of two different sets of DNA from two different individuals. A Chimera can be created when a pregnant woman absorbs a few cells from her fetus. These cells from two different humans travel into the mother's bloodstream and migrate into separate organs. A person can also develop chimerism when, during early stages of development in the womb, non-identical twins merge into one person. And no, not conjoined twins, but ONE SINGLE PERSON! The DNA found on the victims was probably DNA from the female twin that was absorbed into Peter's body in utero. Think about it. They are both tall, slender, athletic, and about the same age.

Randall, since you're Sandy's partner in the championship, try to find some way to lift up her shirt, just high enough to see if she has a darkened pigmentation on the left side of her stomach."

"It will be nearly impossible to lift her shirt up without looking like a total pervert in front of as many as a hundred or more spectators, Elijah."

"Sorry, Randall, but it's the only way. Figure it out."

Randall then pointed out, "Up until this tournament, Sandy has been playing 3.5 pickleball. What would be her motive to spend time playing at a much lower level than she has been if she just stuck with playing as Peter?" It doesn't make any sense, Elijah."

"I don't know anything about pickleball, or sports period, for that matter, but can either of you think of any reason that acting as Sandy could make his game as Peter better?"

"No," Keisha and Randall both answered.

"You're the one who played with her, Randall. Can you think of anything?" Keisha asked.

"No, no, not really… um, um…oh my!"

"What, Randall? What are you thinking?" Keisha queried.

"She played left-handed. Peter plays right-handed, which explains the amazing, left-handed shot Peter made yesterday to help him and Rusty win the 5.0 Men's Doubles Championship. And it explains the crazy, right-handed shots Sandy has made in this tournament!"

Keisha then added, "Meaning the creation of Sandy was to practice becoming ambidextrous, thus eliminating using a backhand. All forehand shots are generally easier and more accurate strokes!"

"You got it, Keisha."

"The love of my life just might be a serial killer. Boy, I know how to pick them."

Keisha tried to comfort Randall by patting him on the back and rubbing his shoulders.

Randall and Keisha then asked Elijah why it was important to find out immediately if Sandy was The Killer. Elijah informed them that Robin had still not been found and that Mathew had gone to Peter's ranch to ask about her, putting them both in danger.

Keisha put her face in her hands and started to cry. "Not now, Keisha. There will be time for tears later; we can't have anyone, especially Sandy, suspect what is going on." Randall pressed.

"You're right Randall," she replied.

He patted her on the back and clapped his hands together. "I'm sure Rusty and whoever-my-partner-happens-to-be are looking for us. Let's go play this damn championship and find us a killer."

Keisha nodded her head in agreement. She then hung up on Elijah and they both ran to the championship court before the match could be terminated due to their tardiness.

CHAPTER 20

Mathew was clinging to Robin for dear life. She was cutting through fields. The speed caused the switchblade-pickleball-paddle to fly out of his pants. He grabbed it with his right hand just before it fell to the ground all while holding onto Robin with his left hand. He nearly fell off the horse reaching for the paddle, and almost pulled Robin with him, but he managed to shift his body back onto the middle portion of Jiffy's back. A few farmers noticed them galloping across the countryside. They all looked awestruck, peering upon an apparently injured woman with a noose around her neck and face covered in peanut butter and a profusely bleeding young man. The onlookers were bewildered at the sight of the boy leaning over the battered girl and holding onto her with one hand and a large paddle with the other. One farmer did call 911 and told the dispatcher the direction they were heading.

Mathew heard his phone ring. He struggled to get to it while balancing on the horse and holding onto Robin and the paddle.

"C'mon, girl! Faster, Jiffy, faster!" Robin hollered.

The thoroughbred picked up speed. Mathew continued to cling to the switchblade-pickleball-paddle with his right hand. The left hand that was holding onto Robin let go.

He fidgeted through his pocket while acting like a trapeze artist in a circus, balancing himself on the horse. He at last pulled out the phone. Mathew did not have the energy to put the phone to his ear. He hit the speaker button.

"Hello?"

"Oh, thank God you're alive, Mathew. This is Elijah. Did you find Robin?"

"Yes, she is with me on a horse."

"On a what?"

"A horse!"

"Are you both safe Mathew?"

"Well, we would be, but Robin insists on finding Peter and killing the son of a bitch or something. We're on his horse with a vengeance!"

"Not understanding all this horse business, Mathew, but if you're looking for Peter, you probably won't find him. Well, not as a man, anyway."

While continuing to guide the horse, Robin asked, "What do you mean 'not as a man'?"

"We think, emphasis on the word "think," Peter is actually Sandy!"

"Have you been smoking crack or something, Elijah? I have two words for you - drug rehab."

"Ha, ha, get somewhere safe, you two, please!"

"I don't think that's in Robin's cards, Elijah." Mathew hung up and went back to clinging to his friend while praying Jiffy wouldn't throw them both into permanent darkness.

......

5-1 SANDY & RANDALL START OFF WITH A BIG LEAD! TIME-OUT CALLED BY RANDALL

Sandy walked up to Randall in a swift and bitter manner. "Randall, why on earth would you call a time-out when all the momentum is going our way? Keisha couldn't hit a ball against a 2.5 level opponent right now, let alone us!"

"I know, baby! I'm not worried about the match. I just called time-out to tell you I'm tired of the flirtatious games. After we win this match, you know what I'm going to do to you, Sandy?" Randall then took his hands and tried to slowly lift her shirt up.

Sandy playfully slapped Randall's hands away. "Oh, Randall, you beast you! There are a ton of people watching us right now. I don't think this is the time. Now let's go back to kicking some booty, dear!"

"I'd like to slap that booty, babe. C'mon, just a slight peek of what's under the bottom of your thin, luscious belly." He again tried to slightly lift up Sandy's shirt. She again slapped his hands away.

"Enough baby, back to work!"

"Okay," Randall playfully grumbled.

During Randall and Sandy's time-out conversation, Rusty apologized to Keisha. He told her that he was sorry for ruining their friendship. He said he didn't even care if they won the championship. He told Keisha that he just wanted her to be happy. He then started to walk back to his side of the court. She walked towards hers, but then she turned around and grabbed his left hand and pulled him to her.

"Just as Caris never gave up on getting her man, Merthin, I'm not going to lose you, either."

Rusty bewildered, responded, "Say what?"

Keisha pressed her lips against his. A sultry, warm sensation, melded with spirited fervor and chemistry, merged the two in a more passionate manner than their earlier embrace in the restaurant parking lot. The parking lot kiss was full of lust and sexual tension. The pickleball court kiss contained titillation but was filled with love and tenderness.

The crowd cheered, especially Debbie and Katy. Grandma Edna was not sure what to think about it. She wasn't bothered by the idea of Rusty and Keisha becoming a couple, but she didn't necessarily approve of the public show of affection.

Sandy whistled, and Randall gave them a thumbs-up. After their kiss, Keisha whispered into Rusty's ear, "I've purposely been missing shots to drag out the match. Randall is investigating Sandy. We have probably already won this match, so it's meaningless anyway because if what we think is true, two men cannot play in a co-ed doubles tournament."

"What do you mean, Keisha?"

"Sandy might not be Sandy at all… but may possibly be Peter. Worse yet, Peter could very well be the notorious Peanut Butter Killer!"

"What?"

"I'll explain it all later, Rusty."

Rusty looked stunned. Keisha then walked back to her side of the court. Rusty stood motionless, trying to process what he had just heard.

Sandy was ready to serve cross-court to Rusty, but Rusty was still standing right by the net, in a near-comatose state, bewildered by Keisha's comments.

Sandy playfully and boisterously commented, "Guess that smooch Keisha gave you was some kind of special kiss. I might have to have her give me one after this match."

The crowd roared in laughter. Rusty pretended to laugh and walked back behind the baseline to prepare for the serve. Sandy bounced the ball three times. She hit it deep to Rusty's backhand, but he returned it with anger and conviction right back at Sandy. Sensing a vulnerable Rusty, Sandy sent the ball back to him. Rusty went to a bangers game, hitting every ball hard and right at Sandy. Sandy's reflexes were crazy good, but the ball was hit with too much speed and power to allow her to strike back with finesse, as all the balls she hit went directly back to Rusty. Rusty hit three more hardcore bang shots in a row at Sandy, until, at last, she hit the net.

Randall then served the ball to Keisha. Keisha hit it right back to Randall. Randall tried a third shot drop that hit the top of the net and stayed at the top. The ball appeared to come to a complete stop before dropping on Keisha and Rusty's side of the net. Rusty dove for the ball but could not get to it.

6-1 SANDY AND RANDALL

Sandy ran up and hugged Randall with a long embrace. While hugging Sandy, Randall looked over his shoulder. He saw Keisha motion with her hands as if to say, "pull up"! Randall then took Sandy's shirt and tried to lift it, but she walked away before he could pull it far enough up.

She then turned to Randall and said to him, "Oh, Randall, you are such a bad, bad boy! Patience is a virtue."

Keisha sweated profusely. Her thoughts continued to drift to her concern for Mathew and Robin and further away from the match. She intentionally missed shots to keep it going, but intentionally losing too many shots would end the match too quickly and give Sandy and Randall the winning Gold. Rusty was not sure what to do. He now understood this match was not about trying to win but about discovering the truth.

Keisha knew she had to keep the match going long enough for Randall to look for the birthmark. She kept motioning for him to do something. Randall purposely missed a dink shot on the next point as he was trying to make it look like he had missed the ball. He was truly attempting to pretend to miss the shot and use his paddle to lift Sandy's shirt. He missed the shirt. Sandy peered at Randall with suspicion. On the next couple of points, Keisha hit superb dinks and cross-court shots, and Rusty was starting to get his mind off the information that Keisha had given him, as he thought there was not much he could do about it anyway. They were on a six-point run and were looking like the better players that they should be.

7-6 KEISHA AND RUSTY TAKE THE LEAD!

The next point saw several dinks. Randall was reaching for a mid-dink shot. He missed it, but he used the lost point as an attempt to run up and bump into Sandy. He then attempted to run into her and lift her shirt without her noticing. She backed up and gave him a frown.
"Get your head in the game, Randall!"
"Umm, uh… Sorry, Sandy."

8-6 KEISHA AND RUSTY

Randall knew that Keisha was getting frustrated with his failure to get a look at Sandy's birthmark. He had been as creative as his soul allowed lead him to be. He was out of ideas and terribly disappointed with himself. Keisha threw a few "gimme" shots to Randall and Sandy to keep the match going. Sandy trounced her opportunities, but Randall's anxiety caused him to miss a couple of the easy set-up shots.

10- 8 MATCH POINT FOR RUSTY AND KEISHA!

Keisha was the first server on her side. She was set to serve cross-court to Randall. To keep the match going, she intentionally served the ball into the net.

10-9 RUSTY TO SERVE FOR THE MATCH

Rusty served cross-court to Sandy. She hit it back to Keisha. Keisha wanted to hit the ball out again, but she did not want to make it totally obvious that she was throwing part of the match, so she hit a third shot drop to Randall. She attempted to hit the ball at the top of the net, hoping it would land on her side. She was able to do so but it landed cross-court to Randall. He dove for the ball. He somehow reached it, but his struggles forced the ball straight up in the air for an easy lob high above the kitchen line to Keisha's side.

Amazingly, the ball flew twenty feet up into the air. Keisha could have already run up to the net to position herself for the slam, but she did not want to win the point, so she stayed back. Then Keisha was sparked with an idea.

She spotted Sandy near the kitchen line, cross-court from her. Instead of slamming the ball to Jupiter for the tournament win, she acted as though she was struggling to get to the ball. Keisha then decided to utilize her Kansas State Champion long and high jump skills. She took three running steps and leaped into the air.

While striking the ball with anger and conviction, Keisha then dropped the paddle and flew diagonally cross-court, over the net. Both legs behind her, Keisha landed on top of Sandy.

Keisha flung her legs open, thrust them in front of her, and wrapped them around Sandy's waist. At the same time, she flung her arms around Sandy's head to protect her from injuries.

Keisha's net jumping flight mirrored the movements of former World Wrestling Champion, Bobby Lashley, who was famous for often leaping off the ropes of a wrestling ring to lock down a three-count on his prey.

The crowd cringed in fear for Sandy and Keisha's safety. Upon hitting the ground, Keisha bellowed, "Sorry, Sandy, I lost my momentum."

As they both struck the pickleball court, Sandy bellowed back in pain, "Spectacular aerial assault there, Keisha."

While lying on top of Sandy, Keisha gently pulled up on Sandy's shirt. Keisha's body was covering her, so the crowd would not notice. She looked down and saw exactly what Randall already had his eyes on; there, exposed, was a deep, purple color that extended from the left side of her stomach, stopping in a near even line from the top of her belly through the middle of her navel and into her waist.

Randall walked up to Sandy and yanked her hair. The blond wig flew off. He calmly muttered, "Hello, Peter. Your time as a cowardly peanut butter pickleball slayer is up."

Keisha then added, "Where the hell are my brother and my best friend, Peter?" Peter stared at Keisha.

"Tell me, damn it."

She then punched Peter in the face. He remained mute, and she struck him again. Peter finally blurted out, "I don't know where Mathew is, but Robin is dead."

Keisha broke down in tears. Peter rose from the ground. He sprang towards his pink, Sandy-style pickleball bag. Randall dove and tripped him, and Peter fell onto the bag and pulled out a 357 magnum. Randall threw himself on top of The Killer. Peter attempted to pull the trigger on the gun, but Randall maintained a tight grip on the hand holding the gun. He squeezed Peter's hand tight enough that he was struggling to get his fingers loose to shoot. Unfortunately, Peter's strength triumphed, and he was able to get his fingers on the trigger, shooting Randall's waist. The crowd screamed, and the vast majority ran for their lives. Rusty charged at Peter, but before he could reach him, Peter aimed the gun at Rusty and shouted, "Don't move, my friend."

Rusty came to a halt and put his hands up. Peter ran behind Rusty and grabbed his neck. Peter held Rusty at gunpoint. "Get back, everyone, or he's dead! Get back!"

Grandma Edna, Debbie, and Katy were sitting together. Edna fainted, and instead of running away, Katy and Debbie bravely stood by her side. Katy grabbed Edna by the shoulders, Debbie took her legs, and they carried her to the other side of the concession building to temporary safety. The rest of the crowd scattered and ran away from the complex. Randall held his left hip as blood poured over his hands and dripped onto the court. Randall tried to negotiate with Peter. He pleaded with Peter that there was good in him, that Randall had seen it.

Randall informed The Killer how depressed he had been until he was able to get to know Peter, Mathew, Rusty, and Keisha. Peter solemnly let Randall know that he could not live the way a prisoner lives. He kept his right arm around Rusty's neck while holding the gun in his left hand, still pointed at Rusty's head, and walked with him to his Mercedes. Peter opened the driver's door and ordered Rusty to get in and move to the passenger's side. He then got behind the wheel.

Peter took the gun and slammed it into Rusty's skull, knocking him on the head several more times, until he was unconscious. Then Peter sped out of the parking lot.

Randall limped to his truck as blood flowed down his waist. He opened the door of his vehicle and grabbed his 9 mm from under his seat. He worked to get the keys into the ignition but struggled as he was getting dizzy. Randall was in such bad shape that he did not realize he hadn't even closed the truck door. Keisha sprinted to the truck and told Randall to move over. He argued with her, demanding her to stay back and stay safe. She made it clear to him that she would not leave Rusty with the psycho peanut butter pickleball bastard!

Randall crawled his way to the passenger side as Keisha slammed the driver's door shut, started the truck, and took off like a bat out of hell. Randall was struggling to stay conscious, but he put his head out of the passenger's side and tried to shoot the back tires of Peter's Mercedes. He wasn't even close. He fell back into the car and slumped over.

Peter drove through the country fields, staying outside the city. The old-but-reliable F-150 followed close behind as the Mercedes bounced through the cut wheat fields.

Although Peter had a new $45,000 sports car, he knew that a tire would eventually blow in the heavy weeds, making it no match for a truck.

Peter knew he had to get to the road quickly. He set the Mercedes on cruise control. He was driving in a wide-open field, so he wasn't concerned with running into anything. Peter crawled out of the window and on top of the car. He positioned himself facing backward and looking straight at the old F-150 coming at him.

He shot directly at the driver-side window at Keisha. But she swerved while Peter shot. The bullet missed the old truck completely. Peter shot again, but as he took the shot, Keisha ducked down under the wheel, still holding onto the bottom of it to steer. Glass shattered in front of her. She closed her eyes just before the shards flew into her eyes. Peter tried to hit the front driver's wheel but missed and destroyed the fender. Peter fired again, directly at Keisha. The bullet missed her head by mere inches as the back window blew out. Glass covered her and Randall, but miraculously did not cut into them.

Rusty slowly regained consciousness. He soon realized that Peter was on the hood after hearing more gunshots. Rusty looked back and saw that Keisha was the driver Peter was shooting at. Peter's ride, at last, reached the end of the open field. A tree was about ten yards to the right. Rusty felt the blood gush from his forehead. He was still dizzy and hurting, but he managed to reach the driver's side.

Rusty buckled his seat belt, grabbed the wheel, and yanked it sharply right, ramming the Mercedes into an old oak tree. Peter flew off the car and into a gigantic pile of hay just to the left of the oak tree in front of the car. The airbags went off. The combination of the seatbelt and airbags kept Rusty secure, cushioning him. Keisha hit the brakes hard, bringing the old 1999 F-150 to a stop.

Blood flowed from the bottom of the pile of hay. Peter, buried in the straw, was not visible.

Keisha checked to see if Randall was okay. He nodded, "yes," and she cautiously exited the truck. She ran to check on Rusty. Keisha helped him out of the car, where they then rushed to the passenger's side of the truck to help Randall.

They could hear police sirens from a distance and saw flashing lights marching their way. They turned their backs to the scene and waved their arms for help. At long last, the two police cars were just a couple hundred yards away, though they struggled to drive through the heavy weeds. Relief set in, knowing how close they were to safety, but then, from behind them, they heard the pickleball voice from hell. "If I'm going down, you bastards are all going to hell with me."

They turned their heads to see Peter standing there, covered in blood, smeared make-up, and hay. He looked like some sort of demonic villain from an old Marvel comic. Peter was still remarkably holding the gun with his right-hand forefinger on the trigger. He was ready and more than willing to fire at Keisha and Rusty.

That is until the only other resident of his own ranch suddenly sprang from the woods. The pupils of Peter's eyes expanded wider than Lake Michigan. Jiffy dashed at her owner. Peter held onto the gun and dodged the horse. He started to shoot at it, but Mathew threw himself off Jiffy while still gripping the deadly paddle. He turned the lever on the switchblade paddle while flying off Jiffy. Mathew landed beside The Killer. He detached Peter's right hand with the switchblade paddle. The hand, still clinging to the gun, fell to the ground.

Peter fell to his knees, screaming in agony. Robin hopped off the horse. She limped to Peter, who looked down at his right hand lying on the ground. He then gazed in horror at his handless right arm. Robin peered with hatred into Peter's defeated eyes. With pure disdain, he said to Robin, "Don't you ever die?"

"No, sorry, sir. I gotta lotta years of pickleball to play." She then punched him in the face, knocking him out cold.

Keisha rushed to Robin and Mathew, "Thank God you both are alive!"

Robin, in enormous pain, struggled but managed to reply, "You didn't think you were going to get out of being my doubles partner that easy, did you?"

Keisha smiled.

Rusty helped Randall get out of the glass-covered truck and walk to the area where the hay was.

The police finally arrived at the scene and got out of their cars. One of the officers started to handcuff Peter before he could regain consciousness. Grimacing in pain, a wounded Mathew managed to work up a slight laugh. He then reminded the officer that you can't handcuff a guy who is missing a hand.

Randall was in too much pain to laugh but smiled and nodded his head. "Well said, Mathew."

Mathew turned to Randall and said, "Just for the record, Randall, after we all get out of what might very well be a long hospital stay, I will be putting you to work, old man."

"What do you have in mind, Mathew?"

"You'll see."

The police eventually helped the EMTs get the injured to a nearby dirt road, where the ambulances awaited their arrival. Mathew and Randall were loaded onto gurneys beside each other. Keisha, who walked away from the trauma astonishingly unscathed, sauntered in between them. She took Mathew's left hand and said, "I love you, brother."

"I love you, too, sis."

Keisha then turned to Randall and gently took his right hand in hers. She looked him in his eyes and, after a short pause said, "And I love you, too, ya grumpy, old fart."

She positioned her body to talk to Robin as the EMT placed her friend on the gurney. Keisha peered into Robin's peanut butter-covered face.

"You are so gorgeous, Robin. I could just eat you." Robin smiled as Keisha took her forefinger and scooped some peanut butter off Robin's cheek and licked it. "On a more serious note, I'm sorry I got you into this mess, best friend."

Robin smiled, looked up at Jiffy, who was loyally standing on the other side of Robin's gurney, and said, "Just take care of my horse, will ya?"

"Absolutely, Robin"

Keisha then walked over to Rusty. "We are a pretty good team, huh?"

He replied, "Yes, baby, but can we try and keep the whole chase-a-serial-killer thing out of our relationship from now on?"

"Sounds like a plan, Rusty." She kissed him on the lips before the EMTs loaded him into one of the ambulances. She, along with the police and Jiffy, watched the medical vehicles drive away. A police officer asked her to get in his car so he could give her a ride home. Keisha politely told the officer thanks, but she already had a ride. Keisha then grabbed a thin rope that was lying near the hay and turned it into reigns for a horse. The police officer helped her onto Jiffy, then asked, "Are you sure you're going to be okay riding this horse without a saddle, miss?"

"Thanks for your concern, officer, but trust me. I'll be home in a Jiffy." It was a pun that was very much intended.

She then rode across the Kansas prairie.

CHAPTER 21

It was the anniversary of the day the pickleball monster was at last apprehended. Fresh air blended with seventy-seven-degree weather comforted the large group of school-age children who pranced around their newly created stomping grounds.

The little humans integrated themselves into their new medieval-themed playground. There were swings, tunnels, slipper slides, monkey bars, miniature playhouse castles... The playground area was highlighted by a splash pad filled with statue animals that sputtered $H_2 0$ out in all directions, creating a cooling point for the little people.

Three-to-four-foot-long oak trees were freshly planted in the soil throughout the park. Each had a little plaque that honored the memory of one of the victims of Peter the Monster. A couple of kids, tired from a hard morning's play, were relaxing. They leaned over the side walls of a walking path that was shaped and painted like a rainbow. It had been built to allow children to walk across a pond filled with foot-long goldfish that mightily swam about their most peaceful home.

The walking path had two words painted across the side rails of the structure. The words read:

MERTHIN'S BRIDGE

A sign a few feet from the parking lot read,

ELAINE STEWART MEMORIAL PARK

If you didn't know better, you would have thought it was General Edna Reynolds rather than Grandma Edna.

"Be careful, Elijah and Mathew. Let it down slowly, especially you, Mathew. We do not want to strain your arm," she said, referring to Mathew's lingering wound from where the switchblade paddle had struck.

"If you boys drop it off Randall's truck, we are going to have to give him our grill."

Mathew then joked, "Well, since it is the exact make and model we have, we *could* just give him ours. I don't think he would complain."

"Okay, smarty pants, then what would we use to grill on at home, a fire pit in the backyard?"

Elijah and Mathew gently lowered the grill off Randall's truck. They then set it down about two basketball goal lengths from a line of tables. General Grandma Edna commanded the boys to retrieve the trays filled with watermelon, twelve pounds of Grandma Edna's world's greatest potato salad, and slices of mouth-watering chocolate cake from her car.

Debbie and Katy soon rushed up to help. Debbie did her best to position herself near Mathew.

For so long, Mathew had looked for every opportunity to court Debbie whenever possible. She was now acting as her own attorney, as she continuously aimed to present her case to be his gal. It wasn't that Mathew didn't still find her attractive, but the events of the past year had forced him to grow up much faster than he might have liked. High school romance was now a trivial amusement in comparison to his pursuit to create a better life for others.

Robin and Keisha soon arrived on horseback. They hopped off the treasured thoroughbred a few feet from Edna.

Edna gave them a hug. "Nice entrance, you two. Jiffy is a gorgeous horse."

"Her name is no longer Jiffy, Grandma," Keisha corrected.

"What, you changed it?"

Keisha looked at Robin as they grinned at each other. "We both decided that Jiffy sounded WAY too much like a type of peanut butter, which we are, of course, sure was Peter's intent. So, we decided to change it to..." Keisha and Robin proceeded to answer at the same time, "FIVE O!"

"A most appropriate name, as it refers to law enforcement as well as pickleball," Grandma Edna replied in agreement.

"Robin and I have more news to tell you, Grandma!"

"What is it, Keisha?"

"I know you were disappointed that I delayed the start of my college career. I was just not up for studies and dorms and all that business after the trauma that Peter put us through."

"Under the circumstances, Keisha, I can honestly say, you probably made the right decision."

"Well, Grandma, the long jump I made to take on Peter/Sandy went viral. Julie Kennedy posted her shot of the leap all over the country. I have been offered hundreds of Division I scholarships for long jump and high jump, but I turned them all down."

Grandma replied, "Oh, honey, with all you've been through, I understand."

"But good news is on the horizon for both Robin and me, Grandma. I turned them down since we have been granted another opportunity. We just received news from Wichita State Tennis Coach Johnson. She is willing to take me on as a walk-on, and Robin has accepted the manager position for the team. And if her ribs continue to heal, she'll be given a try-out to make the team at some point as well."

Edna again hugged them both. "That is fantastic news! I am so proud of you two. I know walk-on athletes, not being on scholarships, can struggle, but we will figure it out, one way or another."

"Thanks, Grandma Edna, but neither Robin nor I will have to worry about money."

"And why is that?"

With excitement, Keisha answered, "Because Wichita State gave us full-ride scholarships in, what else, other than criminal justice!"

Grandma beamed with pride. "There's no way any two people could be more qualified." She hugged them once again and declared, "Now, let's get to work. We have a lot of food to set out yet."

Edna saw Rusty showing Randall a new pickleball paddle. It was longer and thinner. Randall had several questions about the effectiveness of the one-inch-longer paddle.

"Rusty. Randall. Get your butts over here and get to work!" Edna cried out.

"Yes, ma'am!" Rusty answered.

Randall grabbed the cane he now needed due to the gunshot wound, and the two of them made their way to the grill.
The two men put on grilling aprons. The aprons had one large word printed on them:

HEROES

Keisha walked up to Rusty and kissed him as she joined him and Randall at the serving tables. "You look hot in the apron get-up, babe."

Randall pretended to act as though Keisha was talking to him instead of Rusty. "Why, thank you, Keisha. I appreciate that."

Keisha and Rusty laughed. "Oh, you look great as well, Randall." She then hugged him before putting on an apron herself.

Also helping at the serving tables were Robin and her parents. Robin was a little surprised that her mother and father were serving together next to her. It felt like the three of them were a family again, even if it was just for a short while before her dad headed back to Topeka.

Edna's surviving son, Andre, and his wife, Peggy were back from Connecticut for the special occasion to help while their children were out enjoying the new park.

The aroma of fresh-cooked Angus beef filled the air, drawing all the kids in for a delicious lunch. As the last of the hamburgers slid onto the top of the trays, Edna picked up a loudspeaker. "All right, kids, hamburgers are ready! It is time to eat!"

Some of the little humans, who had heard their stomachs roar, flew to the paper plates in a quest to be first in line. Other children ignored Edna's command and continued to play. At one time, Edna would never have allowed youngsters not to obey an elder's instructions, but after the turmoil she had experienced over the past couple of years, allowing children to continue their art of having fun was quite fine with her.

Shortly after the Crew started serving the kids, Randall heard a most familiar voice, "Hi, Grandpa!" He teared up as he flipped the hamburger off his spatula and onto his granddaughter's plate. Beside her were his daughter, Samantha, and his son-in-law, Rudy.

Randall then put his spatula down, hobbled around the table, and hugged them all. Tears rolled down both his and his daughter's faces. "Fourth visit from all of you in five months. I am impressed."

Samantha turned to him and said, "Dad, when we found out that crazy man shot you, I felt responsible. I have not done my part to look after you. You truly are a hero, dad. I'm sorry we haven't been there for you."

"Don't apologize. I could have been a more affectionate father when you were a kid. I put too much into my work."

"Well, dad, being a hero takes work."

"Thanks, Samantha. That means a lot to me."

Soon after the last of the children ate, Julie Kennedy and her Star Action News crew arrived. Mayor Jensen also pulled up, and his chauffeur opened the back door to help him out of the car. Other officials, dignitaries, and police officers gathered behind the playground. A ten-foot-long ribbon floated five feet above the ground, each side tied together by a thin pole. Mayor Jensen placed a mic on his suit and asked everyone to gather around.

"This is Julie Kennedy live from Star Action News. We are here at the ribbon cutting for a most special ceremony. Let's listen in."

The mayor called Robin, Randall, Rusty, Keisha, Elijah, Mathew, and even the horse to join him. Robin guided Five-0 (formerly known as Jiffy) by her reigns as they all walked up to the area where Mayor Jenson was located.

He then spoke. "First of all, let's all bow our heads in a moment of silence in memory of those who lost their lives to the madman."

After a moment of silence, the mayor continued, "Today marks the one-year anniversary of the day the Peanut Butter Killer was captured. I am now happy to declare that we are here to present these fine, heroic citizens of Wichita with a reward for their courage and honor. It was the six of you, now famously known as "The Crew," who not only solved the Peanut Butter Murders but also personally apprehended the monster. And we are not only here to thank you for your heroics in capturing a killer but also for your most gracious donation. Robin Lebbin, Rusty Collins, Randall Baines, and Elijah, Keisha, and Mathew Reynolds, and of course, Jiffy the horse; the city of Wichita most graciously thanks you all for taking the entire 2.5-million-dollar reward money and using it to help build this gracious, breath-taking park now known as Elaine Stewart Memorial

Park!" All cheered, especially the family of Elaine Stewart. She had touched many lives in the community.

The mayor continued, "All the children have already been enjoying the west half of this sensational park, but the other half has not yet been opened... until now."

The mayor's colleagues then brought a large, human-sized pair of scissors up to the mayor and "The Crew." "Crew, it is now time for you to do the honors." The six of them then walked up and cut the ribbon together. The crowd cheered.

Mr. Jenson spoke, "Ladies and gentlemen, boys and girls, welcome to the Sedgwick County Family Pickleball Courts!" As "The Crew" cut the ribbon, the crowd cheered louder.

"Now go play some pickleball!" The crowd continued to clap and holler as they walked out onto the sixteen bright, baby blue courts, outlined with golden strips of paint to mark the lines. Hung along the fence that surrounded the courts were canvases with murals painted by local artists depicting castles, jugglers, jesters, kings, and queens.

Randall, Robin, Mathew, Keisha, Elijah, Debbie, Katy, and Edna all gazed upon the courts in wonder. Randall turned to Mathew, "Well done, Mathew, AKA Merthin." The rest of The Crew agreed and praised him for his architectural creation.

Cluck Putoo Puh - Cluck Putoo Puh - Cluck Putoo Puh

"Ah, that's music to my ears! Randall declared.
"I remember a time when an old, next-door neighbor despised that sound," Keisha remarked.

"In my defense, I was trying to get some good quality Follett reading time in when you were banging that damn, hard-as-a-rock, Wiffle ball against the garage on a Saturday morning."

The Crew all laughed. "Speaking of which, I have gifts for all of you. Gifts did I say? Let me rephrase that, I have a product I would very much like to barter."

Randall had his pickleball bag hanging over his shoulder. He put his cane down, took his bag off, and pulled out several copies of the book *Pillars of The Earth*.

Randall tossed a book to every member of the "Crew." He even included Debbie and Katy. "The book *Pillars of the Earth* for our entire Crew. This happens to be the first book of Ken Follett's Kingsbridge series. I'm hoping one of you will give me one of my three copies of *World Without End* back, so I can at last finish the dern thing. It would be a nice, gracious gesture."

Keisha smiled and said, "You got it, Pops."

Mathew said enthusiastically, "There's a first book? Is there something else built in it, equivalent to Merthin's bridge?"

"Yes, Mathew, something much, much, much larger; the entire Kingsbridge Cathedral!"

"I can't wait!" Mathew exclaimed with excitement.

Debbie walked up to him and said, "Not sure what the Follett Kingsbridge series stuff is all about, but perhaps we could relax and enjoy this delightful book together, Mathew?"

He blushed, put his right arm around her shoulder, and said, "Um, uh...sure, Debbie."

Elijah chimed in,

"Thanks for the book, Randall, but no thanks."

"I know, I know, Elijah. You'll settle for the footnotes."

"You got it, old man."

Edna then asked, "Are there two people in there that create a hotter, steamy, and juicier romance than Caris and Merthin had?"

"Grandma!" Keisha shouted with shock.

Everyone laughed.

Grandma Edna looked up to the sky and said, "Oh, Lord, I'm sorry. I'll pray the rosary twice tonight, but dang, that book had some major hot stuff. Whew!"

All laughed again as Grandma Edna fanned her new treasured Follett book in front of her face to get some air.

Rusty then turned to Randall with his head down and remarked, "I am sorry, Randall that your pickleball bag is filled with books rather than paddles."

"Yeah, me too," Keisha added.

"It's okay. I might have had a short-lived pickleball career, but with all of your help, I certainly made the most of it."

"You certainly did, Randall, you most certainly did," Grandma Edna agreed.

Keisha then proclaimed, "Okay, guys, what do you say we go join the kids and play some PICKLEBALL!!?"

The "Crew" most exuberantly agreed.

Aside from Randall, they all stepped onto the courts. Randall stayed back with his family while he tended to Five-O. The special horse was a real celebrity with all the kids.

Tasha walked up, tapped him on the back, surprising him, and asked, "Got a book in there for me?"

"Tasha, thanks for coming. It's great to see you!"

"Are you sure? Some have said that during your investigation, your crime-fighting pickleball club suspected me of possibly being a killer?"

"Hey, we were competing for the heart of the same person! I had to try to eliminate the competition!" Tasha, Randall, and Randall's family all laughed.

"I reckon our love lives haven't been doing so well, Randall."

"Yeah, I'd say we could get together, but quite frankly, I'm done with younger women from now on."

Tasha and Randall both laughed.

Randall introduced Tasha to his family. She hugged and kissed him on the cheek and walked on.

Just a year ago, Edna had despised Pickleball. Now it was her favorite sport. She had already worked her way up to a 4.0 level in all age group categories, and 5.0 in her respective age group.

She was the last to step onto the new courts, but just as she did, she happened to look over at her Weber five-burner grill with a side smoker. She stared at it for quite some time.

She suddenly ran off the courts and up to Randall as he was starting to walk to the playground area with his granddaughter.

"Wait, Randall. I need to talk to you."

"Sure, Edna, what's on your mind?"

Edna informed him that it had dawned on her that it was quite the coincidence that they both had the same make and model grill. She then kissed Randall on the cheek and said, "I reckon you thought of Edward and me after we lost our son and daughter-in-law, after all."

Randall blushed, "I guess the secret's out."

"Just for the record, Randall, you know you haven't really seen the last of these here pickleball courts. You and I can really tear it up in the 5.0 sixty and older category, and I'm not that far away from seventy. Hell, we could be world co-ed champions."

"I'd love that, Edna, but Peter has ensured that I will be limited to the role of pickleball supporter for the rest of my life."

"Oh, honey, you are not getting off the hook from being my partner that easily. You know there's an entire fitness room in our basement. I expect you to be at our house by 7 a.m. tomorrow morning to do some hard-core rehab."

"I don't know, Edna. This gunshot wound is pretty bad."

Samantha then chimed in, "Edna, he will be there – DAILY. We will make sure of it!"

"Good," Edna replied.

She then walked back onto the court.

Cluck Putoo Puh - Cluck Putoo Puh - Cluck Putoo Puh

Edna looked back at Randall once more before beginning to play. "You're right, Randall; that is a beautiful sound."

Cluck Putoo Puh - Cluck Putoo Puh - Cluck Putoo Puh

"Yes, it is, Edna. Yes, it is."

EXCERPT FROM:

THE GHOST OF PICKLEBALL PAST

BOOK II OF THE PICKLEBALL CHRONICLES

    Peter Weatherford had been locked up for over two long years. He had known that he would hate prison, but he did not know that the hatred for prison be as strong as it was. Peter thought that, at the very least, he would be able to grasp the rewards of some sort of cult-like, villainous, celebrity status. But even if that status existed, he had no way of reaping any type of benefit from it. The warden at Lansing Prison in Kansas, kept Peter secluded as much as the policies of the prison allowed.
    Peter was confined in solitary confinement twenty-three hours a day. He was allowed a one-hour break, twice a day, to go out onto a forty-yard radius outdoor area, surrounded by eight-foot-high walls. Aligned on top of the walls was barbed wire

fencing. The walls did have four, two feet by two-foot square windows that he could use to see the general prison population enjoying a much, much larger yard. Calling it an outdoor area was a complete exaggeration. He could look up at the sky, but this was painful for him, as he often viewed airplanes flying across the Kansas sky.

Peter's mind wandered imagining the airplanes moving their patrons to sandy beaches, beautiful mountains and cities filled with major league ball parks, with exquisite food entrees.

Peter decided to further torture himself by looking through one of the two-by-two windows. There he saw pickleball courts, filled with prisoners enjoying the most popular prison game there is, next to basketball. A part of him wanted to get out there and play with them so. But the other part told himself, "What is the point? I'd still obliterate those idiots, even with just my left hand."

Peter then looked down at his right arm and seethed with anger. The same thought entered his mind every time he gazed upon the invisible space that occupied the end of his right arm. "That damn Mathew Reynolds! He took my prized invention and desecrated it by using it to defile me!"

After his hour was up, Peter begged the two prison guards for just a few more minutes. One of the prison guards instantly turned down the request. "Just so you know, asshole, Elaine Stewart was the grandmother of one of my best friends and the kindest lady I have ever known. Now get your ass back in your cell before I crush your fucking brains in."

After being placed back in his ten-by-eight-foot cell, Peter sat in the barren, right corner of his cell. He placed his head down in his hands and sulked. Peter daydreamed of being back in his mansion's hot tub, drinking a cold one. He thought of sex with Tasha. Before prison life, he had thought of her as nothing more than a co-ed doubles partner who he banged occasionally.

Peter now thought of her as a former lover and recognized how deeply lucky he had been to have shared his life with her. Peter then thought of Keisha. Peter loved her like she was his own daughter. He regretted that he had tried to kill her. Peter looked around the cell for something, anything that he might find to use to kill himself with. He did this daily after his "outdoor" sessions. Peter was not allowed any possessions in his room other than two books.

The boredom was destroying him. Later in the evening he ate his very bland, tasteless meal. It still left him hungry. A middle-aged nurse came to his cell at about 9 p.m. that night. She gave him an Ambien. He hesitated to take the pill. He wanted to sleep to escape his dreadful existence, but he also knew what would come with his darkened unconsciousness. Reluctantly he went ahead and took the Ambien.

With the assistance of the pill, it did not take long for Peter to fall asleep. The siesta provided but temporary solace, before the nightmares soon began. The dreaded, horrific dreams always consisted of reliving images of his mother screaming at him as a child, his hand being detached by Mathew, and worst of all, the demons that haunted him during his ghastly dreams.

The demons were large beasts. They stood upright like humans but had the bodies of a mixture between a pig and a cow. Their heads looked like bulls with large horns sticking out of their skulls. They always appeared to him with fire surrounding them.

The monsters taunted him nightly. Some even had pickleball paddles with triangular blades around the edges that resembled his own pickleball switchblade weapon. They swung the bladed paddles coming inches form his face. And every night Peter screamed, not only in his dreams, but aloud, so that other prisoners in the seclusion and guards could hear his verbal pleas for peace.

The screams made Peter the most hated man in seclusion. The prisoners yelled from their cells for him to shut up so they could sleep, but their commands for his silence were never heard. The dreaded demons would not allow him to wake up until their torturous fun had played itself out. This was the same hell-driven life that Peter had led for his two plus years of incarceration.

But on this night, one thing would change.

His screams to the monsters begging for compassion continued to fall on deaf, demon ears. Peter knew that their nightly, emotional torture session with him would last for an extended period that seemed to be endless.

But then something happened. Peter felt a hand on his shoulders. The demons taunted him but had never actually touched him. He thought that they had finally been granted permission from their commander, whether that be an evil angel, God or even Satan himself. Peter did not know what hell was, but figured he was going to find out soon enough.

The weight on his shoulder became heavier. He crawled up into a fetal position and cried in fear. And then suddenly, he woke up. There before his eyes, was an elderly black woman.

"Uh, uh, um…who are you? How did you get in my cell?"

The elderly woman did not answer.

"Again, I say, lady, who are you?"

"Do you not recognize me, Peter?"

"NO, NO! PLEASE GET OUT OF MY CELL! PLEASE GET OUT OF HERE!"

"Sorry, Peter. I can't do that."

"Hey, listen, lady, how do you know my name? Who the fuck are you?"

"Peter, you must watch your language. Angels are listening. I am terribly upset that you do not recognize me. You should recognize all of those that the good Lord has ever granted you time to pray with."

"NO, NO! THIS CAN'T BE! I KILLED YOU! I KILLED YOU DAMN IT!"

"Oh, Peter, did I not tell you that only the body dies. Your soul lives forever. It is now time that you pay society back for your ominous sins."

"H-h-h-h-how-w-w a-a-a-m-m I s-s-supposed to do that? L-l-l-look where I'm at lady!"

"Goodbye, Peter, I will give you further instructions on another night."

Rob MUNDEN

Peter's face expressed shock and bewilderment as he watched the spirit of Elaine Stewart fade until she was no longer seen by the naked eye.

PEANUT BUTTER PICKLEBALL AND MURDER

NOTE: The expediency of finishing and having a release date for Book II of the Pickleball Chronicles depends on how well sales go for Book I. If you enjoyed PEANUT BUTTER PICKLEBALL AND MURDER, please encourage your friends to purchase the book from Amazon.com or from Rob Munden directly.

AUTHOR BIO:

Although this is Rob Munden's first venture into novel writing, he is an established professional playwright. Rob has had over 20 ONE ACT plays and 4 FULL LENGTH plays produced or had special readings in Kansas, Florida and Minnesota. Rob has plays published by LSH PRINTING PRESS, PRAIRIE ARTS MAGAZINE and AMAZON.COM. You can purchase two of his FULL-LENGTH plays on AMAZON.COM titled, WHAT 2 R U? and JACKSON THE INVISIBLE FLYING DOG.

Rob is also known for his Public Speaking skills. He was an Associate Professor for 12 years for public speaking classes at Barton Community College. In 2000, he was the Kansas State Jaycees Public Speaking Champion and the United States Jaycees Public Speaking Champion Runner-up.

Rob is a solid pickleball player. In men's doubles, Rob, with a variety of partners, has won medals and a couple of championships in all levels all age group city tournaments. He is also a solid singles player. He won the bronze medal, taking third in the state in the 2021 KANSAS SENIOR OPEN CHAMPIONSHIPS, in the 50-54 - 4.0 and below category and the silver medal in the 3.5 - 50 and older 2022 Wichita Riverfest tournament sponsored by Nahola Pickleball Club.

   Rob holds a bachelor's degree in communication from Fort Hays State University and an Associate of Arts degree from Barton Community College. He graduated from Hoisington High School in 1988. He is currently the SPTP Education Supervisor at Larned State Hospital.

   Rob is married to Julie. They have three children - Dallas, Maverick and Mia, and a son-in-law, Ritchie. The family also has two chocolate labs, Jackson and Pluto.

ACKNOWLEDGEMENTS

A book can't be finished without another set of eyes. Thank you to Daphne Norez and daughter Dallas Richardson for proofreading and editing this book.

   Next, it would be difficult to write a pickleball novel without playing a whole lot of pickleball. I would like to thank first those that have been my partners in men's and co-ed doubles in tournaments throughout the years,
Jim Smith, Antwome Topps, Kara Ratzlaff, Robin Lebbin (mom), Monte Linton, Matt Delong and Devon Fuller.

I would also like to acknowledge fantastic tournament opponents. Great battles and rivalries helped contribute to the storyline in this book.

Justin McClung, Shawn Clark, Bryce McClung, Blake McClung, Dave Delong, Jeret Johnson, Austin Zammaripa and Shannon Schartz

Also, one can't get better at pickleball without practice. Below are classic practice partners who have contributed to this book through their stellar play:

Debbie Munz, Justin Clark, Jeff Murphy, Chris Perez, Marcus Herrera, Craig Neeland, Travis Reed, Chris Humphries, Rick Bealer, Sandy Walters, Lexi Nettleingham, Logan Marshall, Austin Weiser, Tony DeLauriers, Patrick and Karisa Cowan, Dan Scott, Larry Parsons, Ramon Lozano, Sharon Steimel, Michelle Dreiling, Cory & Molly Sager, Dave Snyder, Scott Marrow, Teresa & Casey Winter, Steve & Cindy Dayton, Kathy Rebel, Kathy Riggs, Judy Turner, Jo Kurtz, Janene Soeken, Rosemary Demel, Marla Davidson, Greg & Alena Hinson, Karla Ayon, Reva Dougherty, Leesa Butler, Donna Moore, Cecile Folkert and Karen Proffitt.

A thanks to those he has supervised at work for their support: Lonnie Hardy, Bob Alford, Natalie Blackwell and Alex Schmidt and Rob's own boss – Keri Applequist.

Book Cover Design and formatting - Mia Munden (daughter)
Formatting – Maverick Munden (Son)
Marketing – Julie Munden (wife)

Rob MUNDEN

And finally, without a supportive cast in my playwriting career, I would not have had the writing experience to eventually write a novel:
Larned Prairie Arts Foundation, Maverick Munden (son), Dallas Richardson (daughter), Karen Gore, Angela Meitner, Pawnnee Valley Hospital, Great Bend Community Theatre, Fort Hays State Theatre Department, Barton Community College Theatre Dept., Tiny Toilers 4-H club,
Hoisington Summer Recreation Program and Randy Willis – High School Drama Teacher.